MW00487704

Dedication

*Dedicated to The Stoop Krewe and to
Kimmie and Marilyn.*

*I thank my son Jack from the bottom of my
heart for walking me through the technical
aspects of getting this to print.*

And to C.B.. ~ there are no more words.

The Changeling

Copyright © 2020 Annie Russell

All rights reserved. No part of this book may be
reproduced or used in any manner without the prior
written permission of the copyright owner,
except for the use of brief quotations in a book
review.

Hardcover: 978-0-578-66663-1
Paperback: 978-0-578-66137-7

First paperback edition: November 2020.

Edited by Emory Whaley
Cover art by Annie Russell
Layout by Jack Russell Jr.
Internal Art by Annie Russell

Printed by IngramSpark in The U.K.

NoMi Press

annierussell.net

Chapter 1

October 31

The bright red sports car flew through the warm southern Alabama night as the radio wailed a song about wolves and hunger with a vocal backdrop of erotic noises. Amber's dark hair whipped past her face as the night air blew through the open windows, bringing the sounds of birds calling each other back home to roost and big rig trucks lumbering past on their way to anywhere else but here. She turned her face to the left and gazed at the boy driving the sleek car. Privilege draped over his entire being: the preppy lavender shirt, perfectly shaggy surfer hair that cost more than Amber made in a week to have cut and styled in a way that suggested no one had ever cut and styled it before, and the just-tan-enough face one achieves from days at the beach but not leathery enough to garner the stamp of a landscape worker. He sat with one arm draped over the back of her seat and the other resting casually by the wrist on the steering wheel, the air of studied nonchalance was complete. And studied it was. Amber was sure that Rodger spent more time than most girls in front of the mirror perfecting the casual slouch, detached chin-wave, and ironic eyebrow lift. She had to give him credit—he had nailed the whole thing.

Rodger caught her watching him and smiled, confident that she was admiring him—he expected nothing less from anyone. Born into a politically and socially prominent old Alabama family, he was raised to have no doubts about the beauty of his physical body or the security of his place in the world. 'The world' was fairly limited for Rodger, and he was fine with that. Southwestern Alabama—and the South in general—was about as large as Rodger's world would be, and his role there was secure; next year he would be fast-tracked into the University of West Alabama and a spot in the requisite Greek house his daddy and granddaddy pledged to. His acceptance into the School of Law was also a given, as was his name on the plaque outside the 100-year-old barrister's office located downtown once he graduated and passed the bar. For Rodger, life was good.

Amber looked past the perfect profile of her boyfriend and out the driver's side window as they cruised too fast down the tree-lined streets of the Norman Rockwell-esque town. Her place within its social structure was not nearly as charmed as Rodger's. Her large family had been there for as many generations as his, but their stature was not prominent or socially noteworthy. Her father, while a brilliant and highly educated man, chose the security of life as a Methodist minister in which to raise his family of three daughters. Amber's mother was the perfect minister's wife with her conservatively coiffed hair, twinsets, and her ability to host a luncheon with less than two hours' notice. Tradition, decorum, and hospitality were all hallmarks of the Foster family. Flashy red Camaro sports cars were not. Amber grinned, recalling the hissy fit her mother threw as she walked out the door that evening, wringing her hands and going on about not getting into 'compromising' positions and maintaining her 'reputation.' Amber had no plans to stick around this tiny town where nothing interesting ever happened, so her reputation here meant little to her. As soon as she graduated this May she planned on going somewhere—anywhere, really—far, far away from here. But for now, Rodger, his flashy car, and his world of easy wealth were too fun to pass up.

The radio switched to Bobby Pickett singing Monster Mash, and Rodger slowed the Camaro down as they cruised into the residential neighborhoods surrounding the center of town. Tiny princesses, ghosts, hobos, and clowns raced from porch-lit house to porch-lit house followed closely by their parents or older siblings stuck chaperoning the annual event. The scent of warm pumpkins from the jack o' lanterns mingled with the smells of burning leaves wafting on ribbons of cool air that held the promise of chillier weather to come. As the bright-red car grumbled and growled its way down 5th Street, Amber hung her head out the window and breathed deeply the scents of Halloween—her favorite time of year. Despite the innocence of the small children laughing and shrieking their way into a candy-fueled stupor, she had always been enthralled with the story behind that facade—a story where unknown denizens of unknown worlds wandered among the kids bobbing for apples or skulked within the cemetery gates. That this time of year allowed spirits to come into this world and roam at will was exciting to her precisely because it was dangerous. Being a minister's kid made that type of thing doubly dangerous which in turn cemented the holiday as her favorite.

She pulled her head back into the car as they rolled out of the neighborhood and turned onto County Road 43 stretching ahead to the horizon. Amber laughed loudly as Rodger punched the accelerator to the floor, and the powerful car shot forward into the darkness of the rural countryside. With the windows still rolled down, and the car exceeding eighty miles per hour on the straightaway, Amber's hair whipped up and around her head and face like a banner. The silent countryside of cow pastures, farmland, and the occasional farmhouse flew past in a blur as she and Rodger sang with Ozzy's 'Bark at the Moon' blasting through the speakers. Rodger smiled a real smile in her direction, and she laughed with delight and abandon as they raced into the night.

As the car chased its own headlights into the darkness, and Amber and Rodger sang along to the radio, a dog bayed in an empty field to the west. Unheard by the two young adults, another answered. And another and another and another. The fields to the west of County Road 43 were alive with the baying of dogs. By the time a massive, black canine shape stepped out from the shadows along the side of the road and directly in front of the car, the occupants inside of it were out of time. Rodger reacted by cranking the wheel sharply to the right to avoid the dog, sending the car careening off the road and over a ditch where it became airborne for enough time to hit the old Live Oak squarely in the center of its massive trunk before falling to the ground like a squashed red bug. Amber—who hated wearing seat belts—was thrown from the car as it sailed through the night sky. She landed, crumpled, on a bed of scratchy field corn thirty feet from the Oak. Rodger never left the car.

The baying and yipping of the dogs coalesced into an undulating miasma of yelps, barks, screams, and hollers alternating between canine and human vocalizations. Shadowy four-legged shapes converged on the tangled mass of red metal and plastic at the base of the oak tree and melted into its shadow. All was quiet for several seconds as the October wind rustled through the oak's branches, and an almost-full Halloween moon continued its slow ride up into the night sky. The human and canine baying and yelling began again as the pack of shadows detached themselves from the remains of the wreck. If anyone had been there to witness the sight they would have wondered at the effects of the moonlight on the scene as the image of the dogs wavered, only to be replaced with that of raggedy clothed men and women hunched on all fours, heads thrown back and screaming at the night sky. But no other humans were present or conscious to marvel at either the pack of dog-like humans or when a tall, thin figure stepped out from inside the trunk of the oak to survey the scene. The pack saw her, though, and ran to gather round her, nipping at each other in order to garner closer proximity to the figure that stood there.

Morag stood nearly six feet tall with

willowy arms and legs. Her features—fox-sharp—were both beautiful and unpleasant. Her matted hair reached below her shoulders and was the gray-green of the lichen found adorning old headstones. Small twigs, leaves, and dead bugs were stuck here and there like a particularly gruesome crown of the dead, the decayed, and the lost. Just barely poking out at the top of her head there appeared to be a set of small antlers. Wrapped in a dark green length of gauze, it was impossible to tell if she was part of the earth itself—a long-forgotten Mystery of this place—or the spirit of the oak that had been brutally assaulted by the speeding car that had hit its trunk so violently. The pack of dog-like humans—called variously The Wild Hunt, The Sluagh Sidhe, or The Host by those writers of unintentional Truth who compiled the Fairy Tales of The Scots and The Irish—jostled about Morag's feet looking to curry favor with the disturbingly beautiful Being standing before them. With a quick clap of her long-fingered hands, she sent them all scurrying back away from her as she surveyed the scene that had drawn her and the Sluagh Sidhe to this remote spot. The remains of the male human were still in the car, splayed up and across the steering wheel and the dashboard. To Morag, Rodger's lifeless body was as interesting as a discarded piece of paper along the side of the road. Glancing back at the cowering mass of hunched human-dog figures she found him—the figure to the far back of the pack had Rodger's terrified face and his bright blue eyes that rolled wildly around in its head. Likely he would be unimaginably terrified until the moon won over, and he became one with the crazed roaming of the Sluagh Sidhe and their hunt for the lost, the dead, and the dying.

Morag did not spend long wondering about the human male—his fate was destined as soon as The Hunt caught wind of his car's crash into the tree. The other human though— the female—that was of great interest to the Faerie. Morag saw that, while not conscious, the girl was not dead either—she floated somewhere in between, just barely aware of this realm's happenings. The energy of her body showed it still held its strength and was not likely to fail so long as the mind stopped its wanderings and came back to be seated within. Any mind would do. Morag shivered with excitement at the possibilities; to be able to play unimpeded in this world—no longer having to follow The Hunt, the moon, or the Great Festivals in order to gain access was deliciously enticing. The Sluagh Sidhe grumbled and paced to her left as she considered her new opportunity. They seemed to sense her thoughts as they eyed her and growled their impatience to be moving on, knowing that without her escort through this place they would be forced to return to their realm, their job unfinished.

Undeterred by The Host's insistence to be done here, Morag turned her back to them and leaned over the still figure. Holding both hands just inches from Amber's head, Morag

closed her eyes in concentration as she moved
her consciousness outward in search of her
place of entry. Suddenly, violet-colored
energy blossomed behind the Faerie's eyes as
her hands moved clockwise over the center of
Amber's head. She had located it. Holding her
left hand still, she moved her right hand into
the swirl of violet and pulled. Amber—having
previously been floating in a warm sea of
unconsciousness—was suddenly and
violently aware of herself even as she was
yanked out of her own body. The Faerie,
grasping the spirit of Amber with her right
hand, shook it sharply like one would shake
out a picnic blanket. Still holding her left hand
over the top of the body's head, she shoved
the essence of the girl into the oak. Then, as
simple as you please, Morag stepped into the
swirl of violet, watching as it spun closed
above her. Amber, having fallen down the
inside of the oak, came to rest on a bed of
bracken and moss in a world that glowed in a
perpetual purple twilight. Massive trees grew
up all around her, and the chime of a bell

boomed deeply. The baying of hounds came from everywhere and nowhere. The Host— deprived of its Attendant—had returned.

On the side of County Road 43 in rural southwest Alabama, the Faerie Morag, now dressed as the human Amber, opened her eyes. The body she had entered was battered and bruised but amazingly still functioning. Carefully she stretched one arm, then the other, and got to her feet. Looking around with—literally—new eyes, she was delighted to see how sharp and crisp the colors and scents had become. Her hearing was not nearly as precise as a Fae's, but with time she was sure that would become bearable. Morag started walking down the road headed west, shivering with anticipation. She could feel the low beat of Blues guitars, neon lights, and Voodoo drums in the distance and knew she had found a place to frolic with others, like herself, who had defected to this human playground.

Chapter 2

New Orleans

Ashlynne stretched her legs and adjusted her position as she watched the waves of humanity roll in and out of the Square, at times in keeping with the rhythm and beat of the brass band playing in front of the looming cathedral that dominated the space and other times seeming to be at odds with the music. Her long, brilliantly red hair was a product of both nature and nurture, a natural amber amped up to the nth degree with fire-engine-red hair glaze. Black leather combat boots with a myriad of buckles ended just below her knees with her short plaid kilt ending a few inches above—leaving enough thigh to be provocative but in no way

14

suggesting that the sign on her table asking
for a twenty dollar 'donation' in exchange for
a tarot card reading was a euphemism for
anything else. Her set-up was simple and
portable: a sturdy card table covered in a
black velvet cloth—upon which sat a stick of
burning incense in a beach stone that had a
natural hole in it, a sign asking for her
donation, her well-worn deck of cards with a
large crystal sitting on top of them, and off to
the side of it all, an empty chair awaiting her
next customer. It was just like all the other
fortune-tellers dotting the flagstones of
Jackson Square except for one thing—
Ashlynne was the real deal. Not in reading
cards, per se. The cards were simply a point of
focus for her customers. Ashlynne did not
need them. She saw all that was necessary,
and sometimes more than she wanted, with
her own two eyes.

It has always been this way; she couldn't
remember a time in her life when she wasn't a
witness to entities and scenery that others

were not. Sometimes it would be the archetypal 'ghost', though they were rarely the translucent, floating figures that drifted through spooky stories. Most times they looked like the living—what gave them away was that actual living people did not see them or interact with them. Other figures unseen and unnoticed by the general public had never been human. Strange creatures with the heads of wolves, the bodies of bears, and the wings of owls were commonplace during her time spent in Northern Michigan as a child. These creatures could be found wherever Native Americans lived and maintained the old stories and practices. The sounds of drums and chanting lured them close to the dancers. They didn't seem to be dangerous to humans and collected their energy from the rhythm of the sacred drums as well as the magic woven from the stories told by the tribe's Elders. Occasionally Ashlynne would find one wandering along the dunes and pines of Lake Michigan and would gently move it back into the mists from which it had

16

originally come. Other Beings found during
her life in the northern reaches of the Great
Lakes weren't as benevolent. These creatures
didn't gather energy from the sacred activities
of humans but from the humans themselves.
Sometimes looking like scuttling spiders,
other times like bat-winged dogs, these things
were parasites, pure and simple. While
naturally living in worlds adjacent to our
own, they were opportunistic and would
come through to our world for a snack of
human energy whenever the way was clear.
The way became clear when a human who
did not understand the rules would
accidentally open portals and doorways by
playing with magic, ritual, or spirit contact.
Most would walk away from their
experiments convinced that nothing had
happened when, in fact, they had succeeded
in opening a path between realms for astral
nasties of all types to wander in and out at
will. Ashlynne found these openings
everywhere from school cafeterias and

deserted beaches to hotel lobbies. She dutifully located any wandering parasites, moved them back through, and closed the openings. Pathways didn't always need to be opened by humans, though. Some are naturally occurring and look like shimmering sections in an otherwise stable scene. These are the 'thin places' that one often hears about in stories and fairy tales. Thin places are most often found in in-between spaces, hollow or forked trees, shorelines, and crossroads. They can also be found in buildings at the beginning and end of staircases, window ledges, and doorways. Though not found very often anymore, the writers of the old tales also knew that both man-made and naturally occurring wells and springs could act as pathways to other realms. Passing by these gauzy, shimmery spaces was like looking through a wavy pane of glass to Ashlynne. Entirely different landscapes and cityscapes rippled just beyond; strange trees with massive trunks whispered to each other like a gaggle of gossipy church ladies, two or more moons hung in a moody, green sky, and towns with squat houses—each capped with a windmill—marched down straight lanes toward an unknown horizon. Other times it was only purple mists swirling in velvety-black space that could be seen through the thin places. These scared Ashlynne the most, causing her to avert her eyes and hurry past in case anything looking out knew she could see in. For that was the key—knowing when to be obviously aware and when to be purposely obtuse. Some things were better left alone, and safety came from them not knowing that she could see. Years of lonely trial and error had allowed her to become savvy in how she presented herself since otherworld denizens weren't the only ones who could react dangerously should they become aware of her abilities. The myriad of foster homes she had been bounced to and from along the western edge of northern Michigan spoke to the hurtful nature in which humans could act when confronted with the

Unknown in the form of a skinny, little redheaded child. Time and time again she would settle in, and then something would happen to disrupt the household: a spirit, an astral creature, or—the worst—her knowing without a shadow of a doubt that an adult was dangerous. Being young, she would voice her fears or knowledge with chaos and anger the immediate result and expulsion to another home quickly following. By ten years old, Ashlynne had learned to keep her eyes open and her mouth shut. Shielding younger children from both human and astral predators that nested in the foster and group homes became second nature to her. By the age of fifteen, she had fled the area, physically sick and emotionally wrung out from the world of state-run group homes and the creatures that held sway within them.

Ashlynne traveled variously by foot and by bus along the interstate headed south. In larger cities and towns, she would stop to gather cash as an anonymous dishwasher in a diner or a housekeeper in some no-name motel. Smaller towns didn't work well with this technique—everyone knew everyone, and you had better have some connection there or the ranks closed around you. So, in larger cities, she would apply for jobs held traditionally by transients; cash was paid at the end of the day, and no names or social security numbers were required. It was during one of these stops in a middling-sized metropolis along the Mississippi River part way between 'midwest' and 'southern' that she acquired her deck of tarot cards. She had been in the city for a little more than a week and was feeling the tug to move along. Deciding on the next day for her self-imposed get-a-way, she took the afternoon to wander the downtown shopping district. The scent of sandalwood incense drifting out of the bright-purple door of a quaint shop drew her in. Crystals, banners, tie-dyed T-shirts, candles, and jewelry filled every square inch. But it was the hand-lettered sign advertising Psychic Readings for twenty-five dollars that caught her eye. That, and the two women standing behind the counter. Only one was alive; the lady with the flower-printed apron had been dead for over 30 years but liked to stay close to her granddaughter, though she wished her granddaughter knew she was there.

Until that moment it had never occurred to Ashlynne that she could charge money for what she could do and see, but with that simple printed sign a new avenue opened for her, and she jumped at the opportunity. Wandering through the section of tarot, oracle, and assorted Angel cards, she finally settled on the simplicity and classic drawings of The Rider Waite deck. Making her way back to the counter—and the granddaughter and grandmother standing there—she added a two-inch clear crystal point and a purple satin drawstring bag to her purchases. Stepping out into the sunlight, she smiled happily.

"So, twenty dollars for a Reading?" The customer's voice interrupted Ashlynne's wanderings down memory lane.

She looked up to see a woman of about sixty-five standing in front of her table. Dressed in the tourist regalia of denim shorts, white sneakers, and a neck-full of gaudy, plastic Mardi Gras beads over a Bourbon Street T-shirt, she smiled shyly.

Sitting up in her folding chair and putting on her most gentle smile, Ashlynne nodded and gestured her hand toward the empty chair.

"Yes, ma'am. I ask for a donation of whatever you're most comfortable with."

The smile that lit up the lady's face broke Ashlynne's heart—it was open and full of genuine warmth. But playing out just over her left shoulder, Ashlynne watched a scene that showed her that the woman's best friend and husband of over forty years would be dead on the floor of their bedroom in less than three weeks' time. She spun her head around looking for the living version of … Emily; her name is Emily… Emily's husband and found him several yards away taking pictures of the brass band. There was nothing to suggest that he would soon depart this world. Ashlynne sighed. *'Let them enjoy their time together,'* she thought—unsure if it was a reminder to herself or a prayer to whatever deity was listening to semi-homeless girls and happy tourists.

Emily sat down across from Ashlynne and slid a twenty-dollar bill across the black velvet. Ashlynne accepted it with a smile and placed it in the jar.

"What do I need to do?" asked her customer excitedly.

"Not a thing. I'm going to shuffle the cards and then we'll see what life has in store for you!"

Taking a deep breath Ashlynne began cutting and shuffling her cards, second nature now after all these years. She placed the deck face down, knocked three times on the top, and cut the deck into three roughly even piles. Flipping the first card upright and facing Emily, she announced, "The Past—Two of

Cups. Abiding love in a partnership. Mutual love and respect." Looking at her customer, Ashlynne smiled and said, "Your husband."

"Oh! How did you know that I'm m—" Emily laughed and blushed then held up her left hand where her wedding rings had resided for so many decades. "Of course! My rings!"

"Yes," agreed Ashlynne, and let it go with a smile.

"The next card in your spread is The Chariot, reversed. This card is in your present—look for a change of plans or a change in direction. Your destiny has only been assumed, not assured."

"You know," said Emily with a conspiratorial smile at Ashlynne, "we were supposed to go on a cruise, but the reservation fell through, so we came to New Orleans instead! I'm absolutely in love with your city! What great luck to not be stuck on a big boat. Do you think that's what the card means?"

"Absolutely. That is one very strong interpretation of this card," replied Ashlynne encouragingly as her heart broke a little more for the cheerful woman sitting across from her.

"The last card—your future—is The Ace of Pentacles suggesting the coming of money or wealth."

"OH! How wonderful!" exclaimed Emily, clapping her hands together. Ashlynne could literally see five-year-old Emily doing that very same thing at her birthday party after she had blown out all the candles on the cake.

"We're headed to the casino after dinner. Do you think we'll win?"

"It's entirely possible," replied Ashlynne gently. "Anything is possible here."

Emily stood up and fixed the young redheaded girl with a radiant smile. "Thank you so much! This has been astounding, you're so talented! I'm really excited about winning money at the casino!"

And with that, Emily dropped an additional twenty-five dollars into Ashlynne's jar and left to rejoin her husband, wandering hand in hand into Pirate's Alley.

Ashlynne turned her attention back to the cards—2 of Cups—love. Chariot reversed—loss of a partner and of a direction. Ace of Pentacles—an inheritance. Not the most ethical Reading she had ever done, but it provided the lady happiness and sometimes that's enough.

As the shadows lengthened and the sky turned a soft lavender, Ashlynne began packing up her things. The cards and crystal stayed in the pocket of her hoodie, but the scrap of black velvet she folded and placed into a plastic milk crate along with the package of incense and its holder. The table was collapsed and placed on top of those. Last in were the two folded camp chairs and the tip jar—its contents now stashed in her boot. Moving the crate onto the lip of the two-wheeled cart and securing it with a bright-orange bungee cord, she looked toward the river and breathed in deeply the gathering night air. It smelled like home.

Tipping the cart onto its two wheels to pull it behind her, she started toward the sounds and lights of Cafe Du Monde. Turning left onto the rough and tumble urban landscape that is lower Decatur Street, Ashlynne walked with shoulders back and head high, in and around the figures sprawled along the pavement and in the recessed doorways of the old buildings currently holding T-shirt shops, dubious art galleries, and one or two really nice restaurants. Attitude was everything. Not wanting to have to deal with the hassle of replacing her table and chairs should she be mugged, she kept her eyes straight ahead and walked with purpose. Not making eye contact had the added benefit of not having to school her face against showing shock, horror, or surprise at the visages of the street kids no one else could see. Green-tinged skin, long pointed ears, rat-like teeth, bare feet with prehensile toes covered in thick, black fur, and eyes of all shapes and every hue of the rainbow. Ashlynne wasn't sure what would happen if they knew she could see them—not as the 'crusties' that other people saw them; homeless (by choice or not) kids and young adults living in the drug and alcohol utopia that is the French Quarter, panhandling and harassing tourists, but as the creatures that they really were—gathered here from god knows where and for god knows what purpose. *'Maybe they like booze and heroin as much as humans,'* she thought to herself as she stepped over another leg that sported busted Doc Martens over yellow-scaled-skin.

Making another left at her favorite coffee bar in this part of town and onto Barracks Street, the darkness of the more residential street settled in around her, and she was able to drop her shoulders—and her attitude—a little as she continued towards home and bed. Five blocks later, and across the busy street of North Rampart, she stepped into her neighborhood.

Once in The Tremé, she felt she could truly relax. The large family of crows that called the spaces between Louis Armstrong Park and Esplanade Ave home cawed and called for their brethren to return to their roost for the night. A few more blocks and a right turn and she was on Ursulines and approaching her house. Muttering at herself for not leaving an interior lamp on, she scooted up the steps, bumping her cart behind her. The sound of the djembe drums calling the dancers together over at the old Congo Square in Louis Armstrong Park always made the blood twitch in her veins, though they were only the echoes of gatherings from long ago. Nodding to the little girl jumping rope and dressed in a faded pink dress—braids standing up all over her head—on the neighboring porch, Ashlynne unlocked her door and stepped into her front room. The young girl continued to jump rope just as she had done every day since she died of yellow fever in 1905.

Chapter 3

The next morning dawned hazy and warm with the promise of an afternoon thunderstorm on the edges of the sky. Ashlynne stretched, yawned, and pulled herself out of the nest of blankets and pillows she had dived into last night after getting home. She stumbled into the tight kitchen at the back of her half the small shotgun house, started her coffee, then returned to the center room—her bedroom—and folded up extra blankets, pulled the sheets up, plumped the pillows, and righted the coverlet. She liked her space to be orderly. Returning to the kitchen, she added cream to her coffee cup, poured in the hot coffee, and opened the back door to the small courtyard she shared with her landlord. A few chairs and a small iron table sat next to a kidney-shaped pool surrounded by overgrown banana, kumquat, and lime trees. Sitting down at the table, she took a deep drink of the coffee and began to feel alive again.

"Hey there, little one! How goes it?" Ashlynne smiled at the small calico kitten that skittled up to wind itself around her ankles. One of many neighborhood cats, this tiny girl was rescued by Ashlynne and was working her way into fitting into the larger colony that called this block home. In payment for keeping the city rats and assorted vermin at bay, the neighboring households left food and water for them. It was a good arrangement for everyone.

"C'mere, Sweets." Bending down and scooping up the tiny purring ball of sun-warmed fur, Ashlynne held her close and crooned endearments to her. "You are getting so big! Look at that tummy on you!" The kitten purred and rubbed her face on Ashlynne's marking her as her safe human.

Sipping her coffee in companionable silence

with the kitten in her lap, she watched leaves fall into the pool and spin around in unseen currents. Her landlord—an elderly retired lawyer—had dug the pool with the help of his partner in the mid-1960's. Ashlynne loved to think about what they must have dug up from the layers of history just below the surface of this old neighborhood. And, while it was a given that they had to have found all kinds of things—pottery, china shards, broken knife blades, more than likely human remains of some sort—Mr. Alvin never told her a thing about any fun finds. There would be no treasure hunting revelations from his partner who had passed away decades ago and had chosen to not visit the courtyard that he had worked so hard on. Some of the dead don't return.

Ashlynne went back inside to get a second cup of coffee before wandering around the perimeter of the pool checking the assorted fruit-bearing trees for their treasures to add to a salad later in the afternoon. Feeling grateful for the single banana, two limes, and a kumquat that the crows had deigned to leave for her, she went back indoors, leaving the kitten to chase its own tail in a puddle of midmorning sunshine.

After depositing the meager fruity offerings into the sink for washing, Ashlynne pulled on a breezy, light-green, ankle-length skirt, a tank top, and slipped her toes into a pair of leather sandals. Winding her long red hair up into a messy top knot, she headed to the minuscule bathroom that somehow managed to contain—not only the necessary toilet and sink—but a full-sized, antique claw-foot tub with shower attachment. Ashlynne adored the fact that there was a window at just about shoulder level that looked out on the courtyard. It was absolute bliss to stand under a cool spray of water with a breeze coming in through the window on a muggy summer night. Privacy wasn't a big concern to her since she wasn't the preferred type for Mr. Alvin's romantic company. It was a perfect arrangement as far as she was concerned.

Having brushed her teeth and rinsed off her face, she was just slathering on moisturizer with the prerequisite sunscreen for a light-skinned redhead when she became acutely aware of the space just behind her. Continuing as if nothing had changed, Ashlynne simultaneously smoothed the lotion up into her hairline while sending her thoughts outward to try and figure out what had caught her attention, or who—usually it was a 'who'. Flashes of images bloomed in her mind as she wiped her hands on the small towel hanging next to the sink: a low-slung, red sports car barreling down a rural highway, a pack of dogs that didn't look entirely like dogs, a large oak tree, children trick-or-treating in a small town. Each scenario burst into view in her mind's eye only to be replaced with the next one as soon as the image registered. Confused as to what she was seeing and why, Ashlynne slowly turned around to face the bathroom door and the kitchen beyond. Curled in a fetal position

just past the bathroom door was the figure of
a woman, about her own age, with dark
mahogany hair spilling over her face. Her
long legs—pulled up almost under her chin—
were clad in faded Levi's, and her purple
short-sleeved T-shirt was splotched with leaf
mold, twigs, and what appeared to be lichen.
Just as she was sure she was seeing the image
of a dead lady, the woman raised her head
and let her hair fall back against her
shoulders. Her eyes—huge and wide—were
black voids in her face, and her mouth
dropped open in a terrifying parody of the
iconic painting by Edward Munch. Though no
sound came out of the grotesquely elongated
mouth, and the eyes remained nothing but
black holes, Ashlynne was forced backward
two full steps by the power of the terror and
despair that the spirit sent out. Watching in a
horror due more to the emotions that she was
being buffeted with than the actual image of
the woman, Ashlynne found herself mirroring
the Spirit—reaching her arm out to the
woman as the woman was doing to her. The

need for help and the desire to offer it coalesced between the two, manifesting in a shimmering bubble that continued to hover in the small kitchen for several seconds after the spirit had faded away.

Feeling shaky and weak, Ashlynne moved heavily through the kitchen, then her bedroom, and finally into the front room to collapse onto the small sofa that sat facing the defunct, yet picturesque, fireplace that had once been the sole means of heating the Creole structure. Staring ahead without seeing what was in front of her, Ashlynne was mentally reliving each detail as it resurfaced— trying to make sense of it all. She was old enough to understand and accept that not every passing image, spirit, or unseen-by-the-general-public creature was looking for her personally or needed her help in any way. Her first impression of this encounter was that it was of that ilk—a passing spirit that she could see simply because she was able to see them. However, as the encounter continued it became clearer to her that this was not only personal but that this spirit needed help. But what kind of help? And what did the images that preceded her arrival mean?

The knock on her front door sent her jumping straight up in an almost comical startle reflex. Her heart's painful beating against her chest was not at all comical, and the hiccups the whole fright gave her were least funny of all. Muttering curse words under her breath, she opened the slats of the tall shutters that served as doors, only to see the openly friendly face of her across-the-street neighbor and best friend, Andrew, grinning at her.

"Hey, my Baby! Come outside!"

She opened the door and was enveloped in the warm embrace of one of the most genuine and good-hearted people she had ever known.

"Where's Chris?" She asked as she grabbed her sunglasses and headed out the door.

"He's gone to Mississippi to help his momma with the yard. I am a free agent for the whole weekend!"

Ashlynne laughed at the jest knowing that Andrew and Chris had one of those secure and comfortable relationships that most people only dream of.

Stepping off her small front stoop and crossing the narrow street to sit on Andrew's more expansive front porch, she accepted the glass of ice water he handed her and looked around their block. The tiny house—next to her own and across the street from where she sat—was curtained and dark now but, in a few hours, would be sending forth the neighborhood's background music of funky jazz trumpet arrangements as James began warming up for his nightly gig over on Frenchman Street. Next to that was the much more ornate double shotgun with its Victorian trim that housed the third generation of the family that resided there; it was also quiet now with Casey at work and the kids at school. Next to Casey's house stood the newly renovated Bed and Breakfast with a startlingly expensive nightly fee given the sketchy clientele that moved in and out at all hours of the day and night. On the other side of Andrew's stood a fully remodeled Double Gallery snatched up by a man from Dallas just after Katrina for a song, now worth quadruple what he paid for it. At the end of the block sat a small apartment complex that housed mostly film industry workers who migrated between New Orleans and Atlanta, depending on the show and the season. This small block, just outside the French Quarter and in the oldest African American community in the United States, was her home. Her friends and neighbors lived here, laughed here, and thrived here. Everyone looked after one another and worked to keep the more dangerous and seedy human elements that roamed the New Orleans' streets at bay.

Ashlynne felt Andrew watching her as she looked around but chose to ignore him until he broke her mental wanderings by nudging her knee with his sneaker.

"What gives? You're all lost in your head."

She smiled at him, and the concern on his face made her heart melt. It was only through these people that she knew and understood the concepts of 'family' and 'love'.

"Nothing much, just thinking about our 'hood (the term used jokingly between the two of them) and how lucky we are. I mean, every night—every. single. night. —there are muggings and beatings and murders and robberies and yet here, on this one small block, we're safe. It's pretty incredible, don't you think?"

"We're charmed, baby. Charmed. We also work hard to keep our 'hood this way, but yeah—you're right—this is pretty incredible."

The two friends sat in comfortable silence and enjoyed the gathering warmth of the late fall afternoon. Ashlynne felt a little guilty about not telling Andrew what happened, but she wasn't sure herself what had happened and couldn't figure out how to tell someone else about it until it was clear in her own head.

As the afternoon wore on, the citizens of the neighborhood began to emerge from their homes to wander to the corner gas station for smokes, the coffee house for a jolt of caffeine, or dressed to head into work. Downtown and the French Quarter moved on their own time and rhythm, with a large segment of the populace working the nighttime service industries. Ashlynne was one of them— Andrew, being mid-management in a chain retail store, was not. He was looking at a weekend off whereas Ashlynne was gearing up for her evening shift at a private Bourbon Street SpeakEasy.

"How did last night go? Were you in the Square or at the club?" Andrew asked her as he watched a lanky man, painted entirely in silver body paint, carry a fake dog and a plastic milk crate down the road headed toward North Rampart Street and the Quarter. The silver man lifted his free hand in greeting with Andrew and Ashlynne responding in kind.

"I was in the Square, and it was OK. Decent money and no real weirdos but a very nice older couple that made me sad."

"Why's that?"

"The husband is going to die in a few weeks."

Andrew could never quite wrap his head around these matter-of-fact announcements that came out of his best friend's mouth. It wasn't that he didn't believe her, but rather that the whole concept was so far removed from anything he had personally ever experienced that it was a shock every time it happened. And it happened a lot.

"Look, there's Mr. Alvin," Ashlynne said with a chuckle.

"Oh my... Is that....?"

"Yep! A rainbow beanie! Nice addition to the outfit!" The outfit in question was a silky Asian embroidered shorty night robe, the beanie, and nothing else.

Andrew looked horrified, but Ashlynne only grinned; 'characters' were what this part of the city was known for, and their block had them all beat.

"Is the dog with him?" asked Andrew, squinting at Mr. Alvin who was watering the cement urns full of flowers in front of the house.

Ashlynne looked at Andrew's screwed up face and crinkled eyes and laughed.

"You can either see them or not, sweetie. Mashing your face up like that won't help anything except to give you wrinkles by the time you're 30. But yes, the dog is with him. He's walking along the sidewalk just to Mr. Alvin's left."

"I hope he stays out of the road."

"Who? Mr. Alvin?"

"No! Beau! The cars go too fast down this street."

Ashlynne shot him an incredulous look. "Andrew Wilkins! Beau has been dead for over two years now, and you know it! Stepping into the street is no longer an issue for that dog. Poor thing should have thought of that a few years back…"

44

"Right," mumbled Andrew. "How am I supposed to get all of the rules straight to this stuff?! I mean, I can't see anything, but you say that Beau is still here and ..."

Ashlynne raised one eyebrow at him, something that she knew he hated because he couldn't do it himself. He mumbled something unintelligible and let the subject drop.

"Don't be upset. I know this can all get confusing—especially if you're lucky enough to be blind to most of it," she said and threw her arm around Andrew's shoulders. "Maybe we can figure out some way for you to see what I see someday."

Andrew shot her a sideways glance full of both curiosity and trepidation as Mr. Alvin in his shorty robe watered flowers accompanied by his ancient poodle who had been dead for two years. He wasn't sure if seeing would be helpful or terrifying.

A bright-yellow Jeep Cherokee pulled up in front of the porch, blocking their view of the man across the street and his deceased poodle. Andrew's landlord jumped out with a 'For Rent' yard sign and sketched a wave at the friends sitting on the porch. He jammed the sign into the small square of lawn to the left of them, jumped back into his car, and drove off down the street in the direction of the 1-10 overpass.

Ashlynne looked at Andrew who only shrugged.

"I guess he's getting serious about getting the apartment below me rented out. Can't blame him, but I really hope he brings someone in who's a good fit."

Ashlynne sat looking at the For-Rent sign knowing she was the only one who could see the dead leaves, twigs, and lichen that were adhered to the metal square. She tried to hide the feeling of dread that bubbled in her chest.

Andrew nudged her and pointed to a man who was dressed as Santa Clause walking a miniature horse on a leash down the street in front of them.

Chapter 4

The jukebox played a continuous loop of semi-obscure garage band songs straight out of the Seattle Grunge Scene as Morag watched the flotsam and jetsam that gravitated towards the dive bar move back and forth from the bar itself to the back room where a sofa that had seen better—and cleaner—days sat. The sofa, along with a few four-tops and some questionable decor, was visible from the bar where she nursed her drink—a strange concoction of a brown, fizzy liquid mixed with clear, sweet alcohol that she was very fond of. From her vantage point, she watched a young man lean over the arm of the sofa and vomit matter-of-factly into the corner beside him. The body she was inhabiting could tolerate what her Fae form could not from this world: iron, bright-neon lights, and alcohol to name a few. After a few mornings of being ill and head-achy, she had learned that, though her human form could tolerate alcohol, there was apparently a limit—one that guy seemed to have exceeded. Not liking the feeling of being ill, Morag sipped conservatively from her evening Rum and Coke. The slight buzz was enjoyable but kept her sufficiently alert to her surroundings. Because Morag was hunting.

She had made her way over the past few weeks from the scene of the car crash and her body-switch to the French Quarter of New Orleans. The energy pulsed ahead of her as she made her way, calling, beckoning, teasing. Along the way she had tested her new-found freedom of being in human form by staying at small road-side motor courts and glamoring the proprietors into believing the handful of dead leaves and twigs she proffered were the cash required to stay. Finding out that she still had her glamory skills was a very pleasant surprise indeed and, once discovered, were used frequently. The concepts of credit or debit cards were not familiar enough to her yet, but cash and money had been used by humans—and copied by The Fae as trickeries—for millennia. She was confident in her abilities to acquire anything she needed or wanted. And what she needed now were allies. With the Sluagh Sidhe being forced to return to their own realm when she pushed herself into the human, Morag was feeling the loss of her leadership position, and she was on the prowl for other Fae, preferably of the Unseelie Court.

"Want another?" The young man's voice broke her from her thoughts. Morag turned toward the sound and saw him—just a boy, really, standing behind her barstool and smiling at her hopefully. He wore the traditional 'my Daddy paid for this trip' attire: a salmon pink golf shirt with an embroidered lizard on the breast, madras plaid surf shorts, and loafers—sans socks. His dark hair flopped purposely over one eyebrow. Morag smiled as she realized that this boy had a remarkable resemblance to her human's ill-fated Rodger.

Seeing her smile, the young man took it as an affirmative answer and nodded to the bartender to replace her almost empty rum and coke.

"Thank you so much," crooned Morag in the syrupy Alabama voice she now had access to with this body. The voice was both promising and non-threatening, and Morag found it incredibly intriguing. Apparently so did the man standing next to her.

"Where are you from?" he asked her with a smile. His voice practically shouted MIDWEST! with its flat, nasally tones. There was nothing syrupy or seductive about it, but Morag smiled as if he had just dropped honeysuckle flowers from his lips.

"Alabama. I'm from Alabama," she answered and watched as he practically glowed. She was going to have fun with this one.

The jukebox began playing *All That She*

Wants by Ace of Base as if in direct defiance of the previous hour of Grunge, and Morag grabbed the boy's hand saying, "Let's dance! I love to dance!" She pulled him toward an empty space on the floor in front of the sofa. He grinned and allowed himself to be pulled. "What's your name? I don't know your name!"

"Amber! What's yours?" she shouted back over her shoulder.

"I'm Steve."

Steve smiled as the leggy, dark-haired girl twirled in front of him and gave him a welcoming grin. He imagined that this is what 'come hither' meant in those silly romance novels his grandma read. He shuffled closer— not being the best of dancers—and draped his arm over her shoulder. She looked up at him and smiled radiantly. Steve lost his rhythm as he noticed that her teeth were the strangest color—almost a moss green. He shook his head in confusion, was it the lights? He's sure he would've noticed that she had mossy teeth at the bar. As he stared in confusion, his vision became blurry, and his stomach lurched painfully. Wondering if someone had put something into his drink, he stepped back with the thought that he should sit down.

"Wow, I'm really not feeling well," Steve muttered in the general direction of Morag dressed as Amber. "I'm not sure what's happened, but I need to sit down."

"Oh no, Sweetie! Stay and dance with me! I love to dance!" trilled Morag as she gripped his hand and swayed to the music. Steve felt himself being dragged forcefully back towards the woman he was now very sorry he had ever talked to. Her eyes were too bright, her grip was too strong for such a thin hand, and her teeth! What was going on with her teeth? There seemed to be actual moss and black patches of mold growing on them. His vision wavered in and out, and he felt his body jerk and shuffle and sway in time with the music. He felt ill and scared and didn't want to dance, but his body seemed to be on a strange autopilot, completely beyond his control to stop. His feet moved to the beat of the song blasting from the jukebox; had someone turned up the volume? Why was it so loud? Steve tried to turn around and look at the lighted display, but he was incapable of turning away from the woman who gripped his hand. She smiled her mossy green smile and, in her eyes, he no longer saw a sweet Alabama girl but rather the cruel watchfulness of a hunting dog chasing its prey to the ground.

Steve opened his mouth, but nothing came out. His body spun, swayed, and moved of its own accord no matter the all-encompassing feeling of nausea and exhaustion that he felt. His vision wavered in and out—sometimes seeing the dirty sofa pushed up against the wall of the club and sometimes seeing a soft, lavender-lit landscape where trees grew to monstrous heights and dark sparkling bubbles bloomed and burst at intervals within their outstretched branches.

"Stop! Please stop!" Steve yelled as loud as

he could and realized two things: that no sound was coming from his mouth and the tears that ran down his face and dripped onto the floor were an alarming shade of red. The woman in front of him grinned wider as his body convulsed.

Gently, Morag reached out one slim hand towards Steve who continued to shimmy and gyrate in front of her, even as his eyes radiated terror, and gently touched him in the center of his forehead. Bright light exploded behind his eyes as he screamed a scream only he and the woman in front of him could hear. His eyes grew wide as he saw not the pretty dark-haired girl but a skinny wraith of a Being standing there instead. Moss, twigs, leaves, and dead bugs were stuck throughout her disheveled hair. He was certain he could just make out small horns sticking through the matted mess before his mind shut down completely and he floated away in comparatively blissful darkness.

Morag—as Amber—walked away from the gyrating young man shimmying to yet another song blaring from the bar's sound system—his eyes wide and blank, his mouth slack. The next morning the old lady that had the unenviable job of swabbing out the mess from the night before found what was left of Steve curled up on the floor surrounded by a ring of moss, mold, and dead leaves. The beetles that were still alive scuttled away from the macabre circle where their fellows lay strewn about like ghoulish confetti.

Chapter 5

A week had passed since Andrew's landlord had put up the For-Rent sign. Many lookers and interested people were going in and out, but the feeling of dread and fear that had taken up residence in Ashlynne's chest persisted as long as the trimmings on the sign of leaves, twigs, and bugs remained. She had a strong feeling that those strange decorations portended a very unusual tenant's arrival—one that would probably not fit in as well as Andrew had hoped. However, knowing that there was little to be done about the situation until it occurred, Ashlynne tried hard to put it aside and concentrate on her everyday world.

"Ouch!" She blinked rapidly to clear the tears welling up in her eye. Her elbow had slipped off the tiny bathroom sink resulting in a sharp poke by the eyeliner pencil. Blotting the tears with a tissue, she reapplied the under-eye concealer necessary after a long night at the Square and a longer night spent dodging nightmares once home and in bed. The eyeliner was expertly applied and winged outward just a tad, her hair straightened and brushed over one shoulder, and her look was almost complete for tonight's job. Donning a black rockabilly dress, ornate choker style necklace, and her favorite Doc Martens; she was all set.

"Not bad," she said to her reflection, showing in the full-length mirror in her living room. "Not bad at all."

"I like it, but..." interjected the older lady standing in the mirror's surface. Ashlynne had seen her right away but had been pretending not to in the hopes that the woman would go away. She didn't have a mean or aggressive vibe, but Ashlynne wasn't thrilled when uninvited dead people showed up in her house. It was rude.

"Can I help you?" she asked in the iciest tone possible.

"No, Dear. I saw your Light and thought I'd see who was here. You're very lovely, but are you sure that the dress isn't just a little too risqué?" asked the elderly lady in the mirror, dressed in a flour sack housecoat with her steel-gray hair pulled back in a bun at her neck. Not a speck of make-up adorned her skin.

"My Light is my own and not a signal to invade my house," snapped Ashlynne.

"Oh now! Don't be upset! It's so lonesome with no one to talk to and no one who can see me. When I saw you, I knew you could do both—it's a rare gift for both of us! My name is Mimi. Mimi Blanchard. What is your name, Dear?"

Seeing the spirit wasn't going to go anywhere soon, Ashlynne heaved a giant sigh full of annoyance and defeat that did nothing to extinguish the eager look on Mimi's face and dropped down onto the sofa.

"My name's Ashlynne Barrow."

"Barrow? Hmmm... That's not a name from here that I recall. Who are your people, Dear?"

"I don't have *people*—it's just me," she shot back. Seriously? How did this woman find her? She was sure she had shielded so that she couldn't be seen, but apparently this spirit could see through that. How annoying...

Grandmotherly concern washed over Mimi's face as she smiled gently at Ashlynne from the mirror. "I'm sorry, Dear. It must be hard not having a family."

"It's actually quite fine. I have done very well on my own and will continue to do so. I need to go to work now, Mimi. Thank you for the visit, but next time please ask before showing up."

And with that curt dismissal, Ashlynne stood up from the sofa signaling the end of the visit. Part of her felt bad for being so unwelcoming, but she had learned the hard way that if boundaries were not rigorously maintained, her home would soon be overrun with all manner of spirits looking to chat, looking for help, or just looking to cause trouble.

"Goodbye, Dear. Have a lovely night at work, but wear a sweater, please. It's going to get damp and foggy, and you'll catch your death of cold. I think we should visit more often—It's been so nice to have someone to chat with, and you having no people and all... well... we might be good for each other." The hopefulness in the spirit's voice broke Ashlynne's heart, and she felt herself caving.

"Good night, Mimi. I've enjoyed your visit, too."

Inside the mirror, the spirit of the older woman smiled, and Ashlynne grabbed a sweater on her way out the door.

Crossing North Rampart and entering the French Quarter, the energy changes abruptly. It takes Ashlynne by surprise every time she's on the Tremé side of the road for more than a couple of days. Deciding to take Ursuline down to Royal Street, she walked briskly and confidently in the gathering twilight. Her

impromptu chat with Mimi-in-the-mirror
caused her to leave the house later than she
planned, though she knew she wouldn't be
late to work; nothing really started on
Bourbon Street until after eight o'clock, and it
was only seven now. Plenty of time.
Remnants of memories and lost spirits drifted
past her face like cobwebs, and she fought the
desire to brush them away. The air was heavy
with them tonight, probably due to the
gathering fog coming off the river. Keeping
her shields up—no need for another chatty
ghost this evening—she walked past rows of
Creole cottages squatting on the flagstone
sidewalks with minuscule stoops leading to
closed and shuttered doors. To anyone else,
the street appeared to be quiet; it was almost
deserted except for the occasional cyclist
headed further into the Quarter or an
exhausted restaurant worker, identified by the
black and white checked Chef's pants,
staggering home to shower and have a beer
after a busy daytime shift. To Ashlynne, it

was anything but.

"What in the world?" she muttered to herself as a sewer rat with the face of an old man scuttled past her and headed into the narrow alley between two Row Houses. Fast on its heels was a creature with the head of a cat but the body of a large palmetto bug. Chills rolled up and down her body, and her arms broke out in goosebumps as she watched the bizarre creatures disappear between the houses. Shrugging into her sweater, and sending a silent *thank you* off to Mimi, Ashlynne started back on her way only to be met with a group of street kids sprawled aggressively across the sidewalk blocking her way. They weren't there before, and she wasn't sure when they arrived. She came to a skittering halt in front of the group. There were about eight of them, five males and three females, or that was her guess based on their clothing. She was positive that most people would see a group of dirty, disheveled young people with unwashed but human faces. Ashlynne wished she were one of those people. What she saw were human figures dressed in ratty jeans, military surplus boots, T-shirts, and army-green jackets. The females were each wearing short denim skirts with frayed hems and sported mermaid-blue dreads. All of this was normal. What was not normal at all were their faces, their skin, and their eyes. Their faces were long and narrow with sharply pointed chins, their skin dry, scaly, and yellow-green in color. Their eyes were horizontal slits with flaxen-yellow irises and death-black pupils. They did not seem to be able to blink. Ashlynne stared at the group while, at the same time, trying very hard to not let on what she was seeing. Unlike the groups that regularly sprawled on Lower Decatur Street, this group seemed not at all interested in letting her walk past them.

"I think Miss I-model-for-Trashy-Diva wants to pass! What do you think, Cam?"

Ashlynne watched as the lizard girl's thin, whip-fast tongue darted out of her lip-less mouth as she spoke to the male next to her.

"So, go ahead, pass!" jeered the lizard-faced male who was obviously Cam. And, while his tone was jovial-almost friendly, there was an undeniable undercurrent of menace that made Ashlynne's stomach lurch alarmingly.

"Yeah! Go ahead, girl! You can pass; we'll let ya!" This boomed from another male wearing an apple-red baseball cap with white block letters across the front.

"Why is the hat so clean?" wondered Ashlynne as the obscene red assaulted her eyes in direct opposition to the frayed and filthy tatters that covered the rest of his body.

Taking a deep breath, she pasted a non-confrontational smile onto her face and walked towards the group of lizard-faced creatures. Looking in their direction but focused past them to the point of the flagstones that were clear, she stepped as confidently as possible into the filthy mass sprawled across the banquette.

"Excuse me, thank you, sorry for that," she muttered as she walked past, and at times on, the Things blocking her way. Their hissing made her skin crawl, and she fought back the desire to turn and look behind her. Bile rose in her throat, and she choked it down knowing that to throw up now would not only be messy and embarrassing if any actual humans happened by but more than likely deadly for her once the Lizard Punks knew she could see them. One final step over the Lizard Girl with the Mermaid hair and she would be past them.

"Nice boots," the words slithered out of the blue-haired lizard's mouth, and Ashlynne yelped in panic as she felt the dry, leathery hand wrap itself around her leg, the long nails scratching at her skin.

"Thanks, I like yours too!" stammered Ashlynne as she tried to move her leg, but the lizard held fast.

"I have to get to work. I'm late, and I don't want to be in trouble. I've only been there a couple of days, and I NEED this job!" finished Ashlynne in desperation as the words flew out of her mouth in a panicked jumble. Her heart fluttered in her chest as she tried to not let on that she could see what they really looked like. As she continued to pull her leg away the lizard girl suddenly let go, and Ashlynne went stumbling forward past them and into a Crepe Myrtle tree planted along the curb. She clutched the smooth bark to keep from falling flat on her face as rude laughter erupted behind her.

"Oops! Sorry 'bout that!" the blue-haired lizard girl hissed from behind her. "Better run along now—you'll be late for work."

Ashlynne was too terrified to feel anything but relief as she moved shakily down the flagstones toward the corner of Royal Street.

"Oh my God, what was that about?" she thought as she concentrated on putting one foot solidly in front of the other to avoid running full tilt to the corner, which is what her body was telling her to do.

"And not just the Lizard Punks but the rat and cat things, too?" One foot, then the other, slow and steady away from the group as the thoughts ran through her head. *"Not ghosts—*

definitely not human." One foot, then the other, and around the corner onto Rue Royal where she slid down the ancient bricks of the building to squat very unlady-like against the wall as her heart boomed and thumped in her chest. She gulped the fog-thickened air and tried very hard to get herself together, which was proving more difficult than she could have imagined.

Finally, taking baby steps towards pulling herself together, Ashlynne scooched herself back up the wall so she was standing, rather than squatting, on the pavement. Taking one more deep breath, she squared her shoulders and turned to walk down Royal deeper into the French Quarter. Just then her phone vibrated against her hip where it was stashed in the pocket of her dress. The text coming in showed Andrew's face next to the number.

Andrew: *New Neighbor Now.*

Ashlynne: *Wait, what? When did this happen? I only just left.*

Andrew: *I dunno, I got home from work and the sign is gone.*

Ashlynne: *IDK, are you sure it's a new person? Maybe someone just stole the sign.*

Andrew: *Nope. Lots of noises and moving around down there. And I think they have a bunch of dogs.*

Ashlynne: *Weird. No boxes or anything? And why do you think they have a bunch of dogs?*

Andrew: *IKR? And because I can hear a lot of yapping and growling, that's why.*

Ashlynne: *OK, have to get to Bourbon and to work, running late. Let me know what else you hear or see.*

Andrew: *Have a good night—love you.*

Ashlynne smiled at her friend's parting line only to have her smile wiped away just as fast as she contemplated the news of a new neighbor. No moving boxes but lots of dogs. Ugh.

With her mind a-whirl with the strange-even-for-her happenings of late, Ashlynne continued into the Quarter to Bourbon Street.

Wandering down Royal past the famously whimsical wrought iron gate of corn, past gift shops both high end and decidedly not, crowned by stately ferns hanging from the upper balconies, Ashlynne enjoyed the relative normalcy of this street. The girl playing an electric violin at the entrance to Café Amalie provided just enough of a boho vibe without any of the threatening weirdness that had presented itself earlier.

Turning onto Saint Ann Street then onto the famous—or infamous—Bourbon Street, Ashlynne felt the energy of the never-ending party wash over her like a wave. Later, as the night wore on, the gentle wave of energy would turn into a tsunami of craziness, but for now, it was low key and benevolent. She waved at a horse-mounted police officer as she stepped up to the entrance of the nondescript Jazz Club in the center of the block. The pretty woman at the door smiled in greeting and let her pass when Ashlynne provided the nightly password. The live band played a traditional tune—heavy on the horns—as people of all shapes, sizes, and ages sat in rapt attention on the no-frills wooden benches lined up before the tiny stage. Drinks in hand, they swayed, tapped their feet, and held up their cell phones to capture it all on video for friends back home. Scooting past the horn player, Ashlynne pushed her way through a set of ancient, wooden double doors and into a charming courtyard completely hidden from the street. These secret gardens within the crumbling structures of the French Quarter never failed to enchant her. Turning to the staircase, she began the climb up to yet another hidden gem where she was lucky enough to have garnered a part-time job as the house Tarot Card Reader, and sometimes, Cocktail Waitress. The semi-private, Vampire-themed club—that guests could only access with the nightly password given to the lady at the door of the Jazz Club—kept the vibe of a prohibition-era Speakeasy and kept the hordes of crazy to a minimum. Leaning down to pet the two resident cats—both gorgeous tangerine Tabbies that lived on the staircase in stunning feline decadence—Ashlynne crooned her hellos and was rewarded with arched backs and deep purrs. Wishing she could hole up on the stairs with the cats for a while, she sighed, stood up, and entered the bar to begin her shift.

"Helloooooo!" she called out as she walked into the front salon of the club. The small bar wrapped around in a u-shape starting in the front salon and ending in the back lounge. Deep-purple velvet sofas and divans were scattered in intimate groups, and fringed lamps cast a low and mellow light throughout. Beautiful antique Persian rugs lay beneath the sumptuous sofas, and on the far wall of windows facing Bourbon Street, amazing purple and gold theater drapes that probably cost more than Ashlynne made in a year muted the party below. Ornately framed classical nudes hung here and there finishing

the look and feel of decadent Old New
Orleans with a Vampire flare.

"Hey, Girl! Good to see you!" called Lee as
she muscled two five-gallon plastic buckets of
ice into the waiting bin.

"Hi! Good to be seen," Ashlynne replied
with a smile. Lee was the main bartender and
manager extraordinaire who kept customers,
live entertainers, and the assorted private
events the owner was so fond of scheduling
running smoothly and successfully.

"Where do you want me tonight?"

"Let's start you out as a Reader. There's a
bachelorette party showing up tonight and
they've all asked about Readings. Sandy is
coming in tonight, too, so she can handle the
waitressing side of things."

"Sounds good, thanks," said Ashlynne.
'And sounds like some good cash.' she thought to
herself as she moved to the small alcove just
to the right of the back lounge. This small
space held the entry to the back of the bar, the
liquor, the doors to the balcony, and the small
table where Readers set up for clients. There

was also a little girl named Christine who played back here, her long white nightgown showing the stains from the illness that killed her in 1903. Most of the workers and quite a few patrons were aware of her and brought small dolls, blocks, a ball or two, and even hard candy for the little ghost who has chosen to stay on in the attic where she and her sisters died so long ago.

Ashlynne shook the black tablecloth off and laid it back on the table, now free of crumbs. Reaching into her bag she took out her cards, the large crystal point, and a dried alligator head. These she arranged in the center of the two-top and turned her attention to Christine. The small girl was sitting cross-legged in the corner, holding a doll from her own time, and singing a lullaby in French. The toys gifted to her from this time period were stacked in a basket next to her. Ashlynne hoped she wasn't lonely, but Christine had so far refused any offer to move on to join her family, so here she stays. She peeked up at Ashlynne from under dark brown bangs and smiled shyly. Ashlynne smiled back and blew her a kiss.

"Here we go!" called Lee as a group of fifteen young women flowed into the club from the bar below, all wearing matching white tank tops dotted with pink glittered lips, pink short-shorts, high heels of various styles, pink and white feather boas, and blinking plastic tiaras. The bride-to-be sat down across from Ashlynne with a flourish, chanting "Me first! Me first!" to her ladies-in-waiting who had gathered at the bar for drinks. Ashlynne smiled at the girl sitting across from her, noting the stuffed penis headband she wore and tried not to laugh out loud. She didn't need to be psychic to know that it was going to be a long night.

Chapter 6

O pening the front door, Ashlynne drew in a deep breath of refreshingly cool air. She wasn't sure how long this lovely fall weather would last but the opportunity to wear a real sweater, even if it was a lightweight cotton, was blissful after such a long, hot summer. November was looking to be glorious.

"C'mon! We're going to be late!" yelled Andrew from the open driver's side window of his little, red VW.

Knowing his next step would be to start blaring the car's horn, Ashlynne hurriedly locked the shutters and hopped down the short group of steps toward the waiting car and her impatient friend.

"I'm coming for heaven's sake! What's the

big hurry?" she asked as she opened the passenger side door and slid into the car.

"Buckle," ordered Andrew as he put the car into drive and shot down the road toward the I-10 over-pass.

"Geeze! What's got you so grumpy?!" demanded Ashlynne as Andrew made a series of sharp stops, starts, and turns and seemed to intentionally hit every pothole in the road.

"Ouch!" she yelped pitifully as the car dropped into a large crater causing her to bite her tongue painfully.

"Sorry," he muttered around a jaw-cracking yawn. "The new neighbor has been pretty loud the last few nights, and we haven't gotten any sleep. Work has been crazy with the holiday sales, and I just really want to get to the Park and inside before the lines get so long that we spend most of our night waiting to get tickets."

Her friend sounded so wiped out Ashlynne felt bad about giving him a hard time.

"I'm sorry. What's with the new neighbor?

Music? TV volume?"

"Dogs, I think," replied Andrew as he squinted at the traffic ahead.

"Dogs? Exactly how many dogs does the neighbor have? And is this neighbor a male or female? You haven't said."

"It sounds like a whole pack of them down there and maybe some other pets too—I'm really not sure. As soon as it's dark, the noise starts, and we can't get any sleep. It's awful. I think she's a she—it's a woman's voice I think, but I haven't actually seen anyone yet."

"You think? How do you not know if it's a woman's voice, Andrew?"

Andrew yawned widely again, "I don't know, and quit quizzing me. It's all so fuzzy as soon as it's dark. So much noise, a few different voices, but when I try to hear what they're saying it just sounds like a bunch of dogs again. I'm just so tired…"

Ashlynne shot a sideways glance at her friend, distressed to note the dark circles under his eyes and the sallow color of his skin.

"Has Chris heard all of this too?"

"Yeah—we both can hear all of it but can't agree on what we're hearing; dogs, a woman, a group of people..." He shrugged with annoyance and turned on the radio signaling, rather obviously, that he didn't want to talk about it anymore.

Cheesy Christmas Carols blared from the car's speakers as Ashlynne watched the changing scenery creep past. Each neighborhood in New Orleans had its own distinct look and feel, just one of the things she loved about this place. Right now, they were rolling into MidCity and toward the immense greenery that is City Park. Just a few miles from her house and yet an immeasurable distance in atmosphere. The houses, while still urban, had larger lawns, and there were more trees and foliage. Bayou St John, where the famed Marie Laveau held her public rituals, offered a serenity not found in the more hard-scrabble lower Tremé and French Quarter neighborhoods. As different as they were, Ashlynne would be hard-pressed to choose a favorite, though she suspected that the Quarter was in her blood now; she as much a part of it as its flagstones and balconies.

Andrew navigated the small car around groups of families and teenagers all moving toward the entrance of the thirteen hundred acres of twinkling lights, storybook tableaus, and holiday characters. By the time he had parked and was swept up in the human stream of holiday revelers, Andrew's color had improved, his eyes were less droopy, and his shoulders had relaxed.

"Feeling a little better?" Ashlynne asked her friend as she slipped her arm under his.

"I am, it's happy here. I love this time of year."

Ashlynne smiled at this because, in truth, Andrew and Chris loved any time of year that involved a holiday. Easter found them throwing stuffed bunnies from the French Quarter Easter Parade float they manned every year, Mardi Gras had them dressed in their most dapper Southern-gentlemen's suits and bow ties attending dinners, cocktail parties and balcony gatherings with equally pretty people that Ashlynne only knew by their first name. These were not soirees that she was a part of, but she adored hearing about the gatherings from her friends. Halloween was a favorite of all of theirs, and they spent hours and hours dressing and securing a menagerie of plastic skeletons to the railings and chairs of the porch. Spooky lights, ghouls, and cobwebs draped here and there and completed the look. Across the street at Casey's family's porch, the decor vied with theirs for its uniqueness and style with a year's long good-natured rivalry having been established. But nothing and no one could compete with Andrew's and Chris's Christmas porch. Ashlynne learned a while ago to just follow directions on this one and in no way get in the middle of the annual bickering between the two men about light placement or tree trimmings. She sat on the stoop below the upper porch—where they argued back and forth about whether the lights were strung evenly—and fluffed the artificial garlands while watching the neighborhood people wander by. It always amused her that they came to almost-verbal blows each holiday, all the while knowing that their porch was going to be breathtakingly gorgeous no matter what simply because the two of them couldn't NOT make it amazing.

Having paid the entrance fee, the two friends moved into the park. The lights that adorned the towering Live Oaks made the already beautiful park a magical place in the gathering twilight. Families with small children moved toward the miniature train and the entrance to Storyland, while young adults on dates strolled hand in hand and kissed in the shadows of the Spanish moss that dripped from the magnificent Oaks. The evening air whispered against her face as the gathering night turned the sky a soft purple that can only be found in New Orleans. Wandering arm in arm through the families and the couples, not fitting in with any of them and yet somehow perfectly a part of them all, Ashlynne thought about how wonderful this city was despite its obvious hardships of crime and poverty. Moving deeper into the park, the air became warmer and thicker. The crowds had died down, having dispersed to the more obvious Holiday displays located in other niches of the far-flung acreage.

Andrew was humming yet another Christmas Carol under his breath while Ashlynne continued her mental musings about her love affair with the city when, suddenly, she came to an abrupt halt causing Andrew to yank her arm painfully.

"What?!" he exclaimed, having been taken by surprise by their sudden stop. He turned around and saw Ashlynne staring straight ahead, eyes wide and mouth open in small O of surprise. Andrew let go of her arm which dropped down against her side and looked to where she was staring. He saw nothing but another of the huge trees that the park was famous for. While certainly awesome, his friend had seen them often enough to not respond like this. That left only one other option for this weirdness; she was seeing something he could not. He stood still and waited. After a couple of seconds where nothing changed, he gently spoke her name. Again, nothing. Her eyes didn't blink, and her mouth remained open in that small O of surprise. He took her hand very carefully and tried to move her off the path, but she seemed as rooted in place as the massive tree she stood staring at.

Ashlynne was vaguely aware of her arm being tugged as she stopped cold at the sight shimmering in front of her. Andrew's voice sounded far away and full of concern, but she couldn't answer. In front of her at the trunk of the massive two-hundred-year-old tree Ashlynne saw the watery picture of the dark-haired girl she had seen in her bathroom a

few weeks ago. Her face was still horribly
distorted—like a picture that had been
stretched lengthwise, confusing her features—
but this time she was standing and looking
around her at other trees in another place. The
limbs were dark and hung low with twigs and
branches that were sharp and dangerous
looking, not soft, and romantic like the moss-
draped trees to this side. The scene wavered
in and out like Ashlynne was looking through
water or a very old mirror that the silver
backing had worn away from. Were the trees
on that side really moving, or did it only look
like that from here? From the way the dark-
haired young woman moved in a panicked
circle, Ashlynne guessed the trees were,
indeed, moving. In fact—they seemed to be
closing in on her. Did trees hunt? And where
was this place that she was seeing? The young
woman in the purple shirt didn't seem to
belong there, wherever 'there' was. As
Ashlynne watched the nightmare scene
playing out in front of her, and Andrew grew
more and more distressed, bright lights began

to gather within the shadows of the predatory trees and float towards the woman. Beautiful as they were, Ashlynne knew without a doubt that they were bad news and moved forward with a choked scream. As soon as she moved in to help, the shimmering space at the trunk of the Live Oak disappeared as if it had never been there. Ashlynne shot forward, her hands pressing against the rough bark of the massive tree muttering, "No, no. No, no—where are you! Where did you go?!" Andrew watched in confusion and no small amount of fear. He had seen his friend trance out (his phrase for it) on more than a few occasions as she saw or communicated with things he couldn't, but nothing like this. He had never seen her be so frightened and confused.

"Stop baby, stop," Andrew whispered in his slow southern drawl as he gently gathered her up and moved her away from the oak. Ashlynne continued to try to move back to the tree but Andrew held her fast. Finally giving up, she slumped against him, her eyes wide, as her mind moved over and over what she had seen: a thin place and opening to somewhere else, and the same girl who had shown up in her bathroom, but where and who was she?

Morag gazed into the mirror above the sink in the small bathroom of her new apartment. It was surprisingly easy to have gained entrance; the landlord's mind was easily bendable, and he currently believed with his whole being that he had a signed lease and a year's rent paid in full from a young woman named Amber Foster.

As Morag watched, the images of her new neighbors wavered in and out of view. The young man who lived above her was tugging on the girl's arm who lived across the street. The girl was staring straight ahead at the trunk of the ancient Live Oak which — to Morag's view — shimmered and sparked with green and silver light.

"Ahhh... she's found one!" muttered Morag as she watched Ashlynne stare into the portal. "I knew this girl would be an interesting human, but I had no idea *how* interesting. This is going to be fun!" The Faerie smiled with glee, her rotted teeth still so surprising in such a pretty human face.

Moving away from the mirror and out into the narrow hallway, Morag stepped on several roaches that had the misfortune to have not moved out of her way fast enough. Their crushed bodies oozed up between her bare toes. Entering the main living room and kitchen in the middle of the apartment, she opened the window and sent out a silent call. Throughout the block mice and rats of all sizes heeded the summons and headed to the house in The Tremé as the mold continued its enthusiastic growth within it.

"I think I'll be liking it here," said Morag to the mangy dog laying by the debris-covered sofa she had brought in by her new-found friends. The filthy furnishing had been spotted sitting by the side of the street in the French Quarter, having been used as a temporary sleeping spot by the homeless and drunks who wandered the neighborhood. The dog bared its teeth in warning as Morag reached down to pet it. Feeling the force of the Faerie's hand on its head, the dog, long a survivor of a street dog's life, erred on the side of caution and gave up its attempt at viciousness. Whimpering softly, it laid its head down on the filthy tiles, closed its eyes, and dreamed of its life as it once had been— green grass in a suburban yard, his own humans to play with, enough food to eat, and a warm, safe place to sleep every night. At least now he was off the streets, but it was dangerous here too. The Being that looked human was not, and he was unsure how to react to it. His whole body screamed out a warning that he should have run far away by now but, like the Faerie, he too could see the shimmering energy around the girl across the street. He had never seen anything like it, and it spoke to him of safety and comfort. He would stay here for now and keep watch on the girl; Murphy missed having a human to care about.

Chapter **7**

Ashlynne woke with a start, sweat beads popping out on her brow and chest.

"What the hell was that?!" she panted as she grappled with her runaway heartbeat and tried to catch her breath.

The thin, early-morning light filtered through the window above her bed, and the sounds of the neighborhood kids walking up the sidewalk towards the school a few blocks away told her it was about seven o'clock in the morning. Glancing at her watch proved her guess to be correct and helped her to feel more grounded and *here*—less a part of the horrid dream that didn't seem like a dream at all.

Once her heartbeat returned to normal, she sat up and straightened the blankets around her legs. She thought she must have been thrashing around quite a bit because the sheets and blankets were all twisted and bunched. Once they were untangled and laying smoothly across her legs which were crossed lotus style, she gathered in a deep breath, held it for a count of three, then slowly let it out feeling her body settle into itself. Closing her eyes, she carefully summoned up the images of the dream that had propelled her so forcefully from sleep.

In the dream, she was in Jackson Square at her table with her cards, crystal, and incense set up as they always were. Tourists milled about under a huge Halloween full moon, and a small boy played a staccato beat using an overturned plastic pickle bucket as a drum under the streetlamp to her right. The sharp, erratic beat made her feel anxious and seemed somehow ominous in its lack of cohesion— like chaos made audible.

The feeling of 'something coming' became overpowering, and still dreaming, she stood up from her chair to look behind her trying to figure out what was approaching and why she was feeling so nervous. Behind her, she heard the scraping of a chair and turned around to see a woman seating herself in the place provided for customers. While the young woman was physically attractive with long dark hair, tall and willowy in a way Ashlynne has always wanted to be, the feeling of absolute dread that washed over her from the woman's physical presence caused her knees to buckle and her stomach to lurch alarmingly. At that moment Ashlynne knew what prey felt like.

The young boy's rhythm continued faster and faster—her heartbeat made public.

The woman smiled, and Ashlynne felt ill. The teeth within the smile were black, green, and sharply pointed. As she watched, the young woman's pretty face shimmered and rearranged itself, the features becoming more angular, the skin losing its olive tan and becoming a gray-green. Her hair lost its mahogany sheen and seemed to crinkle upon itself, becoming ratty and tangled. Small horns poked their way through, and twigs, dried leaves, and dead bugs seemed to materialize within the mass of tangled hair.

While the image was disturbing, it was the feeling that Ashlynne had from the presence of this woman that was by far the worst: pure dread. The feeling of being found again, and that she wouldn't be able to escape. It settled into her like molten lead, making her heart race painfully with its fight or flight reaction, but her limbs and brain became dead-weight. She was like a car stuck in park with the gas pedal to the floor—if cars could feel terror, that is.

The woman reached across the table and very carefully moved the crystal off the top of the deck of cards, yet it promptly cracked in half. Centipedes flowed out and over it, racing off the table and out of the pool of light from the streetlamp. The young boy's sharp drumming became impossibly fast, and as Ashlynne watched, the Faerie turned over the card at the top of the deck. The Tower card flew upwards as if it had wings of its own, flapping and twirling in the space between them. The Faerie smiled, and a huge oak tree pushed its way up through the flagstones behind her, its branches alive with rats. In the ringing silence where the young boy's drumming used to be, Ashlynne began to scream as the Faerie laughed…

Ashlynne opened her eyes and drew in a deep breath. *'Just a dream,'* she said firmly to herself though she wasn't feeling it. The symbolism was too specific, the feelings too defined to be 'just a dream' though that is what she desperately wanted it to be.

Making her way into the kitchen to start her much needed coffee, Ashlynne continued to wonder about it, especially the feeling of having been found *again.* To her knowledge she had never seen nor encountered anything or anyone like the Being in the dream—*'the Faerie',* her brain corrected her. Yes. The

Faerie. And that was another thing, how did she know it was a Faerie? She'd never had any interest in fairies; those new-age, winged cherub things that flitted from flower to flower held no appeal for her in their saccharin, never-ending sweetness. But this Faerie was none of those things; there was no fake saccharine sweetness, no wings, and certainly no flitting.

"Hell, if that woman touched a flower the petals would probably turn black and fall off," muttered Ashlynne as she added cream to her coffee and headed out to the courtyard.

Seating herself at her normal place at the courtyard table, Ashlynne spied the rescued Calico, now more cat than kitten, playing with a small lizard under the banana tree. "I feel ya, dude," said Ashlynne as she stood up to shoo away the tiny predator. The Calico shot her a withering glance full of betrayal as the lizard raced away, up and around the trunk of the tree to safety.

"Sorry, honey," she said to the cat as it

threw its tail upward in a haughty display of annoyance and walked away toward the gate separating the courtyard proper from the ally that led to the street out front.

Settling back down with her coffee, the dream still front and center in her thoughts, Ashlynne shuddered at the memory of the fluttering, flying Tower card. She knew—and often counseled her clients—that while a ruthless energy, The Tower ultimately made room within one's life for new situations and fresh growth. However, this did not bear out the feeling of the dream—the Tower card-come-to-life seemed to embody the worst of the card's attributes: destruction, upheaval, chaos, and terror. Getting up to pour herself another cup of coffee, she saw the, now safe, lizard watching her from a large leaf on the banana tree and sketched it a fast salute with the empty coffee cup, "Cheers, little one."

Three cups of coffee later, Ashlynne began to feel less betwixt and between: less a foot in her dream and more both feet in the here and now. She didn't have to work until later tonight, so she decided a neighborhood outing was called for. Pulling on a well-loved pair of Levi's, a seen-better-days Nirvana t-shirt, and her trusty flip flops, Ashlynne moved over to the full-length mirror to pull her hair back and put on her sunscreen. As she smeared the white lotion over her forehead and down her cheeks, she caught sight of a gray-haired woman peeking at her from around the interior of the mirror's frame—Mimi. Closing her eyes, she took a deep breath and said, "Hello Mimi, I can see you in there."

"Oh! Hello Dear! I was just passing by and saw you were at home."

Ashlynne laughed, "You were just passing by my mirror located in my house and saw I was here?! That's a good one, Mimi!"

"You know perfectly well that this side of the mirror is not in your house," replied the spirit with a wounded tone of voice. "I would never invade your privacy, Dear!"

Ashlynne hid a smile because invading her

privacy was exactly what Mimi had been doing, but the older woman was growing on her and she had little energy left right now to banish a wayward spirit.

"You look tired, Dear. Did you not sleep well?"

Ashlynne gasped in amazement as the very proper woman in her mirror pulled up a straight-backed chair from just outside the mirror's frame and had a seat. Having situated herself, she took a pack of unfiltered Chesterfield Kings out of her housecoat's pocket, flicked a match against her side of the mirror—producing an interesting flame on Ashlynne's side—and lit her cigarette. Inhaling deeply, the spirit said, "Close your mouth, Dear—flies will get in."

"Wait! You smoke?!"

"Well, I *did* and so I *do.* Why are you so surprised?"

"I've never seen a ghost smoking," replied Ashlynne as she eyed the mirror suspiciously. "You are a ghost, right?"

"Ghost, Spirit, Specter—sure. Most of us

enjoy the same things over here that we did on your side, the same foods, drinks, vices, colors, music, and people. Why do you think altars are set with flowers and incense and pieces of jewelry? Even cigars, food, candy, and wine? It draws us to this realm, Dear. Not all of us are as lucky as me to have found someone with a Light. Though it wouldn't be missed to have a bottle of root beer show up in your house occasionally, you know."

"Gotcha—root beer. Sure you wouldn't want whiskey or rum?"

"Oh no! A lady wouldn't ever drink in public! What are you thinking, Ashlynne?!"

"Gee, I have no idea. Perish the thought," replied Ashlynne looking hard at Mimi's cigarette. Apparently, standards were a bit different from Mimi's time because the spirit seemed not to notice the very pointed stare at the smoldering paper-wrapped tobacco she held in her right hand.

"So, do you want to tell me why you look so tired?" asked Mimi between deep inhales and leisurely exhales. To Ashlynne's dismay, she seemed to have settled in for a very long chat.

"I don't right now, actually. I need to get outside and shake some of this off then get ready for work."

"Ok, Dear—next time we can chat longer. We have things to talk about, I think," mused Mimi who seemed suddenly distracted and not at all chatty like she was just a few minutes ago. The older woman watched a cloud of smoke disappear above the top rim of the mirror's frame then she stood up suddenly, ground out her cigarette on a non-existent floor, and looked directly at Ashlynne for the first time in several minutes. Her gaze stopped Ashlynne cold. Her voice, a very un-Mimi-like and monotone droned from the mirror,

"She's here. The rats and roaches follow her. The lizard-faced ones are her own."

And with that, the older woman turned and walked off past the left side of the mirror's frame and out of Ashlynne's view. The stubbed-out cigarette still smoldered slightly next to the empty chair in the middle of her mirror.

Wishing that by now she was immune to the craziness of ghosts, strange dreams, and visions, Ashlynne turned away from the mirror and headed out her front door. Turning left, she ambled down to the corner passing several Creole Cottages similar to the one she lived in, a building of small apartments, and a single shotgun home covered almost entirely in kudzu vines with the faded Katrina numbers still showing painted in once-vibrant orange on the clapboards to the right of the front door. The numbers told the tale of the one body found within. The gentleman that used to occupy that body still occupied the home and could be seen, day in and day out, sitting on his front stoop with his cats surrounding him — some perished in the storm with their human, while others were alive and well, living in the otherwise abandoned home.

Turning left onto North Robertson Street, Ashlynne began to slow her pace and calm down a little. Moving always helped, be it walking, yoga, or dancing. Concentrating on her physical body helped to get her out of her head and think more clearly. After several more blocks, she made another left to stand in front of a nondescript building with the door situated at a corner angle. The veve of Erzulie Dantor was painted on the interior of an open wooden slab door standing out garishly in its bright red against the teal blue. The perfect symmetry of the ancient symbol filled Ashlynne with equal parts comfort, respect, and fascination. While not an initiate, or even a regular practitioner of Voodoo, she felt a real affinity and closeness to several of the Spirits of that Path and often visited this small neighborhood botanica for candles, incense, herbs, or to simply touch base and feel part of something larger than herself. She crossed the threshold and felt an immense weight bear down upon her; her vision became blurry, her head throbbed with pain, and her limbs felt leaden. Ashlynne shook her head and tried another step but simply had no strength. As she stood there, rooted in place and trying to figure out what had happened and how to fix it, Mambo Michele came rushing towards her from the back room. Without a word, she gathered Ashlynne up, shuffled her over to a small wooden stool, and plopped her down upon it. With her head hanging below her shoulders and her arms hanging limply by her side, Ashlynne seriously wondered whether she had the strength to stay on the wooden seat, but somehow she managed it.

Muttering to herself in Haitian-accented English, Mambo Michele circled Ashlynne. She stopped, ran her hands over the space just aside from Ashlynne's physical body, nodded, circled, muttered some more. Ashlynne lost count of how many times Michele circled her, stopped, felt outward, and circled again, but after about 2 minutes of this, the older woman stopped in front of Ashlynne and clapped her hands sharply in front of her face.

"Where you been at?!" Michele demanded.

"Where have I been? I've been at home. What's going on? I feel sick, and you're acting like a crazy person!" Ashlynne shot back at her friend.

"This space is protected—you know this. And still, you try and come in here with ... With this... This..."

More arm waving from the fierce Haitian, "*dirt* all over you!" she finished in a rush.

"Dirt? I am not dirty! I showered this morning!" Ashlynne replied, feeling both hurt and annoyed.

"There is dirt. And bugs. And dead leaves. Where you been?!"

"I have not been anywhere!" Ashlynne swiveled her head around trying to see where dirt and leaves and bugs might be on her but could see nothing. "*Really,*" she thought "*this is crazy, and more crazy is NOT what I need today!*"

"You can't just look and see it," snorted Michele to Ashlynne. "It's around you but from somewhere else. Again, where have you been?"

Ashlynne's eyes got big and round, and the color drained from her face as it sunk in—dirt, dead leaves, bugs. All these things she had seen around the For-Rent sign at Andrew's. All these things she had seen gathered in the Faerie's hair in her dream.

"Oh Michele," groaned Ashlynne, her voice low and full of dismay. "I think there is real trouble happening, and I don't know what to do."

The Priestess watched the young woman in front of her, usually so full of sass and fire, sink further within herself and become less than what she used to be. "*Unacceptable. This is unacceptable,*" she thought as she watched the dirt and leaves swirl around the room.

"Come!" she announced and pushed Ashlynne ahead of her toward the back of the shop. "We are going to fix you up. Whatever is happening can't be worked with until you are clean." Pushing the young woman through the beaded curtain and into the back room, Michele put on a brave face. What she was seeing, and feeling, was strange, powerful, and very much not a part of here. It made her wary, but a cleansing could be done, and that would be the best way to start.

She plopped the young woman down onto a chair and began bustling about gathering supplies: candles, a large feather, salt, a lime, a sharp knife that made Ashlynne cringe and Michele laugh in response, and a cut crystal bowl that was filled with spring water from a labeled plastic bottle.

Michele turned her back to Ashlynne and began arranging and preparing the gathered items that she had placed on a small table covered in a white cotton cloth. Lighting the candle, she began reciting the old prayers and chants, entreating her Spirits to come and help with the cleansing. She deftly sliced the lime in half, dropped it into the water, and added additional herbs and flowers that would be most useful. Finishing her preparations, she turned to the once fiery young woman, and holding the crystal bowl in front of her, said firmly, "We will begin."

Ashlynne watched as her friend moved toward her carrying the bowl and the feather and wished she felt more confident in what this would accomplish. Sighing heavily, she closed her eyes as Michele began chanting and singing in her musical Haitian cadence—the words unknown, but the power of them cascading over her as the lime-scented water tickled her arms.

As the Priestess continued her ministrations, Ashlynne felt herself enter that place between sleep and wakefulness, floating along with the soft chanting yet incredibly aware of every sensation—from the sharp citrus scent of the limes to the soft brush of the feather against her legs. Images played out against her closed eyelids: the small boy beating his plastic bucket drum from her dream, the lizard faced homeless in the French Quarter, and a small dung-colored dog she had never seen before. Ashlynne continued to float along carried by the rhythmic chants. She watched each scene come together from mist then dissolve like the same only to be replaced by another. The faster Michele chanted, the faster the images floated in, coalesced, and dissolved again until suddenly the image that gathered behind her closed eyes was of the dark-haired girl—features still horribly distorted. Ashlynne caught her breath but didn't open her eyes. Michele noticed the change in her young friend, and now client, and chanted faster and with more force. For Ashlynne the image became incredibly sharp. The young woman could have been standing physically in front of her for all the detail that could be seen. Michele's chanting, now severe and commanding, continued faster and faster, and the image began to waver as if a pebble had been tossed into a small pond disrupting the reflection within, her features becoming even more distorted. As the original image wavered out of view, it began to be replaced with another. Ashlynne's heart pounded rapidly, and Michele's chanting became impossibly fast as the visage of the Faerie came into view. The gray-green skin, sharp and pointed features, and the rotted teeth all bloomed in Technicolor behind Ashlynne's closed eyes. As she watched with a feeling of mounting dread, the Faerie focused her eyes and looked directly at Ashlynne. Reaching out one narrow arm, she pointed her finger and smiled, and Ashlynne knew without a doubt that the Faerie could see her.

With a loud shout and a command in a language that Ashlynne didn't know, Michele clapped her hands and the image of Morag winked out of existence from behind Ashlynne's closed eyes. It did not dissipate into a cloud of mist like the others but was gone in a second with the command from the Priestess who was now standing in front of her, hands raised in victory and power.

"What happened?!" demanded Ashlynne as she jumped off the stool in a panic. "What is that thing? Who is that woman?!"

"Shhh, be calm, be calm," replied Michele while gently taking a hold of Ashlynne's arm and guiding her to a more comfortable armchair covered in floral fabric. Moving her into a sitting position, Michele knelt in front of Ashlynne and looked closely into her eyes.

"What did you see?"

"I saw the drummer boy from my dream, the dark-haired woman that I've seen in other visions, and the Faerie from my dream."

"And how do you know it is a Faerie?"

"I don't know," answered Ashlynne. "I woke up from my dream, and I just *knew*."

"Have you seen or encountered one before? This is important, Ashlynne!"

"No, I don't think so. I mean—I've seen lots of things, but I've never known of any of them to be Faeries." Ashlynne's eyes welled up with tears, "She saw me, Michele. I know she did. I'm really scared! What does she want?"

"I don't know just yet, but I pushed her back for now. For right now you are safe, and you are clean. We'll figure the rest out soon. Rest now."

Sipping on the tea the Michele handed her, Ashlynne felt her eyes grow heavy and her limbs grow warm. She felt Michele take the teacup from her and drape a cotton throw over her body as she floated away in a blessedly dreamless sleep.

Morag screamed in pain and anger as the powerful command shot through the bathroom mirror and struck her squarely between the eyes,

"BE GONE FROM HER!"

The energy, a dark pulsing red with shots of thunder-cloud blue, was potent and old, and Morag was taken completely by surprise by its power. That it was wielded by the small human woman dancing around the neighbor girl was even more surprising. A human throwing this kind of magic around was not what she had ever experienced outside of the old Celtic lands, and she was not prepared for it.

Frustration bloomed in the Faerie's human chest as she stared hard into the mirror, but only gray smoke swirled there now. It had taken her longer than expected to be able to reach the girl's mind, and therefore her dreams, and now she was cut off completely. The Light from the girl was too strong to ignore, and it made Morag very uneasy. This was one that could not be glamored, and that was unacceptable. She must find a way back.

Inside the mirror, Mimi inhaled deeply from her unfiltered cigarette and exhaled in a long slow stream of gray, filling the space completely with the swirling smoke.

Chapter 8

As the smoke obscured the Faerie's vision Mimi stepped back and grinned. "That should teach her," she muttered with more bravado than she felt. The shimmering space that designated the mirror-opening into the apartment that Morag inhabited became more and more indistinct the further Mimi moved away from it until only a small, wavering space remained to differentiate it from the rest of the moving ribbons of fog-like air that made up this in-between realm where she spent so much of her time.

Wanting a comfortable armchair covered in pretty chintz upholstery made it be so and Mimi sank gratefully into the overstuffed cushions. When she first became aware of Ashlynne's Light she was so overcome with

excitement she never stopped to consider the
ramifications of one so bright. Now that she
was up to her eyeballs in those ramifications,
Mimi was almost wishing that she had not
ever stepped forward to the mirror-openings
in the girl's home. Of course, it was not only
intriguing but easy since the girl shone so
brightly that the usual shimmer became a
beacon for any spirits passing through like
Mimi. Fortunately for them both, not many
inhabited the misty space she called the In-
Between. Most spirits stayed within their
realm or that of the living, only moving into
the In-Between to go from one to the other.
But Mimi preferred the softness and solitude
of the mists. The realm of the living was as
loud and boisterous now as it was when she
was one with it herself, and the realm of spirit
was so mutable, with its ever-changing colors,
skies, and times, that it made her dizzy and
her head swim. She knew that she could pass
through it into what the living called The
Light and what Spirits called The One, but she
was afraid of the finality of it all, and so she

chose to stay here where the mists caressed her, time moved as she was used to, and an occasional person shone bright enough for her to talk to. Pulling her pack of Chesterfield Kings from the pocket of her housecoat, Mimi settled in to rest; the emergence of the Faerie and her, so far, successful means of keeping her from Ashlynne had spent more of her energy than she thought possible. Taking a long, leisurely inhale, she closed her eyes and went back to when she, too, lived in Ashlynne's realm and walked the streets of the French Quarter.

Mimi was born Miriam Louis Blanchard in New Orleans in 1882. The small cottage that the family lived in on Saint Ann Street in the French Quarter was dark and cramped with her arrival, bringing the family number to 8. Her father, a rough and tumble sort, new to the city and the continent, chose the winding streets of the French Quarter as home due to its proximity to the docks where he offered his brawn to whatever crew leader would take him on for the day. He was usually tapped to off-load fresh fish and seafood which would be packed in ice to be sent to the fishmongers in the market a few blocks away. The smell of fresh seafood never failed to set Mimi's stomach on edge, less from the pungent stench and more from the violent memories of her childhood.

Charlie Blanchard was a hard worker, and none could deny it. He was strong and didn't tire easily, and this made him well suited as a day laborer on the docks along the Mississippi River. Charlie was wiry, pale-skinned, and had striking dark hair which made his blue eyes spark from his face in a way that held many a young woman rapt in his presence. Charlie Blanchard also liked his drink. The money he made from the docks was spent almost as fast in the bars and saloons that were an easy walk from the river's edge. Mary O'Neil should have paid more attention to Charlie's drinking than to his blue eyes, but by the time she was heavy with his first child and traded her name for his (in that order), it

116

was too late. Five more babies arrived like clockwork—the final being Mimi—as Charlie and Mary fought and drank their way through each fit of colic, new tooth, and skinned knee that occurred within the cramped space. By the time Mimi was four years old, Charlie rarely showed himself at the door and brought his pay home even less. By the time Mimi reached the age of seven, she was roaming the Quarter in a dirty pinafore and even dirtier bare feet, snatching what fruit she could from distracted street vendors to ward off the hunger that gnawed at her belly. It was after one of these excursions that she returned to the small cottage to find that her mother and siblings had all been removed and sent to Common Street to the new Charity Hospital there. The Sister that stayed behind in the small, dark cottage awaiting Mimi's return fully intended on taking her as well, but Mimi turned and ran back into the warren of streets that she knew so well. Sending up an exasperated prayer that the filthy child didn't have the Fever, the over-worked Sister departed leaving Mimi to her own devices. Mimi was nine years old. For the next several years her father would make the occasional appearance at the small cottage bringing a basket of bread, some fruit, and the now-detested fish. He taught his one remaining child to cook and to clean, more for his benefit than for any real thought to her future. Weeks would go by, and he would not show, but Mimi had learned to be resilient and strong and made due. A stolen potato and an onion would be soup, a maggoty apple could be cut up and cooked down for a small bowl of stewed apple sauce. There was no money, but she possessed an uncanny ability to know when she could safely remove an apple, a pear, or a turnip from a cart without being caught. She didn't necessarily thrive, but she survived, and she didn't know anything else, so it didn't occur to her to complain.

Mimi took another long drag from her cigarette as the memories of her life continued to wash over her. Being here in the In-Between allowed for her to feel safe from the true horror that was her early years, while at the same time reliving the sights, the sounds, and most especially the smells of the French Quarter of her youth.

When she was sixteen years old, Mimi decided to find a job. She had a pair of shoes (stolen), a semi-clean dress (brought to her from her father but its original owner unknown to her), and a pretty comb for her hair (also stolen). She had heard talk about the new District around Basin Street where men could purchase 'favors', listen to piano players pounding out Jazz, and drink and eat whatever their wallets would allow. It was to this area that she would look for a job—not in one of the 'houses,' the very thought terrified her, but perhaps in one of the cafes or restaurants that popped up around them. A quick swipe of her hands on the rag that stood next to her washbasin and she headed out the door and through the narrow walkways toward Basin Street. The balconies and galleries on either side of her throughout her walk were strung with all manner of linens, foodstuffs to dry, and potted plants for medicines and cures; the smells of wet cloth, overripe fruit, and spicy herbs blending with horse dung and human urine mingled into an olfactory miasma not found anywhere else in the Americas.

Safely ensconced within the bright chintz fabric of her created armchair, the spirit Mimi stirred uncomfortably with the memory. Her Chesterfield long since smoked away, she stared off into the swirling mists as the memories continued to wash over her.

She got the job. Not as a cook as she was hoping; they wouldn't hire a woman for that—it wasn't right. The irony of that prim and proper mindset just steps away from the house called The Mahogany wasn't lost on Mimi, but she still took the waitress job with hardly a peep of protest. She needed money. Charlie hadn't been around in months with his meager rations of food or coins, and no one in the neighborhood had seen him—or so they said. Whether he had jumped a ship to some town further up the Mississippi or was laying at the bottom of it made no difference to Mimi's circumstances. Gone was gone, and she had to eat. Her spirit-self felt badly for her young, living self; a woman so neglected and mistreated that mourning her own father was never a passing thought.

"How sad," murmured Mimi from her chintz chair. A chair exactly like the one her younger self saw through the tall leaded glass windows of the elegant brothels. The opulence enchanted her but the way in which the money was made terrified her, and she gave the houses a wide berth, staying instead to the side of the street that contained the saloons and cafes.

Her walk to and from her small cottage on Saint Ann to the cafe where she worked in The District—later nicknamed Storyville for the local politician who had conceived of the ill-fated red-light area—wasn't without its perils. Some were run of the mill and common to the Quarter; commodes being tossed over the edge of the balconies with no warning to the pedestrians below, pick-pockets and thieves, and the men and women who trolled for the rich Madams who ran the large houses in Storyville. Having grown up on the streets and being an accomplished pickpocket and thief herself, most of these things were merely annoyances to be aware of. However, there always existed an undercurrent of uneasiness within the French Quarter, the feeling that one was watched from the alleys and courtyards. Occasionally, Mimi was certain that she saw men walking into buildings without first opening doors, and on more than one occasion, she jumped out of the way of the contents of a midden pot being tossed out of a doorway by a woman who wasn't there the next minute. No woman, no pot, no garbage. These things Mimi chalked up to being tired or that perhaps the sandwich she helped herself to at work had gone over—just a bit of bad meat causing her to see things. Food poisoning aside, the evening walks home could be the most concerning. She often saw figures huddled in the dark recesses of alleys and corners. Tall and thin, these creatures were gaunt and pale though their eyes blazed into the darkness as bright as any candle that flickered in the upper windows. Most had patches of brittle hair sprouting in sickly tufts along their pale and sunken scalps. All of them that she had been unfortunate enough to see had teeth that appeared alarmingly long within gums that had receded far into the jaw. Whether suffering from a plague or a fever, Mimi didn't know, but she always pretended to not see these creatures—averting her eyes and walking quickly into the middle of the street to keep as much distance between them and her as possible.

The weeks, months, and then years rolled on, and Mimi continued to serve wealthy tourists their evening meals or breakfasts in between their visits to the Madam's 'girls,' the jazz players' shows, or the gambling dens that made up the blocks and blocks of Storyville. She pocketed her wages, and not a few coins and gold watches of customers that didn't know enough to stay aware, and slowly she was able to purchase not just one but three sturdy pairs of shoes, two good quality dresses, and three white aprons. By the time Mimi was twenty years old, she had saved— or stolen—enough to have gas installed in her little cottage. By twenty-three she purchased a small bed with a lumpy, but clean, mattress and a small table with a straight-backed chair to replace the meager furnishings that both she and Charlie had sold off over the years. She coveted the gorgeous chintz-covered chairs of the opulent brothels but refused to enter.

When Mimi turned twenty-five she had furnished the cottage on Saint Ann with a few comfortable pieces of furniture, lace curtains (stolen from an unattended wash line several blocks over), and a colorful rug to cover the scrubbed pine boards that made up the building's floors. She had a pretty chamber pot, a Blue Willow plate and bowl, and a small green water glass with just the tiniest chip on one side. The silver knife and fork were her most prized possessions, and she kept them hidden beneath a loose floorboard in case Charlie should return. The gas lights played off the lace-paneled curtains making the inside seem misty on lavender-colored evenings. Except for the occasional worry of Charlie's reemergence, the terror and hunger of her childhood had been put to an uneasy rest.

Mimi was courted by a few young men—all dockworkers—but none stayed. Mimi knew too much about things that they never actually shared with her, and each was either frightened away or left in anger. By the time Storyville closed, and the cafe where she was employed with it, she was content knowing that she would be on her own. It was comforting, almost. Depending on others had never worked out, and least she knew she could count on herself to get done what needed to be done.

Though she had saved her earnings and small trinkets that she had stolen, Mimi knew she would need another job soon. It was on her way back home one softly colored evening that she passed a small shop on the corner of her street and Rue Royal. The hand-lettered sign said simply 'Fortunes'. Mimi stepped inside and peered through the candlelit gloom. A table with an elaborately fringed cloth covering it sat in the middle of the empty room. On the table was a deck of well-worn yet vibrantly colored cards—they sparkled for Mimi. Without a second thought, she reached out and pocketed them in one swift motion and was out the door and down the street before the proprietress returned from the back courtyard.

Mimi listened to the deck, and its attending Spirits talked to her. She learned much and acquired many clients that paid handsomely; some paid in money, some in cigarettes (which she loved until the day she died), and some in liquor which she never drank but

used it to trade for such luxuries as fine china
and fragrant teas.

As her abilities grew and the Spirits talked
on, Mimi became aware of changes happening
within the French Quarter that most other
people were not; they had neither the eyes to
see nor the ears to hear. More and more
transients moved into the neighborhood, but
these were very different than the men who
rode the rails in years past. These Beings had
lizard faces, reptilian eyes, and cruelly jagged
teeth. Based on the utter lack of response from
other passersby, Mimi accepted that she was
the only one seeing them, though she had no
idea who or what they were nor what they
wanted. She carefully schooled her face into a
visage of non-expression when she
encountered them—mostly confined to the
doorways and sidewalks of lower Decatur
Street, her preferred method of non-
engagement.

One evening, while snuggled up in her
cottage, she selected a book of Fairy Tales that

had been her mother's and her mother's mother's before her. While Mimi had not many fond memories of her parents, she was forever grateful that they had deigned to teach her to read. Opening the blue, cloth-bound volume, she flipped through looking for a good story. Instead, she found a list of warnings and descriptions for handling and staying safe when a human meets Faeries.

The spirit of Mimi in her flowered chair smiled ruefully at the memory of her younger self who was so surprised to not have found a volume of Grimm's tales or something similar. Instead, her thirty-something self had stumbled upon a grimoire about The Fae. Not fairy tales but Faerie Tales—accounts, spells, and protections about those Beings that live within and beside our world. Her family was, after all, Irish, and the Irish take the precautions of otherworld Beings with all seriousness. She wished she had as well; she might have lived past the age of sixty-five. She might have learned better how to stop the Thing stalking Ashlynne now.

Chapter 9

As the pleasantly cool November days moved into the damp and foggy December nights, Ashlynne continued to sleep fitfully.

Looking up at Andrew and Chris fussing endlessly over the placement of the Christmas lights, she could see that neither of them was getting much in the way of a good night's sleep either. 'Fluffing' the artificial greenery and garlands was no one's favorite job, but Ashlynne took it on to avoid being at ground zero of the verbal picking and poking that the two men engaged in whenever the porch needed a holiday dressing. The Christmas decor was the most contentious since both men had an interest as opposed to Halloween which was Ashlynne and Andrew's thing.

Trying to ignore the faint itching the poky, plastic greens caused, Ashlynne kept one eye on arranging each section to look as real as possible while surreptitiously watching a group of rowdy holiday 'carolers' shuffle down the middle of Ursulines headed toward them and into the Quarter. Red and Green striped rugby-style shirts, perfectly imperfect jeans, and broken-in loafers proclaimed the group of men to be in the later years of their college experience. The cases of beer carried by one and all would have tagged them as being over the age of twenty-one anywhere else. As they got closer Ashlynne decided that, yes, they were all in the early to mid-twenties and wondered what the next ten years would be like for men with so much opportunity available to them from birth. Would they parlay it into a successful career, marry the blond cheerleader, or would at least one wind up with a record of DUI's and lost promotions? The group of merry men's good-natured jeering at each other was suddenly in

stark contrast to the verbal jabs and sharp
tones of her friends. Andrew was standing
with one hand on one cocked hip, the other
hand held straight out with a pointed index
finger several inches too close to Chris's chest
to be anything other than confrontational. In
response, Chris threw both arms up shouting,
"Fine! Have it your way, but it's going to be
completely wrong, and I will not come back
out here to fix it!" to which Andrew yelled at
Chris's retreating back, "Good! I don't like
how you decorate anyway!"

Ashlynne's eyes widened in shock. The two
have always enjoyed a good-natured tit-for-
tat, but she had never seen a real argument
between the two over the porch decor. And
for Andrew to have said that he didn't like
Chris's decorating style?

"Them's fightin' words!" muttered
Ashlynne as she put down the hated plastic
greenery and went up the steps to where
Andrew stood, still glaring at the closed front
door to their apartment.

Laying a hand gently on Andrew's stiffened back she asked, "What's going on with you two?"

"Nothing," said Andrew, shrugging off her hand. "He's just too bossy, and it gets to me."

Raising her one eyebrow, knowing how much it bugged him, she looked at him and said, "Chris is too bossy? Really?" leaving it purposely open-ended for Andrew to backtrack on the accusation. Before he could, however, the good-natured jeering and carrying on of the Christmas-striped college men suddenly turned to a lower-pitched grumbling, and Ashlynne and Andrew watched as the cases of beer were dropped and an all-out brawl began in the street in front of their porch.

"What the hell?" began Ashlynne as she moved down the steps toward the group of previously happy college friends.

Andrew's iron grip on her arm stopped her from moving any closer as he whispered in her ear, "hold up—we don't need to be a part of this."

Ashlynne held her ground as suggested
and watched the sudden turn of emotion
below erupt into pushing, shoving, and
shortly thereafter, punching and hitting. Lots
of crazy situations wandered past their stoop,
but this one seemed strangely out of the
norm. As she stood with Andrew watching
the heaving pile of striped shirts, Ashlynne's
heart sank—one arm that reached out from
the bottom of the pile to throw a punch at a
dark-haired young man whose attention was
on the blond guy he was pummeling had
scaly gray-green skin. The 'hand' was a three
'fingered' claw with a shorter thumb of sorts
ending in thick black nails. As the scaly,
clawed arm made its contact and the owner of
it stood up, Ashlynne felt faint; the gray-green
scales extended up to the neck and face. The
thin, lipless mouth was a horizontal gash
across the lower portion of the inverted
triangular-shaped face, and as she watched, a
black forked tongue flicked out as it raised its
clawed hand to her in greeting.

As Ashlynne stood rooted in horror and the fight continued below her, the sound of scrabbling and a low whispering began behind and below her to her left. Looking down over the poured cement railing of the main porch, she could see a wave of roaches, rodents, crickets, and spiders spilling out from under the wooden gate that led to the side of the building and front door of the newly rented apartment. Fleas jumped up, onto, and above the wave of vermin, and with a disgusted shudder, Ashlynne realized that the sound she heard was that of tens of thousands of wings, insect legs, and scurrying rats against the pavement. The plague inducing, nightmarish stampede rolled its way down the driveway and into the roiling mass of college men leaving Ashlynne's view of the spectacle looking like the largest and most violent dust bunny in the world. Green and red-clad arms would show themselves briefly before being reabsorbed into the roiling mass only to be replaced by a large river rat making an appearance or the flight of a roach as it moved from one head to another. Here and there, scaly, green arms and black-tipped claws could be seen, and Ashlynne wondered if anyone in the group had been human to begin with.

The sound of the wooden gate opening to the lower apartment startled Andrew and Ashlynne away from the spectacle on the street below them. A tall mahogany-haired young woman walked through, leaving it to bang loudly closed behind her. At the firecracker sound of the slamming gate, the brawling tangle of men, and the few that were not men, came to a slow stop until there were no more tangled limbs and legs, just dazed and bleeding college students. Interspersed between them were three lizard-faced 'gutter punks' and piles of dead and dying rodents, roaches, and assorted other insects. It was the strangest aftermath of a street fight that Ashlynne had ever seen.

"Where did they come from?" whispered Andrew in her ear, gesturing to the three street kids with a barely perceptible movement of his chin in their direction.

"I don't know," replied Ashlynne under her breath. "How do they look to you?"

"Look? What do you mean *look?* They look like bloodied street kids."

"But do they look human?" asked Ashlynne quietly.

"What else would they look like?" replied Andrew. Giving his friend a side-eye, he said "Wait, what do they look like to you?"

Before she could mutter her response, a ringing laugh came from the tall young woman standing on the sidewalk below them. She clapped her hands and called into the group in the middle of the street, "Oh my! Well, bless y'all! Look at this! Boys will be boys, I guess, but let's just stop this now." She strode into the street, treading on the dead and almost-dead insects as she continued to tease the group in a thick-as-honey Alabama accent. As sweet as it was, the college boys visually recoiled from her touch while the lizard punks jostled and shoved each other out of the way to receive it.

Reaching around one particularly dirty lizard-faced boy, the dark-haired young woman took a beer from the ripped open case that a ginger-haired college man was clutching to his chest like a security blanket. His eyes rolled in his bloodied face as she moved closer to him. Watching him like a cat watches a mouse, she popped the beer open and laughed as he jumped at the sudden noise. Two small, gray rats chased each other round and round her bare feet though she paid them as little attention as the dead roaches and spiders that were lodged between her toes. Smiling coyly at the tattered lizard boys, she purred, "Come back inside and clean up, y'all. I think we're done here."

Standing as still as statues on the porch above this bizarre scene, Andrew and Ashlynne watched as the group of once happy-go-lucky college men wandered in a daze toward North Rampart Street and the French Quarter beyond. The young woman and her group of scaly thugs walked back up to the sidewalk. Just before she followed them through the gate she turned and said breezily, "Oh hey, y'all. I'm Amber—your neighbor!" And with that, the wooden gate slammed shut behind her leaving the two friends to stand staring at each other in amazement.

"What in the world?!" exclaimed Andrew as Ashlynne's legs gave out, and she sat down with a jaw-rattling hit to the salmon-colored cement step.

"I have no idea," she replied in a daze. She was still trying to wrap her head around how the group had turned on itself so suddenly and wondered when the lizard punks had shown up because she was sure she had not seen them before the fight began.

"Where do you think all those insects and rats came from?" she asked Andrew, glancing at him over her shoulder.

"What insects? And what rats?"

"Seriously Andrew! There was a wave of those disgusting things—you had to have seen them!"

"Well I did not, and I think I've had enough for the day. I'm going inside to talk to Chris."

"Um, yeah—OK. I have to go to—"

"—work." she finished as Andrew shut the front door on her.

Ashlynne stepped gingerly around the drifts of smashed, dead, and dying insects and rats as she made her way across the street to her own apartment. As she unlocked her shuttered front door, she could hear sharp words and arguments coming from Mr. Alvin's place next door.

"What has gotten into everyone?" she asked to no one as she walked into the quiet, peaceful space she called home.

Chapter 10

Ashlynne closed the shuttered door behind her and drew a long, shaky breath. The late afternoon shadows slipped in from the shaded courtyard behind the house where evening spilled and puddled as the sun moved westward. Soon the moon would rise over the roofs and banana trees over the courtyard, its soft glow giving life to the shadows, making them dance into shapes only just recognizable from the corner of the eye. As she moved to her comfortably worn sofa, she could hear the neighborhood crows calling and cawing their nightly announcement that it was time to return back to the roost, while James' horn started its warm-up of notes and scales next door. The sounds of evening in the Tremé—her Tremé, anyway, were soothing. The normalcy of it helped to smooth out her jangled nerves, and after a few minutes, she felt her shoulders drop away from her ears; the space between her eyes at her forehead relaxed and smoothed, and her jaw unclenched with an audible pop. *'Wow—you were wound tight as clock there, girly,'* she chastised herself as she got to her feet and stretched her arms up over her head to release the tension in her back. She had seen plenty of fights and brawls in her time, one doesn't hike across the country or live in this city for long without that experience, but this one was like nothing she had ever seen—or felt. The suddenness, the extra participants, the bugs, and rats... it was just too much, and her head began pounding even as her shoulders hunched back up at her ears again.

"OK! Enough!" she said out loud and strode purposefully through her bedroom and into the kitchen—shoulders decidedly lowered and loose. Opening the fridge, she chose her favorite organic yogurt, a bunch of kale, and the bowl holding the fruit collected from the trees lining the courtyard. Selecting bananas, a kumquat, the kale, some strawberries from the farmer's market, and a generous dollop of the yogurt, she pressed the button and watched it all whirl together in her blender—the kale disappearing behind the sweetness of the fruit which was the only way she would eat the leafy-green stuff. Pouring the army-green drink into a glass, she stepped outside into the courtyard to sip her fruity concoction and watch the crows fly toward Armstrong Park behind her walled oasis. Making herself relax further, she could hear the drums in the park begin their echoed cadences from ages past, and if she had time, she would be able to go deeper in and hear the chanting and laughter of the slaves that danced the rhythms of their Ancestors. Instead, she finished her fruit and vegetable smoothie and headed back inside to get ready for work. She was scheduled as the Reader at the Speakeasy, so she needed some time to get her 'look' together, interesting, and a little bit spooky—but not intimidating or scary. Intimidated and scared people don't pay for Readings, and this job helped keep her several additional steps ahead of homelessness.

Selecting a pair of black leggings, a black tank-top, and a sheer-black, flowered and flowy dress to wear over them, she pulled her red hair to one side and plaited it over her right shoulder. Fixing a black ribbon choker with a bright-red, jeweled Fleur de Lis strung on it around her neck, she added winged black eyeliner and a wine-colored lip to finish the look. Interesting and spooky in a slightly vampiric way but not scary enough to frighten off paying customers. Perfect. Slipping her feet into simple, black ballerina flats and grabbing her backpack in one motion, she headed to the front door and off into the gathering purple of the misty night. As she closed the door behind her, she smiled to hear Mimi call out, "Don't forget your sweater!"

"Got it," she replied softly to the Spirit as she pulled her black sweater from her bag and draped it over her shoulders.

Walking down the sidewalk to the corner of North Rampart, with its new champagne bars, streetcar lines, and short term rentals doing battle with the old school homeless and prostitutes slumped against the brick wall that enclosed Louis Armstrong Park, Ashlynne felt almost back to herself, or rather, as close to herself as she had felt for the last few weeks. Dodging traffic to get to the neutral ground in the center of the busy street, she tried to remember when this nightmare of craziness had begun. Arriving at the Quarter side of the four-lane thoroughfare, she decided that it had to have been about three weeks ago when she saw the vision of the woman in her house. Then there was the For Rent sign with its crown of dead leaves and bugs, the lizard faced street kids moving out of their normal hangouts on Decatur Street, the second vision of the woman in the oak, nightmares, street brawls... "Wow! It's been a busy less-than-a-month!" she exclaimed out loud as she rounded the corner onto Rue Royal and was rewarded with side-eyed glances from a forty-something couple laden with shopping bags. Making a rude noise in the back of her throat she said, "If one girl talking to herself gets your knickers in a knot, you might want to go home now!" to the retreating couples' backs. Regret, mingled with surprise at her behavior, washed over her immediately, and her face flushed with embarrassment. Turning to apologize she could see they had already stepped into the front door of an expensive 'boutique hotel,' and the idea of running in after them wasn't advisable—unless she wanted to be arrested for trespassing and assorted assault charges.

"Get it together Ashlynne!" she whispered to herself and moved at a slower pace further down Royal. Snapping at total strangers and being sarcastic to the city's visitors wasn't like her at all. Was it stress, she wondered? Lack of sleep?

"Both and more," she said under her breath then caught herself. If she didn't stop talking to herself in public there would be more issues coming her way than she had the energy for. Shaking herself out of her internal lecture, she became aware of the joyful cacophony that could only be created with such soul and style by the Queen of the Clarinet, herself. The talented woman and her band of equally talented merrymakers were in their preferred spot on the corner outside of Rouse's Market playing a spirited rendition of *When the Saints Come Marching In*. Literally. As Ashlynne drew closer she could see several spirits standing amongst the living spectators who were all blissfully unaware of the ghosts in their midst. She smiled at the joyful toe-tapping of one long-deceased gentleman. His bare feet, tattered trousers, and dirty linen shirt suggested he had been enslaved in the area at some point in his and the city's history. The wide grin that lit up the Spirit's face as Queen belted out the old Spirituals lyrics

made Ashlynne's heart swell with emotion. All the pent-up fear, stress, and worry of the past few weeks melted away as she watched the gentleman listen, enraptured, to the musicians' performance in front of him. As the song came to an end, a small girl of perhaps seven or eight carried a white plastic pickle bucket covered in hand-drawn dollar signs through the crowd. Ashlynne watched as visitors and locals alike dropped ten- and twenty-dollar bills into the bucket. As the girl stopped in front of Ashlynne's segment of the crowd, she dug into her backpack and found a lone ten-dollar bill which she gladly added to the growing pile of cash. Queen Clarinet, her band of happy horn players and drummers, and all those like them made this city what it was. Ashlynne couldn't imagine a New Orleans without its street musicians.

Breaking free of the crowd of both the living and not, she made her way down the street to Jackson Square. Passing the venerable Muriel's—on her bucket list to afford to dine at—she turned onto Saint Ann

Street and entered the small building housing 'The Boutique,' a hole-in-the-wall gift shop and resource for all those interested in Vampires of both folklore and reality. Only once—and only here in New Orleans—had Ashlynne run across a being calling itself a Vampire. Unlike the TV shows and books so popular right now, this creature was not romantic, sexy, or suave, and Ashlynne hoped to never run into it again.

The minuscule Boutique and the Bourbon Street Speak Easy shared an owner and employees, with several girls doing double-duty between waitressing at the Vampire speak easy and selling Vampire wares here. Ashlynne only worked at the Bourbon Street location but stopped into the Boutique to clock in and get any last-minute instructions for her shift on Bourbon.

Her entrance was announced by the tinkling of the small bell attached to the door; the raven-haired young woman at the desk looked up and smiled, "Hey, you."

"Hey, back," grinned Ashlynne. She and Misty had a wonderfully friendly working relationship but didn't really socialize outside of the Boutique or the bar.

Moving past the too-big-to-be-missed center display of backpacks and purses sporting appliqued bat's wings and fangs, Ashlynne scooted behind the desk and wrote her name and the time in a small notebook that held several other names and times—all people that worked either casually or more regularly for the themed company.

"What's new at the bar for tonight that I need to know about?" she asked Misty.

"Not much up there. The password for tonight is 'Bloodbath,' and the live music is from Mr. Simon."

Ashlynne grinned, "Bloodbath? Seriously?"

"You know it! I figure we have about six months of blood-themed passwords, and then she'll start crafting bat phrases. Anyway, it's almost nine. I'm going to bring the sign in, turn off the lights, and do the till. See you at the bar soon? I think I need a shift drink."

"Of course! See you in a bit."

Stepping back outside onto Saint Ann and around the ornate black iron sandwich board that signaled to passersby that The Boutique was there, Ashlynne rounded the corner onto Bourbon as the waves of lights, smells, and sounds washed over her.

"Bloodbath!" she yelled gleefully to the lady at the door of the jazz club.

"Get in here," Carolyn laughed and stepped out of the way for Ashlynne to pass.

Making her way past the club's patrons and around to the courtyard, Ashlynne stopped. Peering out of the gloom was a large sewer rat with the face of a fox and human hands and feet. Ashlynne squeezed her eyes shut tightly and counted to ten. She opened them again to see the creature had moved out of the gloom of the shadows and closer to her. Taking a deep breath, she pulled her energy in and centered it at her solar plexus. Planting her feet firmly she held out her right hand and began moving it in slow, circular motions.

When a swirling lime green energy became visible, she moved her left arm in a quick sweeping arc, back and out again to the creature. Her own energy shot out, picked up the rat-thing, and threw it into the swirl of green. As it disappeared Ashlynne stopped the circular motion and held her hand-palm out- in one spot and sealed the portal closed. It didn't bother her in the least that she didn't know where she had sent the thing. In her experience the energy of the entity that needed to be moved out of our realm matched with the energy of the portal, guaranteeing that it went to where it belonged. Ashlynne didn't need to know the specifics any more than she needed to know how the electricity lit the bulb when she flipped the switch to 'on'.

Grinning a triumphant grin, Ashlynne felt in control for the first time in weeks. How had it not occurred to her before now that she could move these creatures out and into whatever realm they came from?

As she climbed the ancient circular wooden

stairs leading up to the Vampire Speakeasy, the two marmalade cats that called the courtyard home watched her with slow blinks and bored yawns. Another evening on Bourbon—they had seen worse.

****

In the gloaming of whatever place she had been tossed into, Amber watched as a bright-green swirl of light opened in the sky above her. With a sharp crackle of energy like that of heat lightning, a rat-like creature broke through the swirl of green and dropped into the clearing next to her. Amber and the rat-thing both scrambled up and moved away from each other at the same time; Amber gasped in alarm and surprise, and the rat-thing hissed loudly. Its hairless tail whipped around with its head and body following as it ran off into the forest of predatory trees. Amber watched in horror as its human hands and feet scrabbled along the forest floor.

Suddenly, and without warning, one of the black-barked trees reached out a limb in a grotesque parody of nonchalance and snatched the rat-thing off its feet. Holding it aloft as if to inspect its find, the tree slowly lowered the squirming creature into a hollow space that served as a mouth. As the sound of the rat-thing's screams reached her, Amber's moans of revulsion turned to screams of terror, and the forest echoed them all back to her with the baying of hounds.

Shivering and terrified, moaning with dread and still hoping that this was all some sort of very bad dream, Amber curled up on the floor of the clearing. The dead leaves and moss made for a poor mattress, but it was better than the hard dirt. A bump on her arm brought her head back up. Lying at her elbow was a small wooden bowl of reddish-orange berries and a rough horn goblet of dark-purple liquid. Tired, hungry, scared, and willing to take comfort in whatever form it presented itself, Amber sat up cross-legged and reached for the bowl. The berries were small and clumped together on a small twig. She sniffed them and was disappointed that there was no smell at all. She picked one from the bunch and placed it carefully on her tongue. No taste. "Well, nothing to lose, right?" Amber said to the grim forest surrounding her. The black-skinned trees rustled and whispered in response, *'Yessssssssss…. Eaaatttttt…...'*

Biting down quickly, and almost hoping to be poisoned to be out of this place, Amber's eyes widened, and she smiled in amazement. If she was poisoned this was a wonderful way to go; the flavors of honey and chocolate cupcakes and fresh thyme all exploded in her mouth, a swirl of flavors yet distinct at the same time. As she chewed through the tough berry's skin, she tasted dark chocolate, coffee with cream, and warm toast with butter. Closing her eyes in bliss, she reached for more berries and chewed her way through childhood Thanksgiving dinners, summertime ice-cream cones, and Halloween butterscotch pudding. Taking a drink of the dark purple liquid in the goblet washed her mouth in the beautiful tartness of blackberries picked from her own backyard and made into wine. With her head swimming in beautiful childhood memories and the potent blackberry wine, Amber laid back on her bed of leaves and twigs and stared up at the sky that glowed purple through the dark branches of the forest around her. Silver bubbles of light bloomed and burst at intervals as her eyes grew heavy and finally closed.

A hunched and mangy-furred hound with uncanny, human-looking eyes approached the sleeping girl and sniffed cautiously. The scattered berries and tipped goblet of wine held testament that her wish for a dream had been granted. Scuttling back into the malignant forest the hound went in search of its fellows to tell of the girl who smelled of berries, blackberry wine, and their mistress, Morag.

Chapter 11

The Yuletide frenzy was in full swing as Ashlynne's days and nights moved one into the other in a fairly regimented, if not bizarre, way. She woke every morning after a fitful night's sleep from sinister yet vague nightmares, had her morning coffee in her courtyard, showered then dressed, and then went to work.

Went to work could mean a few things; it could mean that she was going to set up in Jackson Square as an independent Reader, it could mean she was waitressing or acting as the House Reader at the speakeasy, or it could mean that she was hunting. The first two jobs were done at night leaving her open to the third during the day—which was preferable since what she was hunting was scary enough in the sunlight.

That morning she was planning on hunting then taking a long, hot bath at home since she wasn't scheduled to work at the bar—besides, she needed a break from the action in Jackson Square. Finishing her coffee, she grabbed her cell phone before the vibration of an incoming text could bounce it off the small table.

Andrew: *Baby, what's the plan for today?*

She smiled to see the text come in. Since the strange brawl in the street a few weeks ago coupled with Ashlynne's semi-secret hunting expeditions, she and Andrew had been less close than normal. The text was a welcome step back to their regular relationship.

Ashlynne: *Not much*, she typed back—left and right thumbs flying over the phone's tiny keyboard.

Andrew: *Come out and visit then—I have ice water waiting for you.*

Ashlynne smiled. Ice water in and of itself isn't all that big a deal, but Andrew knew her obsession with staying hydrated being a

Northerner by blood, and his having it there and waiting was the sweetest olive branch she could think of.

Pulling her favorite black and gold T-shirt over her head and hopping one foot after the other into a very disreputable pair of cut-offs, she headed to the front door.

"Good morning, Dear!" chirped Mimi from the full-length mirror as Ashlynne passed by.

Groaning inwardly but not having the heart to be mean to the spirit, Ashlynne stopped in front of the glass. "Good morning, Mimi. How are you doing today?"

"I'm fine dear, but we need to talk."

"Um—I was on my way out—"

"It's very important, Ashlynne."

"Mimi, I'm sure it is, but I really have to go now!" Ashlynne turned her back to the woman in the mirror to stop any further conversations and rushed through her front door and across the street to Andrew and his proffered glass of ice water.

"Good morning, my baby," said her friend

as he kissed her on the cheek.

"Mornin'," she smiled back, gratefully accepting the glass held out in her direction.

Taking a long drink of the cold water, Ashlynne watched her friend over the lip of the glass and was distressed to see the dark circles under his eyes. As he yawned a jaw-cracking yawn, she set her water down next to her on the wide cement rail that served as her bench and asked, "What gives?"

"What, what gives?" he countered.

Raising one eyebrow in the hated gesture she replied, "What gives with the bags and yawning?"

"No sleep for ages—neither Chris nor I can get more than a few minutes before that crazy woman below starts a party or her dogs start howling or both at the same time. I swear it's not quiet down there until two minutes before our alarm is set to go off." And with that Andrew's jaw dropped and his eyes closed in another momentous yawn that seemed to go on forever.

"Have you tried knocking on her door and

telling her to be quiet?"

"No. We're not sure what's going on down there or how many people are there; it seems dangerous to go knocking on the door at two in the morning, don't you think?"

"Yeah, I suppose so. But there's got to be something to do so you and Chris can get some rest."

"It wouldn't be so bad except for the street kids we see coming and going. I can't imagine what kind of person has them in as house guests!" said Andrew with a dramatic shudder.

"Wait, what? She has street kids down there till all hours of the night? What do they look like?"

"What do you mean *'what do they look like?'* They look like street kids. Dirty clothes, ratty hair, broken boots..."

Ashlynne sipped her water and thought on this newest development with their neighbor-from-hell. She had not told Andrew about her hunting—partly because he could not see what she saw and partly because they hadn't seen much of each other in the past several weeks. When Ashlynne had once again begun using her ability to move other-worldly creatures back to wherever they belonged, beginning the with fox-faced rat-thing in the speakeasy's courtyard, she became a one-woman cleanup crew. Dozens of scurrying rat-things, legions of roaches with human faces, an army of cats with bat wings, and the occasional large moth with a human skull for a head, had one and all been sent back through the swirling lime-green lights that signified their place of origin. And this is what Ashlynne found to be most terrifying: all these creatures seemed to have come here from the same place. Why were they here, and how did they come through? Answers to these questions had so far eluded her, and that elusiveness helped to keep her up at night—that and knowing that when she slept the dreams would come.

But the lizard punks, she had not considered them since she had seen them

sprawled along the sidewalks of Lower
Decatur Street from the first night of her
arrival in the Quarter. She had assumed they
were spirits of this place. Andrew's
revelation, her assault by them on Ursulines
in the Quarter, and the fight in front of their
stoop meant that they may never have been a
part of this realm. It also meant that they
could now move freely around the French
Quarter. What had changed to allow this?

As she gulped the last of the water and
Andrew fiddled with a game on his phone, it
hit her like a ton of bricks: the new neighbor!
That is what had changed since the beginning
of this craziness.

"Andrew, who is she?"

"Who?"

"The neighbor," said Ashlynne with an
obvious tone of irritation. She didn't play
games on her phone and resented when
Andrew checked out of their visits to crush
sweets in some strangely addictive visual
playing field.

"Beats me. You were there when she introduced herself—she said her name is Amber. And, that accent is pure Alabama so there you have it. Amber from Alabama," and with that, he looked back down at his phone.

"Really, Andrew!" she spat out in annoyance that she didn't even try to hide. "I'm serious! Who is she? Where did she come from, and don't you dare say 'Alabama—' Why is she here? Something is very wrong about her and what's been going on since she had shown up!"

"You're over-thinking things, my baby," said Andrew pocketing his phone in the face of his friend's irritation. "She's a strange person who associates with other strange people, and we have the unfortunate luck of her living close to us."

"I don't think so, Andrew. Something is not right with all of this. I really wish you could see the things that I do…" and here she trailed off. A long-standing habit of not telling all of what she could see and hear kept her from finishing. The very real danger of losing

164

friends forced her to keep much of what she knew to herself. Knowing that Mr. Alvin's deceased dog still wandered around with his living owner was one thing, but being told that some of the street kids were part lizard was quite another.

She stood up and gave Andrew back the glass that had held her ice water. "Gotta go and get some things done, thanks for the water and the visit."

"We good?" Andrew asked.

"We're good," she replied, reaching out to hug her friend.

Walking back across the narrow street to her apartment, Ashlynne had never felt so alone.

"Hello, Dear," said Mimi as soon as Ashlynne has stepped one foot into her apartment.

"Hello, Mimi," she mumbled as she pulled the tall green shutter closed behind her.

Shuffling over to the sofa, she dropped onto

it and looked towards the mirror to where the spirit was.

Mimi was sitting on a wooden chair, smoking her unfiltered cigarette, and looking at Ashlynne with a worried expression on her normally cheerful face.

"Time to talk," she declared. Ashlynne raised one shoulder in a shrug that could have meant an acknowledgment to that statement, a dismissive gesture to the same, or it could have been twitching a fly from her arm. Mimi chose the first and continued, "We need to talk about the woman across the street, Ashlynne."

This certainly got Ashlynne's attention, and she sat up on the sofa and leaned in toward the mirror and spirit residing there.

"What do you mean, Mimi?"

"You know what I mean. You know that there is something wrong over there, and I think you know in your heart of hearts that it's not a human woman—the signs have been there all along."

Ashlynne felt like singing! She jumped up

off the sofa and took two quick strides across the room to the mirror with her arms outstretched. Realizing just before she jammed her fingertips into the glass that she couldn't physically hug Mimi, she switched instead to clapping her hands together excitedly like a small child at the circus.

"Yes! I *have* known, but I didn't want to see it—you're right, Mimi!"

Surprised to see the happiness on the young woman's face but pleased that the slump-shouldered morose was gone, Mimi continued, "And that is why we need to talk. Do you know how mirrors work, Ashlynne?"

"Um, no, not really, I mean, you look in them to see your reflection...."

"They're doorways, openings if you will."

"For spirits?" asked Ashlynne.

"For anyone or anything," replied Mimi. "In fact, you could use this mirror to look anywhere you desire."

Ashlynne's forehead crinkled up in thought, "Me? I could look through it like a magic mirror in a Disney movie?"

"Why is it so hard to believe when you are currently talking to a ghost who is in your mirror?"

"I don't know!" laughed Ashlynne. "I guess I just take for granted that spirits can do things that I can't."

"You are capable of so much more than you know. Unfortunately, the thing across the street knows this, and that is why we must start planning. To begin with, you must know what is going on over there."

"OK, how do I do that? Andrew said it's not safe to just go knocking on the door."

"Andrew is correct. That's why you're going to peek through the mirror."

"But I don't know how to do that!" cried Ashlynne in exasperation, dropping into a crossed-legged heap on the floor.

Mimi eyed the young woman with consternation; for someone so strong she sure was prone to pouting. This would not do. Mimi hadn't the time nor the inclination to coddle, and she wasn't going to start now.

"Stop it, Ashlynne," she demanded sharply and clapped her hands together in rapid succession inside the mirror.

It had the desired effect on the girl who snapped her head up and glared at the older woman.

"Good. There you are, now let's proceed," said Mimi briskly. "Stand up and come in closer to the mirror."

Ashlynne did as she was told, still feeling a little miffed at Mimi's sharpness.

"Now hold your right hand out. You are right-handed, aren't you?"

"Yes," replied Ashlynne holding her arm straight out with the palm of her right hand facing the glass.

"Very good, now think about your hand moving through the glass of the mirror and *feeling* outward for the woman across the street. Really concentrate on how she felt to you; hear her voice, see her face, and move further and further into the mirror."

Ashlynne looked into and through the glass

as Mimi stepped so far to the left that she was no longer visible—just a disembodied voice coming from somewhere beyond the mirror's edge.

"Keep going Ashlynne, keep going." came the soft, encouraging voice as Ashlynne continued her journey through the mirror. Suddenly a noxious smell like rotting meat assaulted her nose, and she startled backward.

"No!" demanded Mimi. "Stay your course. You're there."

"Ugh!" thought Ashlynne. *"If this is what the goal smells like, then I'm not sure I want to see it."*

Ashlynne noticed the glass beginning to cloud over just as her arm began to shake in earnest from its prolonged position of being held straight out in front of her.

"You can put your arm down now, Dear. The connection is made," whispered Mimi.

Ashlynne dropped her arm gratefully and peered through the swirling gray mist of the mirror, blinking away the tears caused by the stench that surrounded her.

Within the mist, shapes and forms began to

move forward; a large white sectional sofa, that at one time in its life had been expensive but now sported green and black mold and deep rips on the cushions. To the right of that, a shabby china cupboard that held chipped and dirty dime store dishes also collected from the side of the roads throughout the French Quarter. Ashlynne gagged in disgust as a large cockroach scuttled over a blue flower printed plate encrusted with what appeared to be dried scrambled egg.

The floor was covered in what should have been white porcelain tile but looked grayer due to the film of dirt and dust that covered it. Drifts of dead leaves and twigs were piled in the corners and cobwebs hung from the stiffened cafe curtains that must have once made the small window seem cheerful. Thinking the window was open and blowing the dust about, Ashlynne shuddered in disgust when she realized that the blowing dust was thousands of fleas jumping from floor to furnishings and back to the floor. She was so entranced by this wreck of space that she didn't notice the small brown dog until it jumped up onto the chair below her mirror and pressed its nose to the glass. Ashlynne jumped back in surprise on her end, and the image of the poor creature grew blurry and indistinct.

"Keep your connection, Ashlynne," advised the voice of Mimi from beyond her mirror's edge.

Ashlynne steadied herself and moved back toward the glass bringing the dog into focus again. It looked directly at her, cocked its head, and wagged its mangy tail in timid greeting.

"Oh, you poor thing!" exclaimed Ashlynne to the image of the skinny and dirty dog on the other side of the mirror.

"What are you doing in there?"

Just then a thin barefoot shot into view and kicked the small dog cruelly in the ribs. With a pitiful yelp, Murphy skittered away under the dingy leather sectional. Gasping in disbelief Ashlynne covered her mouth with both hands as the mirror's surface filled completely with the face of the woman from her first nightmare.

Morag grinned into the mirror as dense gray smoke filled the space between the two pieces of glass obscuring the view for both. The Faerie growled into the smoky haze "Who's there? Who's peeking through my mirror?"

"Enough!" came the robust and throaty command from the far left of the mirror's edge, and the smoke, along with the terrifying visage of Morag, dissipated as the mirror once again reflected Ashlynne's own living room back to her.

Mimi strolled in from the left; *'enter stage left,'* thought Ashlynne trying to hold back hysterical laughter, holding her spent cigarette. Dropping it on whatever passed for a floor on her side of the mirror, she ground it out with the toe of her lace-up black Spectator style pumps. Ashlynne noted with surprise that Mimi's usual frumpy housecoat had been replaced with a smartly tailored suit and skirt and her hair coiffed in the standard rolled style of the late 1930s and early 1940s. The powerful voice that banished Morag was perfectly realized in this younger version of Mimi.

"I like it," drawled Ashlynne nodding her head in approval of Mimi's look.

"Thank you, Dear. The softened me of my later years wasn't going to work for what's ahead of us."

"What is ahead of us? What happened? Who was that in the mirror?"

"That was your neighbor. That is what we're up against. You've seen her before, haven't you?" asked Mimi.

"Yes, she was in my really bad nightmare that Mambo Michele helped me with."

Mimi nodded. She knew this; she wanted to make sure that Ashlynne recognized her.

"What does she want, Mimi?"

"She wants what she wants. To play, to enjoy the chaos she causes, to call the others to her, to feel powerful, and most of all to stay here—all at the expense of any humans or animals that she comes in contact with. She is alien to this realm, and we must send her back. Her and all of the others that she has called to herself."

"The lizard punks?"

"Yes. They've been here a long time—began showing up in the Quarter when I was alive. On their own, they are a nuisance and tend to stick to the shadows. With the coming of this Faerie, they have been empowered and now feel free to roam well past the confines of the streets they used to call home.

"Why did she look like that and not like our neighbor, Amber?"

"The mirror is most likely to show one's true self. There are ways of hiding it, but they are long and complicated rituals. Suffice it to say that when Overlooking with a mirror what you see is what you get."

"So how does she manage to look different in person? A spell? Magic? What?"

"She's a Changeling."

"A what? I thought she was a Faerie?"

"She is, at her core. But she has found a human body to step into, and that is how she looks like 'Amber' while still being a Faerie."

"I'm so confused!" wailed Ashlynne. "How can she look human and be a Faerie? And what has happened to the person who was Amber before the Faerie stepped in? Is she dead?"

"I don't know where she is or how she is, Ashlynne. The Fae are complicated and tricky when they play by their own rules, but when one breaks them and heads out on its own it's complicated to understand the what's and why's of the situation."

Ashlynne's head hung low as exhaustion and fear began to take over.

"You mustn't do that, Dear," chided Mimi gently to the young woman on the floor in front of the mirror. "I said it was difficult, not impossible. We have tools—some you know of and some that will be new to you, but we DO have them, and we will use them. Now, let's start with the questions about the human with whom the Faerie switched. Have you had any other dreams about a young woman during this time? Dreams that haven't made sense about a woman that you don't know?"

"No," answered Ashlynne glumly. "The only dreams are about the lizard punks and the Faerie…." Here she trailed off as her eyes gazed beyond the mirror. "Do they have to be dreams, Mimi?"

"No, not necessarily. Why?"

"I have had some visions…" admitted Ashlynne shyly. She was never sure how new people would react.

"Of course, you have!" laughed Mimi. "What was I thinking?! I should have asked that first! Tell me what you've seen, Dear."

Relieved that Mimi didn't laugh at her or dismiss the idea of visions, while at the same time strangely oblivious to the fact that she was worried that a ghost living in her mirror would judge her for having visions, Ashlynne relayed them to Mimi. The young woman who reached out for help while Ashlynne was getting dressed and seeing the same woman in the 'thin place' at the Live Oak in City Park.

"But she doesn't look like the neighbor—like Amber," said Ashlynne.

"How do you mean?" asked Mimi.

"Her hair is right, and her body size and proportions are the same but, in my visions, I can't see her face."

"Her face is gone?"

"No, it's there, but it's stretched out, and the eyes are just black circles and the features are all—well—wonky."

"Wonky?" repeated Mimi, trying the word out herself. "Wonky. What is wonky?"

"Out of proportion, not right, weird," replied Ashlynne. "Her face looked like that famous painting, *The Scream*."

"Ah...I understand what you mean now. Thank you."

"You're welcome, but why does her face look like that in my visions when the Faerie looks normal across the street?"

Striking a match on her side of the mirror's glass, Mimi lit a cigarette and inhaled then exhaled slowly and deeply. Twice. Looking out at Ashlynne after these two long, meditative breaths, she said, "I can only take a guess, but I believe it has to do with how humans identify with their true self, which is by how we *look* as opposed to who we *are*."

"I don't understand."

"Who you *are* has very little to do with how you *look*, but our human world hasn't made that shift of awareness yet. There are some small pockets of humans who are starting to understand this, but people are still hopelessly stuck with what their eyes can see dictating the reality of the whole. The Fae, on the other hand, have lived a life of mutable reality for millions of years and aren't stuck in this cage of 'what is visible is real.' Humans with gifts such as yours can also step outside of this human cage."

"So, the essence of Amber is showing herself to me with her face distorted because she identified her true self with how she looked, and her body is no longer connected

179

to that true self?"

"Yes. I think that's about the gist of it."

"My head hurts," sighed Ashlynne flatly with a long gaze past the mirror into the darkening recesses of her house.

"I'm sure it does. As much as you've seen in this short life of yours, this is a real mind-bender. There's more, though."

"Of course there is," whimpered Ashlynne, "why wouldn't there be?"

"We need to get the real Amber back."

"Back from where? We don't know where she is, how she got there, and where we can bring her to since that Faerie-woman-thing is in her body!"

"Exactly," replied Mimi succinctly.

Waiting for more, Amber sat staring at the image of the dressed-up version of Mimi in her mirror and yet there was no response.

"Mimi?"

"Yes, Dear?"

"*Exactly*, what? What do we do and how do we do it?"

"Go take your bath, Ashlynne, and I'll get

to work on this."

And with that, Mimi sauntered out of view to the left of the mirror's frame.

Ashlynne's head pounded, and her thoughts were spinning. Her heart pounded quickly, with no small amount of fear.

"Go take a bath?" she grumbled. "Sure, a bath. That will fix everything," she continued with her sarcastic monologue as she walked through her bedroom, into the kitchen, then on into the tiny bathroom.

She opened the window to let in the late afternoon breezes and, dropping the plug into the drain, cranked the hot water open as far as it would go. Watching the steam rise and move out of the screen reminded her of Mimi's cigarette, and she wondered if it was that smoke that obscured the images in the mirror or something else the ghost could conjure.

Adding some cooler water to the jet she shook a generous amount of Epsom salts into the water and found a clean towel in the basket that held linens which she kept under the sink. Slipping out of her clothes and tying up her hair, she stretched her arms over her head and touched the after-thought-of-a-bathroom's ceiling with her fingertips. Stepping gingerly into the deep tub, she sank down into the hot water with an audible *'ahhhhhh'*.

Across the street in the apartment below the two nice men, Murphy peered quickly around the edge of the sectional when the sound of the door opening reached his hiding place. The movement caused a deep ache in his ribs to bloom, and he held back the whimper that threatened to call attention to him. The monster that looked like a lady was the last thing he wanted knowing where he was. Seeing two sets of broken and battered army boots walk through the front door, Murphy watched closely. The voices attached to the boots were so caught up in arguing over who got to drink the last beer that was left on the counter, that the door was never kicked shut.

Ignoring the ache in his side, Murphy scurried and skittered as fast as he was able around the sofa, past the counter dividing that room from the tiny kitchen, and slipped out the door. Breathing the fresh air as deeply as his injured ribs would allow, he ran down the sidewalk and pushed open the wooden gate to freedom. Limping across the street, he crawled under the chain-link gate that led into the red-haired girl's courtyard. Feeling safe for the first time since he had entered the monster's house, Murphy stretched out on the sun-warmed flagstones outside of the back door and fell fast asleep.

Chapter 12

Murphy trotted along beside Ashlynne, enjoying being leashed and collared, bathed, groomed, and fed. His feet didn't hurt so much because the vet had trimmed his toenails, so they no longer dug into the pavement. His patchy fur from the mange was beginning to grow back in as his skin healed, and his broken ribs from the monster kicking him had healed enough to no longer need wrapping. Life was good. Of course, his dreams of green grass and fenced yards hadn't been realized, but he would gladly give those up for sunny spots in the courtyard with the small calico cat, Ashlynne sharing her bananas with him, and being able to sleep curled up at the foot of her bed whenever he wanted.

Murphy was out hunting with Ashlynne.
He didn't like this very much; he didn't like to
see his savior put in danger. Several times he
had lunged at a rat-faced creature, snapping
and growling, only to have Ashlynne pull him
back and scold him. He could see not only the
bright light around her—it had attracted him
from the beginning—but he could see the
sickly green light playing out around the
creatures she hunted, and he knew they were
dangerous to her. She was strong, though,
and no matter how much he tried, she didn't
welcome his help. An outstretched palm and
a quick flick of her wrist and the creatures
were sent back through the swirling green
lights to where they had come from. Murphy
was both afraid for her and proud of her.
Even if she thought she didn't need his help
he would remain on guard and watchful
because a good dog was a loyal dog, and a
long time ago he was told he was a good boy;
he intended to live up to that title.

Ashlynne walked at a brisk pace and smiled at the small brown dog who walked easily along beside her. Over the short time that she had him, it became obvious that he had belonged to someone at some point in his life. He knew basic commands like sit, stay, and come. He took his dog biscuits very politely and was completely potty trained. When she had discovered that he had made his escape from the Faerie and her tribe of creatures, she was beyond happy and spent all her meager savings at the vet to get him treated for mange, fleas, and broken ribs. A thorough grooming and updated shots completed the transformation from derelict street mongrel to the cutest little schnauzer-mixed dog she had ever seen. Dr. Rob scanned her new pet for a chip to see if the previous owners could be found, but there was nothing. Ashlynne was secretly thrilled. While she would have, of course, made sure he was returned home, she had become attached to the small dog and was more than happy to offer him a home with her.

It was several weeks before 'Dog' received a name, or rather told her his name. From day one, she had run through a host of different monikers for the small canine: Ben, Snoopy, Scooter, Jake, and Cooper were all top contenders, but when she looked at him and said any of these names he simply walked away. One day, as she prepared to give the wood floors in her apartment a good washing, she was struck by the name. Holding her favorite cleanser, she smiled and called, "Hey Murphy! Come Here!" and like magic, the small brown dog came running from the living room, through her bedroom, and into the kitchen barking enthusiastically. He leaped onto her lap and licked her face with joy.

"Ha! That's your name, then?" laughed Ashlynne as she extricated herself from the frolicking ball of fur. "So, how are you, Murphy? It's so nice to meet you!" Murphy pranced in a circle at her feet, gracing her with the biggest doggy grin ever.

And now Murphy, formally known as Dog, accompanied Ashlynne during her daytime hunts; she liked his company and suspected that he could see what she could, and he liked to be on hand to protect his new human.

Having exhausted herself from a full afternoon of moving-along-the-not-from-here-creatures Ashlynne, with Murphy beside her, crossed the busy expanse of North Rampart Street and headed up Ursulines on the Tremé side and home. The drums played on within the depths, and darkening shadows of Armstrong park to their left and the usual colorful clientele of the tattoo shop on the corner stood outside, enjoying a late-afternoon smoke between sessions with the artist inside.

"Hey, Baby, how you doin'?" drawled the woman with the small black mop of a dog.

"Hey, Candice, doing well. How 'bout you? Everything good?" replied Ashlynne to the older woman who swayed and danced in place as if low voltage electricity were running from the pavement up through her feet. Her equally animated dog hopped and bopped along with her, making Ashlynne feel tired just to stand with them. Murphy yawned and lay down next to Ashlynne, not at all concerned with the woman or her bouncing black mop.

Candice, a long-time fixture of their block, was equal parts local character and do-gooder. Rumor had it that she had spent her youth in the Haight Ashbury neighborhood of San Francisco enjoying herself a bit too much during that infamous time in the district's history. This would explain the jittery and flighty habits of her neighbor, but Ashlynne didn't know if this rumor was true, and Candice had never confirmed nor denied it. Maybe she didn't remember. Aside from the specter of a hippie past, Candice was most known for her one-woman trap and release program that kept the block's cat colony in check. How and why she took this chore on herself was anyone's guess, but over the years she had perfected her technique, and the entire block benefited from it.

"Took another young male into the Vet's to be fixed this morning," said Candice to Ashlynne, though her eyes bounced and danced from Ashlynne to the trees over her shoulder to the building across the street. Ashlynne resisted the temptation to look at all of the places that Candice was, and instead replied, "Another one? Where do they keep coming from? I thought if the females were fixed, the males wouldn't come around anymore."

"That's how it has always worked, but starting this past fall our block has been over-run; cats, rats, opossums, raccoons, you name it. 'Course I'm not getting anywhere near rats and raccoons, so they come and go when they feel like it," continued Candice as her feet shuffled, and her hands shimmied of their own accord. "But the cats we know what to do with, and more means more need to get 'em fixed. Hopefully, they'll take care of the others."

"Others?" echoed Ashlynne.

"Yeah, others. The rats, raccoons and such," replied Candice with an obvious rolling of her eyes that left Ashlynne feeling a little annoyed with the older woman. It would be easier to follow a conversation with her if she weren't also having to follow her shifting eyes, shuffling feet, and dancing hands.

Swallowing her irritation, she reminded herself that crazy or not, Candice was, at heart, a good person who helped keep their block habitable.

"Thank you for everything you do, Candice. I really appreciate it," smiled Ashlynne as she held out a twenty-dollar bill to the small woman in front of her. Either not familiar with polite objections or not caring, Candice quickly snatched the money and stuffed it into her pocket. Reminding herself to have Andrew take care of these transactions in the future, she bid Candice and her bouncing black fluff ball goodbye and continued up the street to her house.

Ashlynne unlocked the green-shuttered

front door and walked into her front room. The house was cool and dark—a welcome respite from the unrelenting sun of the early spring day. While not yet hot, the sun was strong and bright without a cloud to be found, and the cold darkness within the home was refreshing to both human and canine. Ashlynne flopped herself down onto the sofa, and Murphy followed suit, laying full out on his now rounded tummy on the dark wood floor next to her. Both sighed in contentment and closed their eyes.

The sound of a clearing throat roused Ashlynne from her late afternoon nap. She sat up and peered around the darkened room, noticing that Murphy hadn't moved at all.

"Some watchdog you are," she whispered to the small brown dog sleeping so peacefully on the floor next to her. She made the comment in pure jest; she had no doubt whatsoever that the terrier would put himself between her and whatever he felt might harm her without a moment's thought to his own safety. Having never had a pet before,

Ashlynne was surprised at the depth of the little dog's devotion.

Stepping over him quietly to not wake him, she moved into her bedroom but stopped at the mirror when she saw Mimi sitting there smoking her cigarette and tapping one Spectator-clad toe against the rung of the wooden chair.

"Hello, Dear."

"Hey, Mimi. What's going on?"

"It's time, Ashlynne."

"It's time for what?" asked Ashlynne suspiciously. Aside from her daily hunting, life in the 'hood had been quiet this past month, but this seemed to suggest that the silence might be over.

"It's time to make plans on sending that thing across the street back to wherever she came from."

Ashlynne groaned loudly, rousing Murphy from his nap. He trotted up to the mirror and cocked his head at the smartly dressed woman sitting within.

"I don't know how to do that. I can send back a rat, a cat, or a bug—but a Faerie who's strong enough to change places with a human? Who knows how to do that?"

"You will know how as soon as you get the book," replied Mimi shortly and exhaled a long plume of gray smoke.

"*The Book*. Really?" countered Ashlynne irritably. "What book, Mimi?"

"The book I left at my house. It's under the floorboards. You just need to go and get it. I believe everything we need to know will be in there."

Ashlynne stared at the woman in the mirror in amazement, her mouth agape. Did she seriously think that whatever book she left in whatever house she had lived in would still be there? And was the house even still there? If so, what about the people living in it now? Ashlynne found it safe to say that her ringing the doorbell, sauntering in, and asking to tear up the floorboards wouldn't be met with open arms and smiles of approval by the house's current occupants.

"Mimi, get serious. How am I supposed to do that?"

"I can tell you the address, and then you need to go in and get the book."

"I don't think it will be that simple. Do you know if the house is still there? When did you die, anyway?" asked Ashlynne as an afterthought.

"1947, and yes, the house is still there."

"How do you know that?" countered Ashlynne.

"Really, Dear! Do you think your mirror is the only place I visit? The house is still there—the smallest cottage on the 1000 block of Saint Ann Street. The book is still there; you just need to go in and get it."

And with that, the mirror's surface filled with smoke. When it cleared, the only things visible were Ashlynne, Murphy, and the room in which they stood.

Chapter 13

Ashlynne added stalking the small cottage on Saint Ann Street to her daily rounds of hunting; she was beginning to feel quite disreputable. She and Murphy would leave the house early in the morning and grab a coffee for her and a dog biscuit for him at CC's Coffee House on Royal before heading further into the French Quarter to track and remove the creatures that the Faerie had called in. As the weeks passed, the creatures had become bolder, attacking the neighborhood cats, pigeons, and dogs that had, until recently, lived peacefully in the more residential areas of the Quarter. Her route was roughly the same every day: coming into the French Quarter down Ursulines to Rue Royal, wandering in and around the narrow streets to Jackson Square, and ending at Saint Ann Street. Here they would stop in the square to sit and sip water, watch the street musicians, and rest. Then it was time to head home, going up Saint Ann to Armstrong Park and North Rampart Street. Once she approached the 1000 block of Saint Ann, Ashlynne would slow her pace until she and Murphy were in front of the small single-family structure that Mimi had said she lived and died in. Like all the houses in the French Quarter, this cottage sat directly on the flagstones and had a narrow 3 step stoop leading to the shuttered front door. The small, single-unit structure seemed squashed in among the larger and more elaborately maintained double resident houses sporting fanciful paint, crisply tinted gingerbread trim, and lush hanging ferns that shaded their full porches. Mimi's former home needed to be scraped and painted, and the one potted plant that sat next to the stoop on the flagstones— the house had no actual porch—looked dusty and neglected. Try as she might, Ashlynne couldn't tell if the home was occupied. As was her habit now, she gazed at each window in turn trying to peer through the shutter's slats to the interior without really appearing to do so. So far, she had had no luck; no lamps could be seen, furnishings, or signs of life.

As she stood there looking at the cottage while trying to look like she wasn't spying, a woman holding what looked like a see-through mailbox, a hammer, and a box of nails approached the house. She smiled at Ashlynne and proceeded to nail the box to the left of the narrow front door's shutters. Placing a sheaf of papers inside the box, she said, "Cute place, isn't it?"

"Yes, very," replied Ashlynne trying to sound as nonchalant as possible.

"It's being sold at a very reasonable price for the French Quarter because of the work it's going to need. Here, take a look, we're having an open house this Saturday."

Ashlynne took the offered flier from the real estate agent and tried not to gasp out loud at the 'very reasonable' price shown at the top of the advertisement.

"Thank you, If I'm not working, I might stop in."

'Don't yell, don't skip, don't hoot or holler, Ashlynne,' she whispered to herself as she sauntered as casually as possible away from the real estate agent who was unlocking and entering the cottage. Ashlynne could not believe her luck and sent a silent 'thank you' up to whatever god or spirit orchestrated this amazing set of circumstances.

As she approached her house Murphy turned his head at the cawing of the crows flying overhead to their roost in Armstrong Park.

"Dinner time," she said to her furry companion as she unlocked the door and went inside. She dropped the flier onto the coffee table and went through her bedroom into the kitchen. Scooping kibble into Murphy's bowl, she put it down on the mat next to his water bowl and smiled at the small dog who tucked into the simple meal with such obvious delight.

"It's the little things," she said as she spooned her favorite dark roast coffee grounds into the filtered basket, poured water into the machine's carafe, and turned it on to brew. Miracle open houses didn't pay the bills, and Ashlynne had her significant monthly obligations looming, as well as needing to restock her little rainy-day savings account, so tonight would need to be a work night.

As the decadent aroma of the brewing coffee filled the small home, Ashlynne gave Murphy his after-dinner cookie and let him into the back courtyard. Pulling off her shorts and T-shirt, she dropped them into the laundry basket and turned the shower on in the bathroom, not bothering to close the door between it and the kitchen.

Stepping under the spray of cool water she lathered up with her favorite bar of handcrafted mint soap. As the bracing scent of mint mingled with the warm steam of the shower, she reflected on the day's events, still amazed at the luck of having an open invitation to go inside Mimi's old house. Breaking in had seemed to be the only alternative, and she had dreaded the thought of being caught. Now that this fear was gone, she could enjoy the idea of exploring where her Spirit-friend had lived.

Rinsing the soap from her body and turning off the shower, Ashlynne wrapped herself up in the towel and stepped over and down out of the deep antique tub. She padded into the kitchen and checked on Murphy in the courtyard. The little dog was fast asleep on the sun-warmed flagstones with Mr. Alvin's dog, Beau, sitting next to him, looking out over the pool. Ashlynne smiled and hoped Beau was happy with the company.

Pouring half and half into her favorite coffee mug, she added the dark liquid and took a grateful swallow of her favorite elixir. Choosing her outfit for the night, she selected a sweater as a silent nod to Mimi and began getting dressed. Black jeans, a white T-shirt, and her black combat boots. The lime-green Gap cardigan purchased at a Decatur Street thrift store was the only bit of color aside from her bright-red hair. Looking into the mirror at her reflection, she nodded in satisfaction; she liked the effect.

"Murphy! Come Inside now!" she called out the door, and the small dog reluctantly left his favorite spot to come inside, where he immediately sat down with perked ears, staring intently at the large cookie jar that held his treats.

"Really? Didn't you just have one, Murph?"

Murphy wagged his tail and gave her a big, sloppy doggy grin that he knew would get him the cookie, and he was, of course, right. Ashlynne reached into the jar, chose a peanut butter flavored cookie, and offered it to the grinning canine.

"Take it nice."

Having settled her four-legged roommate into his favorite bed—hers—Ashlynne left the house pulling her two-wheeled cart down Ursulines, across North Rampart, and into the

French Quarter. Work tonight would be Reading in Jackson Square since she wasn't scheduled at the bar. As she made her way towards the open-air theater that was the Square, she hoped tonight would be lucrative but uneventful.

Chapter 14

The sun was slipping below the horizon, and the evening sky began to glow with the incandescent light found only in the French Quarter as Ashlynne began unpacking her tote and setting up her station. The regularly attending Readers who called Jackson Square their office had agreed upon spots which were not mandated by any city ordinance but rather by seniority and consistency. Ashlynne's regular spot was catty-corner from the double entry doors of Muriel's and along the fence. There were Readers who insisted that being situated in the center of the walkway was best, but Ashlynne found that being visible, yet a little secluded, ensured that her clients were mostly sober and therefore pleasant.

With her black velvet tablecloth in place, she set her deck of cards down in the center with her crystal point on top of them. While it did look witchy and mysterious, the crystal served two important functions: the first being that it absorbed excess energy from her cards that might affect her reading. She didn't really need the cards to see the answers to her clients' questions, but if the after-effects of every client were stuck in them during sessions, it would jumble the images that came to her. The second purpose the crystal served was as a beautiful paperweight. The clear quartz was just heavy enough that it kept the occasional river breezes from blowing her cards off the table and scattering them around the Square's flagstones where there wasn't enough cleansing in the world to make them right if that were to happen.

Scooting her chair up to the table and facing the front of the cathedral, she lit a stick of incense that stood upright in a stone with a small hole in it. She had had this stone for several years and found it on the beach at Lake Michigan before she began making her way south. It had felt 'right' in her hand when she picked it up all those years ago and it had stayed with her ever since. When she first set up shop in Jackson Square, she had noticed that the other Readers all burned a stick of incense at their tables. Not having the money for both incense and a holder she had improvised with her stone. It worked perfectly and her plan to buy a 'proper' incense holder was set aside.

As the spicy/sweet scent of her favorite Nag Champa incense curled upward, Ashlynne looked around. It was early and most people- tourists and locals alike- were only passing through the Square to get to one side of the Quarter or the other. Further down and closer to Chartres Street a group of Buskers were huddling up and working out the beat of a song they planned on performing, as the night continued to creep up from the River's dark waters two blocks away. One girl with bright

blue dreads and a prairie-print dress tapped a
homemade tambourine against her thigh
while across from her a young man who
appeared to have taken his look from a
Where's Waldo cartoon strummed a tune
from a banjo that was in almost museum
quality condition. Ashlynne closed her eyes
and received flashes of images; an older man
in a suburban living room playing the banjo
for his five-year-old grandson. That same
older man, now with the grandson at ten,
teaching him to finger the notes and chords to
coax a tune from the instrument, and finally,
the grandson at eighteen standing at the
newly inscribed headstone of his
grandfather's grave strumming 'Amazing
Grace' on the banjo that now belonged to him.

Ashlynne opened her eyes to see that the
singer of the small group was beginning a
tentative hum, her voice moving in and out of
the notes and beat provided by the other two.
By the time the man with a make-do pickle
barrel drum began his portion of the musical

medley, the small group had already begun to attract tourists armed with cell phones, taking pictures and videos. Ashlynne smiled; it looked to be a good night for them.

"Excuse me, can I get a Reading?" Ashlynne turned to see a woman about her age standing in front of her table. Gesturing to the empty chair, Ashlynne smiled, took the offered twenty-dollar bill, and began shuffling the cards. As Jackson Square began to fill up with tourists wandering through the Readers' tables, listening to groups of musicians, or waiting under Tour Guide signs for haunted history and vampire tours, Ashlynne thought that perhaps it would be a good night for all of them.

The hours passed quickly, and the small bag hidden in her cart began to fill with cash. The various musicians scattered around her had long ago switched from cheery banjo music to the deeper thrum of brass horns as the shadows melted into inky black patches where the streetlamps couldn't reach. Ashlynne was equal parts wired and

exhausted, running now on whatever energy
that each client left behind and the caffeine
supplied from her now almost empty thermos
of coffee brought from home. The Readings
had been par-for-the-course as far as Readings
go; lost loves, cheating spouses, new homes,
and pets that had passed but were still
walking along beside their living humans. No
unusual tragedies or surprises, just the
everyday miracles that make up the act of
living.

Lighting another stick of incense, Ashlynne
rummaged in her cart for a bottle of water. As
her fingers closed around the aluminum
container her stomach knotted painfully, and
a line of cold energy snaked down her back
like an invisible finger running from her
hairline to the waist of her jeans. As the
goosebumps moved up and down her body in
waves, she stood up very carefully. Standing
directly in front of her table was Amber—who
was not Amber—the Faerie from across the
street. Her neighbor from Hell. Here. In the

Square. Smiling at her.

Ashlynne took a deep breath and smiled as normally as was possible given that her body had gone into 'flight or fight' mode. Wondering at how her body could be smarter than her mind she said "Oh, hey there! What's going on?" hoping against hope that her smile didn't resemble a cadaver's fixed grin and her voice wasn't as high and squeaky as it sounded to her own ears.

"Well, I was just wandering around enjoying this lovely cool night when I noticed you sittin' here," purred her neighbor in the sickly southern drawl that made Ashlynne's skin crawl.

"It is nice out, isn't it?" asked Ashlynne, at a complete loss as to how to respond to the woman who was not the person she appeared to be. Who was not, in fact, a person at all.

"You've been busy," her neighbor said as a flat statement. Ashlynne had the sinking suspicion that she wasn't talking about her night of card reading.

"It's been fairly steady," she agreed as

blandly as possible.

Looking around the square, the thing masquerading as Amber said, "Usually there are so many of my friends out, but lately I can't seem to find a one." Her pretty face pulled a theatrical pout as her eyes watched Ashlynne's. Understanding now that the conversation wasn't about her job as a Reader Ashlynne replied carefully, "Well, you know, Quarter folks come and go pretty regularly."

With a surprisingly deep laugh, she sat down in the empty chair across from Ashlynne and said, "Well, since I'm here, how about giving me a Reading?" and held out two dead leaves. Not quite understanding but knowing it was in her best interest to play along, Ashlynne took the leaves, placed them under her thigh, and began to shuffle the cards. As the cards arced and rearranged themselves into new locations Ashlynne's thoughts raced faster and faster. What was she supposed to do? This thing looked human, but she knew it was not. That being said, she wasn't sure what it could do or what it wanted. Mimi's response to that question of 'she wants what she wants; chaos' was vague and unhelpful. Knowing she couldn't just sit there shuffling the cards all night, Ashlynne placed the deck face down between the two of them and reached to turn over the first card. Quick as a snake, Morag crushed her hand in a vice-like grip. Gasping in both pain and surprise, Ashlynne looked up and moaned in dread and dismay. The Faerie was there. The image of the pretty, dark-haired Amber had been replaced by the gray green-skinned being from her nightmares. Trying to jerk her hand out of the Faerie's grip only resulted in a bone-crushing hold. As tourists wandered by, seemingly oblivious to what was happening at her table, Ashlynne's heart began to beat painfully fast in her chest.

"They only see a woman getting a Reading from a pretty little redhead," laughed the thing holding her hand.

Ashlynne looked at her and noticed, once again, the small horns sticking out of the tangled mass of hair stuck through here and there with leaves, twigs, and bugs. Just like her dream. Wondering if she had fallen asleep and was dreaming now, the Faerie laughed and said, "I'm afraid not," showing off black and green pointed teeth in a cruel, thin-lipped mouth. Everything about this creature was hard, thin, and mean, and yet it was strangely beautiful. Watching, enchanted, and terrified, Ashlynne saw the Faerie flick her free hand at the cards which took flight, flapping, and swooping around their heads.

"I think it's time YOU received a Reading!" she laughed as Ashlynne closed her eyes and fell headlong into the images that the Faerie conjured.

Ashlynne found herself standing in a large crowd of people at what was obviously a party. As she looked around wondering where she was, she noticed a woman coming down the stairs to her right. Ashlynne caught her breath and turned to leave but it was too late; the woman had seen her—she was caught again. Knowing exactly what a mouse feels like when an owl swoops down, Ashlynne stood in mute terror as Morag moved through the crowd and approached her. Unable to cry out or move on her own, Ashlynne was helpless as she took her by the arm and led her out a back door and into a yard strung with outdoor lights. Pretty settees and potted plants were scattered here and there, and a small bar had been set up in the corner, a perfectly normal outdoor party. Except it wasn't. While dressed in the business-casual slacks and pretty summer dresses of people who would attend such events, the partygoers weren't human. Some had the lizard-skinned faces of the lizard punks she saw throughout the French Quarter, some had the gray-green skin of the Faerie who had brought her here, some looked almost human except for the strangely elongated noses and ears on their beautifully alien faces.

A fire pit was situated roughly in the center of the lawn with a fire burning enthusiastically despite the warmth of the summer night, which struck Ashlynne as odd, even for here. The Amber look-alike pushed her forward through the crowd, and a female with a pointed fox's snout wearing an understated Ralph Lauren frock hissed at her as she stumbled past. Roughly shoved and prodded toward the brightly burning fire, Ashlynne's face began to bead with perspiration as waves of heat and fear rushed over her.

"No, no, no, no, no…." She moaned as a male dressed in chinos and a golf shirt with an orange pig's face moved aside to reveal Murphy trapped in a small wire cage sitting dangerously close to the flames. Straining to be free of the woman holding her, she cried out to her small dog whose eyes rolled in terror in his head.

"Let me go!" Ashlynne hissed at her tormentor. Pulling her arm out of the iron grip, she turned on the woman who was now in full Faerie form. The crowd of party-goers sighed in pleasure as the Faerie stood to her full six and a half feet tall. Her wrappings of green gauzy fabric blew gently around her stick-thin arms that were just a bit too long. The Faerie smiled cruelly down at Ashlynne and whispered, "I saw you in my mirror, spying on me. I know you took what was mine," waving one skinny arm to the dog she had trapped by the fire, "and I know you've been sending my friends and companions away."

Ashlynne took several steps back from the being who towered over her. The murmurings of the party-goers were a waves-on-the-beach counterpoint to the Faerie's throaty voice.

"You will stop, Ashlynne, or I swear I will make your life, and the lives of those you love, as miserable as I am able. I will do it for fun, I will do it for sport, and I will not stop until everything and everyone you love is gone."

As sour panic rose in her throat and Ashlynne tried desperately to move, the low murmur of the other Fae suddenly stopped only to be replaced with a unified and confused gasp. Ashlynne saw her captor whip her head around and look to the very back of the yard where the hedgerow gathered the darkness to itself. As they both watched, a portion of the dark separated itself from the rest. Standing in the shadows was a figure taller than the Faerie that had brought Ashlynne to this place. Though very tall, he was slightly built with long thin legs, a narrow chest, and stooped shoulders. His skin was a dusky brown, and he carried a wooden staff. Skeleton keys of all sizes and styles hung from a cord around his neck. The thin black man exuded incredible strength and power- and he was old, almost as old as The Faerie if Ashlynne was to guess. The Faerie squared her shoulders and faced the man as the other fae backed away slowly into the house leaving only the 3 of them. Aside from the terrified dog in the cage, there was not another living thing in the yard.

The black man stepped forward and, using his staff, scraped an equal-armed cross in the lawn between them. The Faerie hissed and took a step back dragging Ashlynne with her. The man raised his staff and brought it down firmly in the center of the sigil bringing forth sparks of gold, red, and black that blinded Ashlynne completely. She could hear the Faerie scream, whether in anger or pain she had no idea, and felt her hand let go of her arm, and then there was the feeling of falling from a very great distance.

Ashlynne had no idea how much time had passed before she became aware of the sound of a brass horn and the chatter of a group of women somewhere to her right. The smells of the French Quarter worked their way back into her consciousness, and as she became fully aware, she jumped up with a scream, hands up to shield her face and feet planted. Morag didn't move a muscle or seem at all surprised by this, but rather sat watching as Ashlynne whipped her head one way then the other trying to get her bearings.

"Y'all musta' fell asleep," she purred as she stood up and stretched lazily. "Of course, I'm sure you've had a long night. This kind of work isn't like a garden party, is it?"

Ashlynne stood there with her mouth hanging open and her eyes wide as her neighbor winked at her and sauntered off in the direction of Chartres Street.

"Oh, hey. Did y'all get a dog? I thought I saw you walking him; he's cute as can be." With a flash of green and black rotted teeth, she turned and walked off into the shadows that pooled between the lamp posts.

Shaking like a leaf, Ashlynne squatted down to pick up her scattered tarot deck. It hadn't rained in a while so thankfully the flagstone walks were dry but cleaning them would still be awful. Maybe she would burn them and start over. She stuffed the cards willy nilly into her bag, added the crystal, and as quickly as she could, dismantled the table and chairs and piled them into her cart. As she took off out of Jackson Square at a run, her heart thudded with a jackhammer rhythm, scared to death about what she would find when she got home.

"Hang on, Murph!" she panted as she ran down Rue Royal, her cart bouncing behind her, "I'm coming. Just hang on boy!"

Ten blocks away in one half of a pink double Creole Cottage on Ursulines Avenue, Murphy struggled against the bars of a cage in this dream that wasn't a dream. The monster had found him and had locked him here, and he wasn't sure how it had happened. The fire that was next to his barred box danced and shone as if to mock him as he pushed harder and harder against the cage's door trying to escape. A shadow settled over him from above and blocked the hated glow of the fire. Feeling immediately relieved, Murphy was just as quickly sent into a panic as he looked up to see a thin black man in rags leaning over him. Unsure about this newest figure, Murphy threw himself against the bars again and again in a panic to be free and away from him, but it was no use. The small brown terrier collapsed in an exhausted heap on the floor of his prison, so spent that he could only whimper as the man reached through the cage's bars and gently touched him between his eyes.

"Sleep," the man growled, and Murphy slept dreamlessly within the dream that wasn't really a dream at all.

Chapter 15

Murphy burrowed further under the blankets and smashed himself as close to Ashlynne as was physically possible, his tiny body still shaking and shivering from the experiences of last night. He had been awakened from his dreamless sleep within a dream that wasn't a dream by his red-headed human grabbing him out of his nest of blankets on her bed and shaking him roughly while crying his name and sobbing loudly. It was all too much for him, and he began to howl loudly which scared his human so much she dropped him onto the hardwood floor bruising his hind foot badly. If they hadn't both been so terrified it might have been humorous.

His howling did serve the purpose of

snapping Ashlynne out of her panic, and she gently picked him up, cuddling him like a human baby and crooning soothing non-words into his ears.

"Whsshhhht, whhhssshhttt... There, there, Murph. You're ok. Who's a good boy? You're such a good boy," and more as she cuddled and rocked him back into some semblance of calm.

Once Murphy had settled enough to lay still in Ashlynne's arms, she began checking the small dog for damage or injury. Aside from his bruised foot, the only physical difference from when she left him earlier that evening until now was a strange mark on his forehead. It wasn't red or swollen and didn't seem to cause him any discomfort.

Ashlynne brushed her thumb over the strange mark, "What is this, Murphy? How did this happen?"

The small dog tucked his head under her arm making tiny whimpering sounds that broke her heart. Gently lifting his head back up so she could see his face, she studied the mark more closely. The fur was rubbed clean in a small patch maybe a half an inch wide. It looked like a child's line drawing of a key.

Pulling her boots off and tugging each leg out of her jeans, Ashlynne scooped up Murphy and crawled under the covers in just her T-shirt and underwear. The chill and terror of the night began to move away as the weight of the bedding and the warmth of the dog worked to loosen her taut muscles. Feeling impossibly heavy and drained, Ashlynne slipped into a dreamless sleep cradling the small brown dog who had fallen back to sleep as soon as they were in bed.

Chapter 16

Her aching head finally roused Ashlynne from her almost comatose sleep, and she was surprised to open her eyes to a darkened room; the sun had risen and set again as she lay curled under the heavy quilt.

She rolled over to check the time, three in the morning, and to find the small dog. She smiled to herself to see that he had slipped out from under her arm and curled up in his customary place at the foot of the bed. Taking this as a good sign for his well-being, Ashlynne sat up, squinting into the room through the pounding of her headache.

Climbing gingerly out of bed and walking carefully to avoid any jarring that would send the ache into a full-fledged bloom of pain,

Ashlynne stepped around the bed, past the now-defunct fireplace and mantle, and into the kitchen. Pouring the cold filtered water into a glass and gulping down a double dose of aspirin, Ashlynne sat down at her small kitchen table and waited for the headache to recede.

As she sat there staring out the small window that faced the walkway into her courtyard, and James' house just beyond that, the sky began to brighten a bit with the coming of the sunrise, and the vice grip along her temples let up enough for her to contemplate coffee. The ritual of preparation helped with the anxiety that the aspirin could not, and once the kitchen was filled with the aromatic scent of the brew Ashlynne felt physically strong enough to begin to think about what had happened the night before. Sipping her coffee and its generous splash of half and half, images flashed in her mind's eye: a young street musician with his Grandfather's banjo, a couple who had stopped for a Reading, groups of tourists

226

gathered around a man in Victorian garb holding a tall sign signifying the start of a haunted history walking tour, and finally the appearance of Amber. Amber who was not Amber. Amber who turned into the Faerie that had been terrorizing her dreams. The Faerie looked like the young woman who seemed to be trapped in a twilit forest. Her head began its dull thumping again as Ashlynne purposely brought up more of the memories of the night: her tarot cards flying and flapping like pigeons, the other-worldly garden party, Murphy in a cage set dangerously and threateningly close to the bonfire, and the powerful, yet elderly, man who showed up at the end. The man who had so frightened the Faerie that she released Ashlynne back to Jackson Square. She didn't know who or what he was, but she sent a silent 'thank you' out to him all the same.

As Ashlynne stood up to refill her mug she smiled to see that Murphy had decided to leave the comfort of the blankets and join her.

Reaching down to pet his head she was struck again by the odd mark just between and above his eyes; it certainly did look for all the world like a key. Letting him out into the pink dawn, she stood in the doorway and breathed in the scent of the green and flowering vines; it was both comforting and healing. She smiled to see that, after having done what he needed to do out there, Murphy was doing the same as her. His little head was held up, eyes closed and nose twitching at the scents that seemed to settle down around the pool and flagstones of their small oasis.

"Birds of a feather," she said out loud and stepped back into the kitchen to indulge herself with one more cup of coffee.

Murphy barked sharply at the back door, demanding entrance. Ashlynne had briefly considered asking Mr. Alvin if she could install a doggie-door but quickly dismissed the idea as visions of errant rats, opossums, feral cats, and heaven knows what kinds of insects invaded her house. The remembered visual was too close to what had been happening with the arrival of the neighbor across the street, and she shuddered in revulsion. Much safer to simply open and close the door at Murphy's request. Having done so and provided the bossy canine with his breakfast, Ashlynne rinsed her coffee mug and went in to straighten the bed and get dressed. The trauma of what had occurred mixed with the over twenty-four hours of sleep had left her feeling discombobulated and out of sorts. Coupled with the radio silence from Andrew, she was in an increasingly foul mood by the time she sat down on the sofa in the living room to tie the laces of her tennis shoes.

"Why don't you call him?"

"Mimi," Ashlynne's response being equal parts greeting and tired sigh, she turned to the mirror and forced a smile for her friend sitting on her chair on the other side of the glass.

"I guess I could," she grumped in response to Mimi's question.

Mimi smiled at the young woman who

looked much the worse for wear with her long red hair a tangled mess of half unraveled braids, partially bleached-out black and gold T-shirt, and jeans with both knees blown out.

"Are you feeling better? That was quite the long sleep you had," she said while blowing smoke rings above her head.

"Yeah, I guess. A little, anyway," replied Ashlynne in a monotone voice as she watched each smoke ring grow larger and larger as it moved further above Mimi's head. She wondered if there was a ceiling on Mimi's side of the mirror then stopped herself; how had her life become so completely out of whack? Hunting strange creatures, spirits in mirrors, flying tarot cards, body-swapping Faeries — it had all become too much. Granted, some of it was normal for her: spirits, visions, elemental type creatures, but what was not normal right now was that it was all happening at once and all seemed to be centered around the Faerie.

"What's her name?"

"I'm sorry, what?" asked Mimi with a

shocked expression toward Ashlynne who had her back to the mirror, rummaging through her tote looking for her cell phone.

"Her name," came the muffled reply.

"Whose name?"

"The Faerie's name," replied Ashlynne as she turned to face the mirror holding her cell phone that had been stuffed under her black tablecloth.

"Well, I don't know, Dear. That's part of what you need to find out. I suspect it's rather important information to have. When are you going to go get the book from my house? I don't think anything else can be done until we have it."

Ashlynne was staring at the screen of her phone, thumbs moving lightning fast over the keyboard, "Uh-huh... Yeah, OK, Mimi," she mumbled—not shifting her gaze from the small electronic device in her hand.

"Ashlynne! Really!" exclaimed Mimi as she ground out her cigarette on her nonexistent floor—the picture of older adult annoyance.

"You must begin to take this seriously, and you must go get that book!" And with that, she stomped out of view to the right of the mirror's frame.

Looking up from her phone at the sound of Mimi's tantrum, Ashlynne noted that the spirit had walked out of the mirror to the right this time. Finding it strange that she had, until just now, assumed that Mimi could only leave from the left, Ashlynne returned her attention to the screen in front of her.

Andrew: *Hey, my baby. Where you at?*

The first text came in from Andrew yesterday afternoon as she and Murphy lay sleeping.

Ashlynne: *Headed to Mississippi for the weekend to visit Chris's mom. Talk to you later. XXOO.*

The second and last text was marked later that day at about dinner time. Ashlynne was still fast asleep with her phone buried under a yard of black velvet in the other room, so she hadn't heard its chimes signaling incoming text messages.

"Damn," she said. "What day is it?" and checking the phone again, her eyes widened to see that it was Saturday.

"Wow! Talk about sleeping your life away! I'm like Rumpelstiltskin!" and immediately cringed at the fairy tale reference. Fairy tales had lost a significant amount of charm for her in the last few months.

Ashlynne: *Sorry I missed you — was Reading in the square. Let me know when you're home.*

Hitting send, she dropped the phone onto the coffee table and began emptying her tote from Thursday night.

The yard of black velvet with its raw edges was tossed into the laundry hamper to be washed and repacked. Pulling her deck of tarot cards out of the small bag into which she had hastily shoved them as she fled the French Quarter, she spread them out and righted each one so that all seventy-eight cards were facing the same direction. Holding them in her hands, she tried to decide if they were salvageable; while there was no visible damage, it bothered her that the Faerie had sent them flying so easily. Her use of them left Ashlynne feeling violated, and she wasn't sure if the cards would ever be truly *hers* again. Deciding that she would think about it before investing in another deck, she reached back into the tote, and her hand closed around two dead leaves. The visual flash of the memory came with such force that Ashlynne sat down so fast it appeared she had been pushed onto the sofa. Why had the Faerie left her with two dead leaves? What in the world could that mean? Studying each one and turning it over to look at all sides, Ashlynne could see nothing out of the ordinary about them. They were slightly leathery, yellowish-brown with an elongated oval shape. "From a Crepe Myrtle?" she mused aloud. Shrugging at yet another mystery, Ashlynne put the two leaves on the mantle of the fireplace and continued to pull her things out of the tote and put them to rights: her green sweater went into the laundry, aluminum water bottle into the kitchen sink, and money from her

Readings into the bottom of a cereal box that was kept in the top cupboard alongside boxes of rice, pasta and mac n' cheese.

"One hundred and twenty dollars. Hmm... Not great, but not terrible," said Ashlynne to Murphy as she walked back through the bedroom and into the living room. Murphy blinked at his mistress but didn't trouble himself to lift his head.

"And two dead leaves," she finished.

Having completed that chore, Ashlynne changed into a nicer T-shirt but opted to keep the jeans. She had noticed Mimi's disapproval, but they were some of her favorite clothes, and she desperately needed the comfort today of a just-right pair of jeans. She brushed her teeth, rinsed off her face, and re-braided her hair before tossing Murphy a dog biscuit. "Here ya go! No, no—don't bother to get up," she said sarcastically to the brown lump of ruffled fur crunching away on his milk bone on her bed.

"I'll be back in a bit, Murph. I have some

things to do," and she headed out the door—
but not before grabbing the flyer for the open
house at Mimi's Saint Ann Street cottage.

Chapter 17

Ashlynne made her way across North Rampart and into the French Quarter, equal parts excited to get into the house and nervous about the whole thing. 'Under the floorboards' seemed easy enough until you factored in almost seventy-five years' worth of restorations, carpeting, tile, or complete removal of the existing floor. So much time had passed that it wasn't a given that the book, or anything from Mimi's time as the owner of the house, still existed within the structure.

She approached the small house and stepped up to enter the open front door behind two other couples and a man dressed in a shiny suit and equally shiny shoes. This would be the obligatory investor interested in spit-polishing the house and then selling it for even more than what was currently being asked. As the others walked into the home and Ashlynne moved up to the front door, the real estate agent who had originally given her the flyer for the open house greeted her with a smile, "Hey! Glad to see you! Feel free to walk around the house and ask any questions you might have. We are entertaining all offers today, so don't wait too long!" she said in a perky salesperson voice that Ashlynne suspected was nothing like her everyday way of speaking.

Smiling in response, she moved into the large front room of the house. There were no curtains or blinds on the tall windows, and the house was free of furnishings, allowing light to stream in on the original wood flooring causing Ashlynne to breathe a little easier.

The living room flowed directly to the kitchen area with no wall or barrier between. The cupboards had seen better days, and the avocado-green electric stove spoke to the last time the kitchen appliances had been purchased. There was no refrigerator, and the counters were cracked and peeling Formica fronted by a strip of dingy metal. Moving into the next room—there was no hallway— Ashlynne found an empty room with cracked plaster walls, boarded up windows to the left, and a utilitarian fireplace with a grimy painted mantle to the right. Consulting her flyer's floor plan drawing, she noted that this room had been used as a bedroom. Beyond it was a small bathroom that had obviously been tacked onto the structure at some point in its history. As she compared Mimi's description with the current layout, one of the couples who had entered ahead of her walked past on their way back out. "Well, it definitely has potential," she heard the man say with the woman's sarcastic reply coming sharp and fast, "For the price they're asking, it better have potential and be able to do my laundry and taxes." The man chuckled, knowing the discussion would go nowhere, and they walked back out into the gathering heat of the day.

Turning back to her flyer, Ashlynne could see that the only change to the basic floor plan of the small house was to remove the wall that had once separated the living room and kitchen, thereby turning the former kitchen space at the back into a bedroom. This made much more sense for modern living rather than having one's bedroom in the center of the home like Ashlynne's current setup. Mimi had said that her hidey-hole had been cut into the floorboards in the kitchen next to the fireplace's hearth. Given the swap around of the rooms that meant that, if it still existed, it would be here in the room that was being listed as the bedroom.

Seemingly enchanted with the cracked plaster which allowed for the second couple to walk back out and into the front room, Ashlynne looked around as nonchalantly as possible to see where the investor had gone. Assuming he was in the back checking out the courtyard, and not wanting to take any more time in case more people decided to come through, she moved quickly to the fireplace, knelt down, and looked closely at the floor on either side of the hearth.

"Nice fireplace," said the investor over her shoulder causing her to jump to her feet and blush darkly.

"Uh, yeah. I mean, yes. Yes, it is. It's really pretty," stammered Ashlynne—inwardly cursing her flushed cheeks and awkward response.

As he walked back out to the combined living and kitchen area, Ashlynne once again knelt at the hearth and looked for any tell-tale signs of the floorboards having been altered. So many years had passed, and the dust and grime were so built up that it took longer than she expected to finally find a small line that moved vertically through the horizontal layout of the wooden boards. Blowing gently on the layer of dirt revealed the rest of the cuts forming an irregular square of approximately eight inches. It was partially concealed by the corner at the base of the wall and the bottom of the mantel just at the edge of the hearth, and if you weren't looking for it, you'd never see it. Ashlynne dearly hoped no one had been looking for this for the past seventy-three years.

Glancing back over her shoulder, she noticed the chipper real estate agent talking with Investor-Man with a pained look on her face. "Low ball offer," Ashlynne said quietly with an internal eye-roll as she turned her attention back to the section of the floor where, hopefully, she would find some answers to what had been happening these last very long weeks.

Moving quickly, Ashlynne brushed her fingers along the square of cut boards looking for a place that would allow her to lift one up and see underneath. With one ear to the conversation going on in the next room, she continued to investigate the space fearing that there would be no easy way to look underneath. As the voices rose behind her, she felt a small divot between the altered section and the rest of the floor. Using what little fingernails she had, she pried up the small section then pushed her fingertip under and lifted the square; it appeared as if Mimi had cut and glued the sections of wood together to make one piece. Reaching inside the dark space and praying that there were no snakes, rats, or roaches, Ashlynne felt around until her hand hit on what felt like heavy fabric. She wrapped her fingers around the parcel, pulled it out, stashed it underarm as if she always walked around with a bundle of rotting rope bound canvas with her, replaced the floorboards, and sauntered unnoticed past the argument still happening in the living room.

Squinting into the bright sunshine, Ashlynne turned back toward her own home and walked quickly down the sidewalk, her heart hammering in her chest, expecting at any moment for the real estate agent to yell for her to bring back whatever she had stolen. After a full block and no shouts of *stop thief!* Ashlynne's pace and heart rate slowed and she began to relax.

Moving the bundle of dirty canvas from under her arm where she had been carrying it like a football, she stuck two fingers through the rope holding it together and walked home swinging what was probably the world's most ugly handbag.

Chapter 18

Ashlynne unlocked her door and entered her home, awash in the half-light of the late afternoon. Dust motes danced around the tall windows with their wrought-iron safety gates designed to keep intruders out but always made Ashlynne feel more nervous than secure; if they kept intruders out, they also kept the residents trapped within. No matter her persistence, no amount of pleading with Mr. Alvin to remove them based on fire safety proved fruitful except for his gifting her a handheld fire extinguisher.

She dropped the bundle from Mimi's house onto the coffee table and walked through the bedroom to the kitchen where Murphy was sitting patiently by the back door waiting to be let out into the courtyard. She pushed the door open for him and watched as he trotted out into the gathering shadows. Spying Beau sitting under the table by Mr. Alvin's back door, Ashlynne wondered again if Murphy could see the other dog who refused to leave the home and human that he had so loved much.

Dumping the used coffee grounds into the garbage can under the sink and filling the basket with fresh coffee, she poured the water into the coffee maker, clicked it on, and let Murphy back inside. After filling his bowl with dry food and a dollop of canned pumpkin, Ashlynne filled her favorite mug with half and half and coffee and returned to the living room to inspect the parcel she had located at Mimi's old house. Feeling proud of herself for not tearing right into it, though her curiosity was at an almost painful peak, Ashlynne took a deep breath, a gulp of the restorative coffee brew, and carefully untied the delicate rope that had held the canvas together for so long. She imagined that it hadn't always been so delicate; the rope was quite thick, but years of critters, humidity, mold, and rot had weakened the fibers.

As the knot came apart, and the rope loosened its hold on the canvas, the whole packet fell open with a puff of moldy dust that moved up and away toward the windows behind her. Ashlynne pressed the age-stiffened fabric flat to reveal the contents that had been wrapped within for almost seventy-five years. A man's pocket watch with the hands stopped at a quarter to two, a matching silver knife and fork—each with an ornate pattern decorating the stem, and a small bound book with a faded navy blue cover and burnished gold script along the spine. Squinting closely, Ashlynne thought it said *Faerie Tales*. She set it aside with a yelp of surprise and held up the next item in the bundle—a deck of well-loved tarot cards. "Oh, Mimi! You never told me!"

"You never asked me," came the soft reply from the mirror to her left.

Ashlynne turned to see Mimi sitting on her customary wooden chair, smoking her cigarette. She was still dressed in what Ashlynne had come to think of as her 'power suit'—a 1940's tailored blazer and skirt with silk hose and laced up Spectator style heels. With the iconic rolled hairstyle of the era, Mimi truly did look to be a force to be reckoned with.

"How long have you been there?"

"I saw that you found my book and thought I'd visit," replied the spirit in the mirror.

"But how did you know? There's no mirror in your old house."

Mimi blew smoke rings over her head and simultaneously rolled her eyes at the young woman who now held the last of her earthly possessions. "Really, Ashlynne? How many spirits have you seen in your life? Have they required mirrors to move about? No," snapped Mimi with annoyance, "No they have not."

Ashlynne's cheeks burned with embarrassment at both her obtuse inquiry and the spirit's harsh reprimand.

"Sorry," she whispered, placing the tarot deck aside to pick up a cracked leather wallet—the last item in the bundle. Opening it carefully until it was fully unfolded to a length of about nine inches, Ashlynne saw it was a vintage men's wallet. The interior held a faded union card issued to Charles Blanchard which had expired over ninety years ago. Snugged into the long pocket that ran the length of the wallet was a sheaf of faded green and white. Ashlynne gently extracted the paper from the wallet and gasped, it was money. Lots of money.

"Mimi! What— "

"I worked my whole life," replied the spirit in response to the half-formed, but obvious question.

"Banks weren't for me," she continued with a rueful chuckle as she remembered both the hardships of the Great Depression and her lucrative pick-pocket escapades. It was safer, not just for Mimi but for a whole generation of people who had watched the largest bank collapse in history, to keep their money and valuables hidden safely within their own homes. "I kept my money at home where I could get to it anytime I needed it."

"Was Charles your husband?" asked Ashlynne, inspecting the union card carefully.

"No. My father." And the response was so curt and so final that Ashlynne wisely chose to not pursue the question further.

Putting down the wallet and turning her attention to the stack of money, Ashlynne very carefully pulled each bill away from the next. The damp of seventy-five New Orleans' summers had glued them together with a mixture of gummy dirt and dark-black mold that was, by this time, more dusty than slimy—a detail that Ashlynne was very grateful for.

"Mimi, there are over five thousand dollars here!"

"Yes, I imagine that would be about right," agreed the woman in the mirror with the same amount of interest one would give to a hangnail.

"Don't you care?" asked Ashlynne looking at Mimi who was still blowing elaborate smoke rings that rose above her head.

"Not really, Dear. There's no need for any of that anymore. I am glad to see my fork and knife made it. I loved those so much! But it's the book that is important, Ashlynne. The book will tell us what to do with the Faerie and how to bring back the woman whose body she's walking around in."

"But this money—"

"Keep it, it's yours now," came the fast reply as Mimi stood up and pointed to the small blue book on the coffee table. "We need that to be our focus. You may have the money to do with as you please, but you must read and study that book. It is of the utmost importance, Ashlynne."

And with that Mimi walked out of the frame and into whatever place she inhabited when she wasn't in the glass.

Ashlynne set the money aside and picked up the small book. The cover seemed to be linen stretched over cardboard. There was no title or author on the front, only the darkened script on the spine spelling out *Faerie Tales*. Brushing the grime and dust of decades off of the cover, Ashlynne carefully opened the book and breathed in the scent particular to old books: ink, wood pulp, sunshine, mold, and a strange sweetness that she could never identify, though all old books seemed to have it to a varying degree. If someone could match this in incense or a scented candle, she might never leave her house again, content to simply sit and breathe in the delicious scent of old words.

The first page was yellowed with age and blank. The paper was thick and unevenly trimmed, and the twine that bound the pages together could be seen at the crease between the paper and the cover. She carefully turned the next page and found a handwritten note in a spidery script that had blurred to a dark gray with age. Squinting at the writing, she thought it said simply *Recipes*. Scattered here and there below the word were dots of ink that had dropped from a quill more than one hundred years ago. Tucked into the crease along the interior edge was the ghost-thin outline of a pressed primrose flower.

The next page had more hand-written notes in no order but did, indeed, seem to be recipes of a sort.

At the top of one page, written in the same spidery script as the cover page was an entry dated 1812. Holding the old book almost to her nose Ashlynne read slowly,

'To Sleep Safe: St John's Wort, Daisies, & Verbena Red -Dry Together & Hang Above the Bed.'

This was signed 'Bridget O'Neil'. A couple of delicate drawings, rudimentary yet charming botanicals, were doodled alongside the little poem which Ashlynne assumed represented the plants in question.

Further down the page was another entry— again handwritten. This one said:

'To escape the Fair Folk That Chase You: Water Run An' Water Flow Keeps the Good Folk Dim

An' Slow. A Stream Moving Toward the Sun
Keeps the Traveler on The Run'.

This one was dated 1815 and signed
'Maggie O'Neil.'

The last entry on the page was titled *A Tea*
and seemed to be a much more normal recipe:

'To one pot of boiled water add one handful of
purple Thyme flowers, a smaller amount of Red
Clover flowers and the leaves of the Elderberry. Let
steep until the water turns purple.' Up to this
point, Ashlynne thought this tea recipe
sounded wonderfully charming and fairly
benign until she got to the last line which
read, *'drink at the black moon to see the Dark*
Host'.

"Wait, what?" asked Ashlynne to Murphy
who looked up at the sound of his human's
voice.

"What is a *Dark Host*?"

In response, Murphy yawned lazily, laid his
head back down on his paws, and closed his
eyes.

Page after page was filled with writing
providing Ashlynne with directions to keep

milking cows safe, stop pixies from entering the home, and the avoidance of Fairy Rings. There seemed to be three women who had composed entries and had a hand in compiling the fifty-odd pages of rhymes, recipes, drawings, and charms.

Turning the pages carefully to not tear them, Ashlynne found an entry with the title *'Barrow'* and stopped in surprise—her last name.

'Barrow: Place of the Sidhe, also a Fairy Mound. These are to be avoided at all costs. The way into the Barrow opens at the great festivals. For the traveler who finds no other recourse but to enter, placing a blade along the threshold will keep the way open so that he may return. Mary O'Neil'.

Ashlynne noted that this writing was less elegant and spidery than what was penned by Maggie O'Neil and the wording less archaic. There was no date, but other entries scattered throughout the book by Mary were written between 1897 and 1889 suggesting that Mary might have been a younger sister or perhaps the daughter of Maggie O'Neil. Ashlynne wondered who any of these women were to Mimi as she continued to flip through the homely book and sip her coffee as the sun set outside of her home.

Unseen by both Ashlynne and Murphy, a large sewer rat with the face of a pockmarked human man clambered up to the side window's exterior sill. As it prepared to slip into the half-opened window, its long tail brushed against the security gate, and the rat-thing let out a hiss of pain and anger—Iron. It could not pass. Chirping and hissing in fear and pain it slipped back down the side of the house and jumped to the pavement from the top of the trash cans that sat against the side of the house. The rat-thing slunk off into the shadows, hoping the Sidhe that had summoned it to enter the human's home wouldn't notice the failure.

Chapter 19

As the night wore on and the second pot of coffee was consumed, Ashlynne had read and re-read the pages of Mimi's book. While the title on the spine, *Faerie Tales*, suggested the stories of the Brothers Grimm, the actual information inside was more along the lines of an old-fashioned herbal or spellbook. "Every Witch worth her cauldron had one of these in the movies," she said as she turned the pages for the umpteenth time. Mimi had been adamant that the book would tell them how to not only send back the Faerie but release Amber. This seemed impossibly complicated, learning how to move the Faerie out of the body and at the same time release Amber so that she could go back to it. The book may have contained information on how to accomplish this, but there were no chapters or sections to narrow down the information; each woman who had written in it simply added what she thought would be useful wherever there was room, chronological order and topic be damned.

Ashlynne's head was swimming with the combined input of too much new information and too much caffeine, and she decided it was time for a break. She stood up and stretched her arms over her head and arched her back trying to release the crick that had settled there sometime during the night. She located Murphy's sweater and after wrestling him into it, clicked his leash onto his collar, and headed out into the cool early morning.

The sky was a smudgy gray with just a hint of orange and yellow peeking up from the horizon as she and Murphy turned left and walked up Ursulines. They passed the corner building that had been cut into a dozen or so tiny condos and smaller single-family homes that had been occupied by generations of the same name for over a hundred years. A block over, on Governor Nicholls Street, these smaller Victorian styled shotgun homes had all been snapped up by out of town investors and turned into swanky short-term rentals for tourists. While they looked pretty, painted vibrant colors with crisp white trim and ferns hanging from the porch roofs, Ashlynne still found it sad that the oldest African American neighborhood in the United States had turned into a series of boutique hotels, now unaffordable to the original inhabitants. Of course, the irony that she was a white girl transplanted from the far north living in the very same neighborhood wasn't lost on her.

As she and Murphy approached the corner of Saint Philip Street, she heard the crows calling off to her right and watched as a dark cloud of them lifted up and out of the trees of Armstrong Park where they roosted for the night. Individual black shapes separated from the main mass and flew off in all directions over her neighborhood and into the French

Quarter. Sending them a silent 'good morning,' Ashlynne led Murphy across the street to the brightly painted coffee shop.

Having decided against any more caffeine, Ashlynne ordered a bagel with lox and an orange juice for herself and a plain bagel for Murphy. Her phone beeped with an incoming message just as she and the dog settled in at a table on the outside patio.

Andrew: *'Heeelllooo.'*

Ashlynne: *'Hey there, you home now?'*

she typed back with one thumb while picking the red onions off her bagel with her free hand. She had forgotten to ask for it without.

Andrew: *'Just rolled in and wanted to check in before I crashed for a little while. You good?'*

Ashlynne: *'Yeah, I'm good. Lots to tell you though, come over when you're awake—I'll make dinner.'*

Andrew: *'Yay! It's a date!'*

Having removed all the onion from her bagel, Ashlynne tore off a bite-sized portion and began chewing slowly as she watched the sky go from the mixed yellows of dawn to its customary blue. Murphy tugged on his leash trying to get to the surrounding grass and hedge, so she let go of her end and allowed him the room to nose around for interesting smells while she finished her breakfast and juice.

Content to sit for a little while and listen to the block wake up, Ashlynne watched as Murphy spooked a group of sparrows from the hedge at the edge of the patio. The fat gray and black birds hopped away then took flight, seemingly cheerful even in the face of a would-be predator.

"Silly things," she grumbled as she gathered up her garbage and threw it away in the can outside the back door.

"C'mon, Murph," she announced as she tugged on the little dog's leash, forcing him away from a pile of god-knows-what on the far side of the patio. "You have to go home and I have to go to the store — Andrew is coming to dinner." And they set off back the way they came, crossing Saint Phillip onto Ursuline and back down the street to their house. The morning light was clearer with none of the murkiness of the early dawn, and both Ashlynne and Murphy walked at a good pace, passing the same houses but with the addition of people sitting on stoops and porches with cups of coffee or tea, smoking the ubiquitous cigarettes that also littered the curbs and planters. While it may not have the swankiness of the made-over short-term rentals or the grandeur of St Charles Avenue, this part of the Tremé made Ashlynne feel safe and at home like no other place she had ever lived.

"All the more reason to get that thing out of our neighborhood," she said to Murphy who had stopped to sniff at the flattened tires of an ancient Fiat that had been sitting in that driveway for decades.

Past the rotting sports car and up another half a block and Ashlynne was back at her own house. She let herself in, took Murphy's sweater off him, and got him settled.

Checking the refrigerator, she noted that she needed basically everything to make a decent dinner and groaned.

She was pulling her hair back into a ponytail and pondering how she was going to manage a full shopping trip with the meager earnings she had pulled in that week when Mimi's unexpected voice made her heart jump painfully in her chest.

"You have the money from my house, Dear. Please use it."

"Don't do that!" yelped Ashlynne spinning around to face the mirror, "Can't you knock or something?"

Mimi's brow furrowed as she squinted at the glass separating them. "Well, I don't know. I don't think so, though. Would you like me to announce my being here? Maybe clap loudly or whistle before I speak?"

Ashlynne narrowed her eyes at the older woman, unsure as to whether she was mocking her.

"Yes. I would like that very much," she

retorted, calling the spirit's bluff.

"Really? You want me to clap and whistle before I speak?" Mimi sounded both horrified and annoyed.

"No, of course not, but could you at least start with a 'hello' before you start making proclamations?"

"Yes, of course. I'm sorry, Ashlynne," replied Mimi in the gentlest voice that Ashlynne had heard the spirit take to date.

"What's that?" she asked suspiciously.

"What's what?" replied the spirit, matching Ashlynne's tone.

"The sweet, motherly thing you just did?"

"Oh, for heaven's sake! You look tired, and I know there's a lot going on. I was just trying to be nice!"

Ashlynne looked sideways at Mimi who had turned herself partly away from her and was lighting a cigarette.

"I'm sorry," she whispered.

Whether Mimi was waving her hand at Ashlynne's apology or to move the smoke away from her face was anyone's guess, but it broke the tension just the same.

"Ashlynne, please use the money from my house. I'm giving it to you, and you're going to need it! With everything you must do you are not going to have time to work like you're used to. This money will allow you to devote your time to the book and figuring out how to get rid of that thing across the street. And, of course, feeding Andrew who you will need to help you with all of this."

Ashlynne smiled at the woman in the mirror trying to decide if she was a friend, a mother figure, or a fairy godmother. Deciding on friend, she nodded her head and extracted one twenty-dollar bill from the wallet.

"Is this OK?" she asked, but the mirror only reflected her own image. Grabbing another twenty just to be safe, she stuffed the money, her phone, canvas shopping bags, and her shopping list into her bag and let herself out into the bright February morning.

She walked her usual route into the French Quarter to Rouses. The small market might be severely lacking in inventory compared to the much larger Super Markets outside the Quarter, but its old-fashioned neighborhood-store feel and convenient location still made it a favorite of hers.

It was still early in the day, so the joyful music provided by the street musicians wasn't part of the Royal Street landscape just yet. She passed perfectly human homeless and street kids splayed out along the brick buildings and flagstones, and while their plight made her heart ache, she was very relieved that none had lizard skin or forked tongues. For now, at least, the lizard punks were holed up asleep somewhere else.

Nodding a greeting to the security guard who was stationed outside the double doors of the market, Ashlynne pulled one open and stepped into the cramped space. Directly in front of her were two checkout lanes with only one being open this time of day. The cashier looked tired, and Ashlynne imagined that she was on the tail-end of a long night shift. To her right were wire racks stretching to the ceiling and filled with a dozen or so variations of the King Cake; there were apple, cinnamon, lemon, raspberry, cream cheese, and more available as fillings in the flaky circular pastry dressed in the colors of Mardi Gras. Ashlynne moved past the King Cakes and turned the corner at the far back of the store.

Moving along the back aisle and shimmying around several other shoppers all trying to move about in the tight quarters, Ashlynne grabbed a wedge of Parmesan cheese and a length of Andouille sausage. Having checked those items off her list, she noticed that she had forgotten half and half and scooted around a woman dressed entirely in purple and gold with the longest fake eyelashes she had ever seen.

"Excuse me, darlin'," drawled the purple lady as Ashlynne moved past her to reach into the dairy case. "This is like shopping in a game of Twister!" laughed Ashlynne, and the woman chuckled in agreement. Adding the last of the necessary items to her basket, Ashlynne headed to the checkout lane.

Hefting the three canvas grocery bags out the door, held open for her by the security guard, Ashlynne began the trek of eight blocks or so back to her house. She passed wave after wave of gold, green, and purple decor; puffy wreaths on front doors, glittering garlands strung from galleries and balconies, and large metallic masks attached to shuttered windows. Mardi Gras season had begun.

The sun was closing in on its noon peak as she schlepped her bags up the steps to her front door and let herself inside. The coolness of the shuttered interior was a relief after the cloudless, sunny sky that presided over her walk home.

She opened the back door for Murphy, poured herself a glass of cold water from the pitcher in the refrigerator, and began to unpack the groceries. Once that was done and Murphy let back in, Ashlynne curled up on her bed relishing the solitude and darkness. She flipped on the fan for some white noise to

block the neighborhood's usual background
sounds and drifted off into a dreamless sleep.

Chapter 20

Ashlynne slept deeply and only woke when Murphy whined to be let outside. She stumbled into the kitchen, opened the door for the small dog, and blinked at the clock on the stove; it was three o'clock.

"Whoa! I slept for three hours!" she marveled aloud as she opened the refrigerator to retrieve the vegetables and other ingredients that she would need to make dinner.

With the water boiling for pasta in her one large pot, she added salt and dumped in the twisted rotini style noodles that would be the basis for their dinner.

By the time she had set the table, the pasta

had been tossed with her homemade white wine cream sauce and was simmering with the sausage and peppers on the stove. Murphy, being underfoot one too many times, had been banished to the courtyard where he was skulking at the back door, not wanting to miss out on any morsels that might drop to the floor.

"Ohhhh! That smells amazing!" called Andrew from the front door as she sliced the French bread and placed it on the table.

"C'mon in!" called Ashlynne, despite knowing that Andrew would always let himself in if the door was unlocked.

"Dinner is gonna be gooooood!" he smiled, kissing Ashlynne on the cheek. "Are you making your sausage and pepper dish?"

"You know it! I'm a one-trick pony when it comes to cooking," she laughed.

Over their dinner of pasta, peppers, and sausage accompanied by fresh, crusty French bread, Ashlynne filled Andrew in on locating the book and how it might help them be rid of the neighbor.

"OK, you stole a book from under the floorboards of an empty house?" repeated Andrew for the millionth time as Ashlynne took a long drink from her glass of wine.

"Again, it wasn't really stealing because the woman who put it there told me to go get it."

"The woman who is dead but you talk to when she's in the mirror in your living room? That woman?"

"Yes. That woman," replied Ashlynne flatly as she gazed steadily across the table at her friend.

"And the neighbor-from-hell isn't from hell; she's a Faerie? Where are those from? And how do you know this?"

"I don't know exactly where Faeries are from, a place sort of next to our world. I think..." Ashlynne trailed off as Andrew listened skeptically.

"But I know she's a Faerie because I've seen what she truly looks like which is so not what we see when she's being the neighbor!"

"OK."

"What?"

"I said *OK*," replied Andrew.

"You don't believe me, do you?"

"It's not that I don't believe you, it's that I don't understand how you know all of this! Faeries, ghosts, hidden books! It's just a lot to take in," said Andrew trying to soothe his friend's hurt feelings. "SO!" he announced with forced cheeriness, "let's go see this book that is supposed to take care of all of this!"

"Yeah, OK. Let me rinse these dishes, and I'll be right in," replied Ashlynne—feeling disheartened. She wasn't sure why she had expected Andrew to jump right into the fantastical situation with no questions asked, but she had, and now she was feeling defensive. She knew what she knew, and she knew it was correct, but she had no way to prove this to Andrew.

"Faith, my friend," She counseled herself as she scraped pasta and sauce from the dinner dishes and into the garbage can, "have some faith."

"I'll be right there!" she called to Andrew as she scooped the yogurt into two cut-glass bowls and scattered chopped fruit on top. A sprinkle of salted pistachios and a drizzle of honey completed the simple after-dinner dessert, and she stashed them in the fridge until they were ready to have the final portion of the meal. Flipping the already prepared coffee pot to 'on,' she moved to the living room, sending a silent plea to Mimi to not be hanging out in the mirror right now.

"Coffee smells good," remarked Andrew as he scratched Murphy's ears and fed him bites of French bread that had been secreted out of the kitchen behind her back.

Ashlynne sat down next to him on the sofa and shot Murphy a withering glance in response to his triumphant look in her direction. Having decided that discretion was the better part of valor, the small dog jumped down with the last bite of bread between his teeth and trotted into the bedroom to enjoy his forbidden treat in private.

The small blue-covered book sat on the

coffee table between them, not looking at all like the key to fixing the craziness that had taken over their neighborhood these past few months. With a nod from Ashlynne, Andrew picked it up and gently opened it to a random page about three-quarters of the way through.

"It's all handwritten?" he asked her in a near whisper.

"Yes," she answered, matching his tone. She was pleased that he seemed intrigued.

As Andrew carefully thumbed through pages containing assorted recipes, quotes, drawings, and musings, she brought in the coffee and bowls of dessert.

"This is amazing," he said around a bite of yogurt and fruit. "Listen to these, Ashlynne!" said Andrew, obviously forgetting that she had already gone through the book several times by now, but she was happy he was as enchanted with the book as she was.

'Of Elder no cradle make lest the Fair Folk the babe do take.'

Andrew looked up at Ashlynne, "what

does that mean?"

"I think it means if you make a cradle from Elder wood then the fairies will come and steal the baby."

"But why?"

"I don't know, Andrew!" she laughed as she took a bite of her yogurt and fruit. "This one is interesting, too," she said and pointed to another entry.

'Nine Ivy leaves place under the head to dream of the living but not of the dead. Eight of the leaves place under the bed to protect you in sleep from fear and from dread.'

"Ivy will stop bad dreams?" asked Andrew as he stirred cream into his coffee and took a sip.

"According to this, yes. I'm more than willing to give it a try if it stops the doozies I've been having lately," said Ashlynne. "*'Faerie Folks Are in Old Oaks.'* Well, if that's true then we should have tons of Faeries roaming around New Orleans—"and he stopped when he saw Ashlynne's face. "Oh no! Wait! There's more isn't there?"

"Yeah, see, I've been meaning to get to that part," replied Ashlynne with a sheepish look.

"Oh, Come ON!" groaned Andrew. "It's not enough to have the weird neighbor not be human, but you're saying there's more?"

"Yes—many more. But they don't look human at all, so they're easier to see. For me, that is."

Andrew stared at his friend, waiting for her to continue.

"Remember the big fight with the college guys out front?"

"Yeah."

"The street kids that jumped in weren't human. I call them lizard punks. I'm pretty sure they're all from wherever Amber-who's-not-Amber is from."

Andrew blinked slowly and deliberately, like a cat trying to decide whether to stick around and watch the birds outside the window or walk away and not be bothered.

"Lizard punks." A statement, not a question. "You're telling me that the street kids living below me and Chris are not human and look like lizards?" With the question, Andrew's voice rose alarmingly at the last word.

"Uh, yeah. Partially lizard, anyway," she replied carefully as she watched her friend try desperately to absorb all of this new information.

Andrew took a deep breath and held it then exhaled loudly.

"OK, spill it, Ashlynne. Tell me everything because I obviously need to be caught up to speed."

And Ashlynne did. She started at the beginning with her visions of dead leaves and bugs on the 'For Rent' sign, meeting Mimi in her living room mirror, the visions of Amber, her nightmares, the cleansing by Mambo Michele, how Murphy came to her, the lizard punks, skull-faced moths, human-faced rats, and the terrible Reading with Amber-who-wasn't-Amber in the Square the other night.

"So, this Faerie, she took Amber's body?"

"Yes. I'm not sure how, but she took the

human body and has left the real Amber in the other place."

"And the Faerie is here for what purpose?"

"Mimi says she has no real purpose, but that she delights in destruction and chaos."

"And we get rid of her, how?" asked Andrew, finishing his now cold coffee.

"The book is supposed to help us with that, but I'm not sure how just yet," replied Ashlynne gathering up the coffee cups and empty dessert bowls. "I know Mimi said that the book would have the information that we need, but it's not organized in any way, and some of the writing is so hard to read that it's been slow-going."

Andrew sat gazing at the walled-up fireplace in front of him, lost in his thoughts. Leaving him to it, Ashlynne carried the dirty dishes into the kitchen and rinsed them off before stacking them next to the sink to wash later.

"So, what is this Faerie's name?" called Andrew from the living room.

"We don't know," she replied, coming back in to sit next to him on the sofa.

"I, for one, want to know the name of the thing that has caused so much craziness, don't you?"

"Oh, yeah. Most definitely," replied Ashlynne with a steely resolve that her friend had never heard from her before. A small smile played along Andrew's lips as he thought to himself that this Faerie had no idea who she had decided to tangle with.

It was well after midnight before Andrew called it quits for the night and walked across the street to his own house, his head swimming with archaic rhymes, strange recipes for teas, and drawings both fantastic and mundane.

Annie Russell

Chapter 21

Ashlynne was finishing up the dishes from last night's dinner when she heard Murphy give three sharp barks at the front door. She dried her hands on the dish towel and went to see what had alerted the dog. Pushing him out of the way, she opened one of the shutter's slats that were at roughly eye level, the New Orleans' version of a peephole, to see Andrew standing on the sidewalk just below her stoop holding a bakery bag in one hand and a notebook in the other.

"Hey, what's going on?" she asked as she opened the door for him to come inside.

"Well, I got zero sleep thanks to our conversation last night and decided that the amount of work we needed to do would require lots of therapeutic carbs and copious amounts of note-taking. So, here, have a donut," he said holding out the bag and adding, "I assumed you would have coffee."

"It's me, Andrew," she replied with a chuckle as she went to put on a fresh pot. "Let's do this in the kitchen!" she called back over her shoulder to him as she arranged the assortment of pastries on a plate and set out two coffee mugs, the half and half they both used, and some napkins.

Andrew pulled up a chair and added a new spiral-bound scholastic style notebook, two pens, and Mimi's book to the kitchen table and breathed in the rich aroma coming from the freshly brewed pot of coffee set between them.

"You make the best coffee of anyone I know," he smiled at her as she poured the warm liquid into both of their mugs.

As they enjoyed their breakfast, Murphy was outside nosing around the foliage with

Beau at his heels. Ashlynne was watching the two dogs from her chair at the kitchen table as Andrew chatted on about a Mardi Gras Ball that he and Chris were invited to attend at some grand ballroom or another on St. Charles Avenue. As always, the two men's social life was interesting but completely removed from Ashlynne's, and even more so now, making it very hard to follow his conversation past certain keywords that floated out past the *'blah blah blah'* of the commentary; *Throws*, *Floats*, and *Beads* jumped out allowing her the opportunity to nod and reply in the vaguely affirmative while allowing her own thoughts to return to the book and what they needed to do to put things to rights again.

"…...and that's how we cooked and ate the glittered shoes!" announced Andrew.

"Wait, what?" exclaimed Ashlynne. "Cooked and ate what?"

"Yeah, I figured you weren't listening to me," he replied around the last bite of croissant. Taking a drink of his coffee, he continued, "Chris and I have several events to attend in the next few weeks, and I don't want to miss them. So, let's get this Faerie removal party started, shall we?"

Scooting her chair around the table to sit next to Andrew, Ashlynne reached for the small book that they were told would provide them with the information they needed to not only send the Faerie back but restore Amber to her human body.

"So, our goal is to get the Faerie out and bring Amber back, correct?" asked Andrew as he held his pen over the first page of the notebook.

"Correct," replied Ashlynne with a firmness that belied her uneasiness. Was it really that simple? There was so much that had happened that it seemed strange that the whole situation could be combined so succinctly.

As Andrew wrote down their goal, Ashlynne realized that this was a perfect way to get her head out of the fuzziness of too much information, and she smiled at her friend's approach.

"OK, next. We should probably go through the book and look for anything about Faeries who take humans or evil Faeries in general. What do you think?" asked Andrew as he reached around Ashlynne for the coffee pot.

"That seems like as good a place to start as any," she agreed while shaking her head at the offer of more coffee. It didn't happen often, but she had had enough for now.

Huddled together, the two scanned the spidery writing of entries and drawings set down over the course of sixty-odd years throughout the middle to the late nineteenth century. There was no explanation regarding any event that may have caused Bridgette O'Neil to begin the journal, but it seems that both her daughter and granddaughter continued the tradition. Why it ended with Mimi was anyone's guess, but Ashlynne made a mental note to ask the spirit about the women who wrote the book and why she had declined to add entries of her own.

"Here's something," muttered Andrew, his eyes squinting at the sepia-toned page in front of them. *'If elf grippet boil together rosemary, thyme, comfrey, and herb grace in a strong ale. Strain properly and add honey. Drink each morning for three mornings between the new and full moon. Maggie O'Neil'*

"What is elf grippet?" asked Ashlynne.

"No clue," replied Andrew as he continued to turn pages and scan the entries. "But the recipe seems to be a medicine."

"Next?" suggested Ashlynne as she doodled suns and moons at the margins of their notebook.

"OK—here. This is something we should look at, for sure. *'To see: From a Black hen take the first egg laid. Boil it well and rinse the eyes of him that wants to see with the sweat of the egg. Bridgette O'Neil.'*"

"Him who wants to see what?" asked Ashlynne.

"I assumed Faeries since that's what the book is about."

"I can already see Faeries, Andrew."

"Well, it's a good thing you're the only one working on this, then isn't it?" he replied sharply.

"You're right, I'm sorry. But that leads to the next issue with that entry; where do we find a black hen, and how do we know which was her first laid egg of that morning?"

"Yeah, you're right. I guess I would like to be able to see what you're talking about, though."

"Well, how about this, then!" exclaimed Ashlynne with a triumphant jab of her finger at the next entry as she read aloud, "*'For him that through the holed stone looks are wonders more than found in books. Mary O'Neil'*"

"Umm, what?"

"It says that if you look through a stone with a hole in it you can see amazing things!" said Ashlynne trying not to sound impatient.

"And where do we find one of those? Or do we need to drill a hole in a stone?"

"I have one already!" exclaimed Ashlynne, her eyes alight and a big grin on her face.

She jumped up from the table and went into the living room where she kept her supplies for Readings in Jackson Square. Rummaging around inside the milk crate, her fingers closed around the smoothness of her incense holder.

She hurried back into the kitchen and handed the pink and green speckled stone to Andrew.

"Isn't this your incense holder?"

"Yep!"

Giving her a sideways glance, he held it in both hands, turning it this way and that.

"You know this is just Granite, right, Ash?"

Ashlynne rolled her eyes at him, not even trying a little to hide her annoyance.

"Granite with a hole through the middle," she retorted in the tone of voice one uses for the purposely slow and hard to teach.

"It's not a very big hole," he muttered under his breath, holding the stone up to eye level.

"The book doesn't say it needs to be a big

hole, just a stone with a hole through it.
Rather than arguing, why don't you try it?"

"Try it?" asked Andrew with a look of part
amusement and part fear on his face.

"Yes, Andrew. Try It. Go outside into the
courtyard and look through the hole and see
if things look any different. I dare you."

"Oh, you dare me?' he asked incredulously.
"Fine. Dare accepted."

Ashlynne watched as Andrew stood up
from his chair, holding the stone in the palm
of his hand. His face was set in studied
nonchalance, but Ashlynne could see the
nervousness like ribbons of blue energy
rippling off his body.

He pushed open the door and stepped out,
Murphy slipping out behind him before the
old metal screen door slammed shut.
Ashlynne looked out from within the kitchen,
not sure what she was hoping for but feeling
excitement zip through her limbs at the
thought of the stone working.

As she stood there watching, unseen by
Andrew, Beau wandered over to Murphy

from Mr. Alvin's side of the house, tail wagging in happiness. As usual, Ashlynne wasn't entirely sure whether Murphy could see the little poodle, but he seemed to acknowledge that he wasn't alone so maybe he could sense him if not outright see him.

Andrew stood still and looked around the courtyard. It looked like it always did; he saw the small, kidney-shaped pool that was the envy of the block, overgrown yet somehow lush banana and kumquat trees, and the small wire table and chairs shared by Ashlynne and Mr. Alvin. He noted that Murphy must have slipped out when he opened the door because the small dog was on the other side of the pool nosing around in the bushes.

Taking a deep breath, and feeling not a little foolish, Andrew held the palm-sized granite stone up to his face and squinted one eye to peer through the small hole that normally held Ashlynne's incense sticks. It took a second for his vision to adjust, but soon he was looking at the greenery to his left that framed the small window of Ashlynne's bathroom. Turning to his right like he was scanning the horizon from the deck of a ship with a telescope, he saw the small utility shed tucked into the corner of the brick wall, and continuing from there, he saw Murphy, still nosing around the leaves and grasses at the back of the courtyard. And this is where Andrew stopped. Because next to Murphy was a small grayish-black poodle. He lowered the stone away from his eye and let his vision readjust. He looked across the pool—no poodle—just Murphy. He lifted the stone back up to his eye and peered through again—Murphy and a poodle.

Ashlynne watched in amazement from the back door as Andrew's arm raised and lowered repeatedly as he looked through the stone then looked across the pool without it. By the time she made it outside and to his side, he was simply standing with both arms hanging limply at his sides, the stone held loosely in his right hand.

"What did you see?"

Andrew just stood and stared. He could hear Ashlynne and felt the weight of her hand on his shoulder, but he was rooted to the spot in amazement. The thought that their places in this scenario had been reversed passed through his stunned brain; usually, she was the one standing in a trance, not him.

"Andrew! What did you see?" Ashlynne repeated with more force and gently shook his shoulder.

"I think I saw Beau," replied Andrew in a dazed voice.

"Small grayish-black poodle standing to the right of Murphy?" she asked.

Andrew held the stone back up to his eye and peaked through the small hole again.

"Purple collar?" he asked.

"That's him. Welcome to my world, Andrew," said Ashlynne with a small laugh as she gently guided her confused best friend back into the house.

As she busied herself with filling glasses with ice and cold water, Ashlynne watched

Andrew from the corner of her eye; she wasn't sure how well he was going to handle this whole situation. To say you want to see what others don't normally see is a far cry from being able to do so. It was an adjustment, to be sure.

Andrew took a grateful swallow of the ice water and a deep breath and looked at Ashlynne.

And then he started laughing. Not polite, small laughs but full-on belly-laughs and guffaws that made Ashlynne a little nervous; this wasn't the reaction she had imagined at all.

She leaned against the sink, sipping her water, and watching as the deep belly laughs slowly subsided to gasping giggles and finally sporadic hiccups as Andrew's hysteria wound its way down.

"Better?" she asked dryly as he heaved a giant sigh and laid his head on his arm, splayed across most of the kitchen table.

"I don't think that's the right word," came the muffled response as Ashlynne replaced the ice and the water in both of their glasses.

"Here," she nudged his arm with the glass, and he sat up to gulp down three-quarters of the cold water.

He wiped his still weeping eyes on his sleeve and looked at Ashlynne who had resumed her position in the chair next to his.

"Wow."

"Yeah."

"What else is out there?" He asked in a small voice.

"More, and more than that," replied Ashlynne and refrained from adding *'curiouser and curiouser'* because she didn't want to sound flippant.

Andrew pushed the stone at Ashlynne with one finger, "Here. You hold onto this. I'll need some practice, but I don't want to do it alone."

"You got it, and you're never alone," she replied with a warm smile in his direction.

They pushed on through the afternoon, sifting through entries and drawings and assorted poetry looking for anything that might help with the chore at hand. By the time Ashlynne had warmed up leftover pasta from last night, they had a working list of items from the book that they thought might be the start of removing the Faerie.

"According to our notes, the stone can help me see what you do and can also help us in seeing other places that are normally hidden. Faeries don't like running water like streams, and they also don't like iron or electricity.

The evil or more unfriendly Faeries are called Unseelie, do you think that is the type of Faerie that our neighbor is?"

"I think so," replied Ashlynne. "But I'm curious if the Faeries don't like iron or electricity, how is the neighbor getting along so well here?"

"I've been thinking about that too. I think it's because it's in human form right now, so these things aren't as bad for it compared to if it was in its real body."

"Well, that makes sense! You're getting pretty good at this stuff," chided Ashlynne.

Ignoring the teasing, Andrew continued, "The book also has a note about names being power; that if you have the true name of a thing then you have power over it. I think it's really important that we figure out the Faerie's name."

"Oh, wait—hold on a minute," said Ashlynne as she turned the pages in the book back to the page where they had found the information on the holed stone. "It says here that the holed stones are also called *'pledge stones'* and that they give the holder the ability to know if another is speaking the truth."

"Yeah?"

"Wellllll…" said Ashlynne, furiously turning pages, "if we combine that with this rhyme that I remember but can't find…." She chewed on her lip as she continued quickly scanning the entries, "Ah! Here! *'Holey Stone and Red Thread Make the Fae Its True Name Will To Spake'"*

"What in the world does that mean?" asked Andrew after trying to fit his tongue around the slippery old cadences.

"I think what it means is that the stone can be hung on a red string, and we can use it to find out the Faerie's real name."

"Well, OK. I'll add 'red string' to our list, but we still haven't found anything about swapping the Faerie for the human."

"Maybe we don't need to."

"Yes, we do. That is literally the point of all of this," said Andrew with a weary sigh.

Ashlynne began telling Andrew about her hunting missions and how she was sending the creatures back to wherever they came from. She detailed the swirl of green light that opened for each one and how she believed that meant they all came from the same place. She finished with her theory: that ever since all these strange things had begun showing up when the Faerie did, that meant that they came from where she did, and that's how she could both call and control them.

Andrew nodded thoughtfully and said, "So you already know how to send her back, we just need to know how to swap them so

Amber gets her body back?"

"Exactly. And I think that happens when we find out the Faerie's true name."

"Alright. Then we need to do that. We have a stone with a hole through it and some red string, any ideas on how to get those to work?"

"I don't, but I think Mambo Michele might."

"Then we'll go see her tomorrow. You bring the stone, and I'll bring the red string. Meet you at the Coffee shop at nine?"

"It's a plan," said Ashlynne, more than ready to call it a night.

Ashlynne and Murphy said goodbye to Andrew as he walked across the narrow street to his house, and they turned right, heading into the French Quarter. It was a long day of sitting, and they both needed to walk off some steam and stress.

"An evening stroll to look at the Mardi Gras decorations is just what the doctor ordered, isn't it, Murph?" she said to her furry companion as they ambled up Ursuline.

Chapter 22

The morning was overcast and chilly when Ashlynne walked up to the coffee shop a little after nine, and she was grateful to see that Andrew had opted to sit inside instead of on the back patio.

"Mornin' darlin'," and her friend smiled and kissed her lightly on the cheek.

"Good morning. Did you get any sleep?"

"Not very much," Andrew grimaced. "Between my head swimming with bad poetry, herbal remedies, and fairy tales, and the so-called neighbor making a huge racket downstairs, there might have been a minute or two of shut-eye."

"Ugh, I'm so sorry," replied Ashlynne,

adding cream to the coffee that Andrew had ordered, ready for her arrival.

"Do you want anything to eat?" she asked, checking out the offerings in the pastry case to their left.

"Naw, I think I'll pass for now and just have coffee."

"What time does Michele's shop open?"

"Ten, I think. We have time to finish our coffee, but then we should head down there. Did you bring the red string?"

Andrew took a swallow of his coffee then reached into his pocket and pulled out a ball of red twine as well as a smaller spool of thread.

"I wasn't sure which one would be best, so I brought both. How about you? Did you remember the stone?"

Ashlynne pulled the speckled granite stone from her bag and placed it next to the red twine and spool of thread on the table.

"Yep, I put it in my bag before I went to bed last night so I wouldn't forget."

"Alright, let's do this thing," said Andrew

with a firmness that neither one was feeling.

Ashlynne always felt a sense of well-being when she entered Michele's shop; the layered scents of the many incenses, the orderly lines of glass-encased colored candles on the shelves, and the amazing beaded flags — called *drapo vodou* — that hung along the walls had all combined to create a calm yet powerful energy.

Michele ushered them to the back of the shop where her office and private consult rooms were located.

Andrew sipped the tea that was placed in front of him, more to be polite than because he wanted it, as Ashlynne began to fill Michele in on what had been happening since her last visit to the shop. Michele nodded and listened and only interrupted when she needed a detail clarified.

"And you found the information you needed in this book that you stole?" asked Michele after Ashlynne's monologue concluded.

"I didn't steal it! Mimi owned it and asked me to go and get it!"

"Did you find the information that you needed then?" asked Michele again, sidestepping the issue of thievery, though she certainly considered the acquisition of Mimi's book sketchy. At best.

"Some of it, yes. There was an entry that said a 'holey stone' could do a lot of amazing things. My incense holder is a stone with a hole in it, and we found out it really does allow Andrew to see things that I do. The book said that the stone could also help us to find the Faerie's real name and said to use it with a red thread or string."

With a glance at Andrew, Ashlynne saw that he was holding up the twine and the spool to show Michele.

"But we're not sure how that works, exactly," finished Ashlynne.

"May I see them please?" asked Michele, holding out her hands.

As they passed their items to Michele, they

exchanged a glance; neither was sure whether Michele believed them or would help.

"Do you have the book?"

"Yes, I brought it along," said Ashlynne, pulling the small journal from her bag and passing it over to Michele.

Michele held the book in both hands, one below it and one above it, sandwiching the covers between her palms. She closed her eyes and breathed deeply through her nose, exhaling gently from her mouth. The Priestess sat like this with her eyes closed while Ashlynne and Andrew watched and wondered.

After a minute or two, Michele opened her eyes and gently placed the book on the table in front of her.

"This is a beautiful book; it has strong female energy and a solid feeling of power to it. It's not flashy, but the women who wrote it weren't either; I'm glad you have this, Ashlynne."

"Do you know how to use the stone and

thread?" Andrew asked.

"I think so, yes. But first, I want to go back to the garden party dream. Ashlynne, please tell me again about the thin black man who helped you escape as well as the mark on your dog."

Ashlynne told Michele about the man in as much detail as she could remember: his slight appearance that was at complete odds with the power that radiated off of him, the staff he carried, and the colors of the light that sparked out of the sigil he drew.

"Ashlynne, I want you to go out into the shop and look around. Bring to me anything that reminds you of this man."

Ashlynne got up and walked back out to the retail section of Michele's shop and began wandering up and down the aisles. She chose a glass-encased candle colored a deep red, a greeting card with an elaborate skeleton key drawn on the front in gold glitter, and a statuette of a very thin black man dressed in rags carrying a tall walking stick. A small dog was at its feet. She carried these items into the

306

back room and set them down on the table next to the book, the red thread, and the stone.

Mambo Michele looked at each of the items she had chosen and then held the small statue of the man dressed in rags up for them to see.

"Papa Legba," she pronounced.

"Who?" asked Andrew

"Papa Legba," Michele and Ashlynne replied in unison.

"Oh my gosh! Of course! How could I not have recognized him?" exclaimed Ashlynne.

"Sometimes what we experience in dreams is so convoluted and so removed from the everyday of our lives that it takes another to show you what you have seen," explained Michele. "Papa Legba came to you in that place."

"Murphy and me," said Ashlynne, pointing the dog at the feet of the figurine.

"Dogs are a favorite of Papa," explained Michele. "The thing threatening you and your dog must have offended him, and he came to you. This is a great honor, Ashlynne. A great honor…"

"Did he leave the mark on Murphy?" asked Ashlynne as Andrew's head swiveled back and forth between the two women trying to keep up with the newest developments.

"Yes, I think so. I'm not sure why, but I do believe he marked him."

"Umm, who is Papa Legba?" interjected Andrew before one or the other could start talking again.

"Papa Legba is a most powerful Loa, a spirit of the Voodou. He holds the keys that open the way between our world and the world of Spirit. Papa is a guardian of the crossroads, meaning he can open—or close—the roads to opportunity. Dogs are sacred to him, and he is very protective of those he claims as his own."

"And this is the man who helped Ash and Murphy to escape the Garden-Party-From-Hell?"

"Yes."

"But why? Why would a Voodoo Spirit show up to help someone escape a Faerie?"

"As I said, Andrew, Papa Legba is very protective of those he chooses to call his own, and in this case, it would seem that he has chosen Ashlynne and her dog."

Andrew looked over at Ashlynne who was staring at the statuette in amazement.

"Will he help us?" she asked in a small voice.

"Oh yes. I think he will most definitely continue to help you, and he is uniquely equipped to do this, Ashlynne," said Michele to the wide-eyed young woman next to her. "He opens the doors between realms."

Ashlynne and Andrew looked across the table at each other for a long moment and then Ashlynne let out a whoop of excitement, "Oh, this is wonderful!" she laughed as she jumped to her feet.

"How so?" asked Andrew. "I think it's gotten much more complicated."

"Nope! It's gotten much easier. We now have a powerful Spirit that can open doors for us and close them, too. We don't have to fight this thing on our own or watch it continue to destroy our neighborhood."

Michele nodded in agreement, "Yes, exactly right. But we still have a lot of work to do. You had asked how the stone and string work earlier. I believe that we can use these together as a pendulum of sorts to find out the Faerie's name. But first, we need to establish what we do with its name once we have it and how all this works with Papa Legba."

Michele gestured for Ashlynne to sit back down and she opened the book.

"Let's see what this has to say about the power of names."

Ashlynne and Andrew flipped through the now-familiar pages looking for an entry that might have anything to do with the names of Faeries. Besides the charm for using the stone and thread, they weren't finding much.

"May I look?" asked Michele, reaching for the book.

"Be my guest," replied Ashlynne, sounding tired and frustrated.

Michele picked up the small book and

turned to carry it to a more comfortable chair to read in when a small scrap of paper fluttered down and settled on the table in front of them.

All three looked at each other in amazement as the quietest quiet that there ever had been descended upon them.

Very carefully Ashlynne reached over and picked up the yellowed paper. Unfolding it carefully she pressed it flat and leaned over to read the faded writing, "*Circle round and flame a bright, say its name to set to right. Say the name again times three to send it far away from thee.*"

"Where did that come from?" whispered Andrew

"I have no idea," replied Ashlynne in a voice low with trepidation.

"Well, it had to have been in there the whole time, look how old it is. You just missed it before now," replied Michele who was trying to be the lone voice of reason.

"No way," said Andrew. "There is no way we could have missed that! We've been over and over that book a hundred times or more. Haven't we, Ash?"

"Yeah, at least," agreed Ashlynne. "We would have seen it by now, Michele!"

"Well, it's here now, and it mentions 'names.' Let's see what it's about," said Michele, trying to stem the look of outright panic that was playing across the other two faces staring at her across the table.

"*Circle round and flame a bright.* So, we need a circle and a candle? Make sense you two?"

Seeing nods all around she continued, "*say its name to set to right. Say the name again times three to send it far away from thee.* In this part, it says to say the name to make things right. Then to say the name again three times to send whatever it is away."

"Do you think that this is what we can use the Faerie's name for?" asked Ashlynne.

"I think that is exactly what this scrap of paper is trying to tell us," replied Michele with a smile.

"OK, let me get this straight: we use the stone and the string to find out the Faerie's name then make a circle, light a candle, and say its name four times to get rid of it. That seems way too simple," said Andrew to the other two.

"I think there might be a little more to it than that," chuckled Michele. "I think the rhyme is talking about a magic circle, not just any old circle."

"What makes a circle magical?" asked Ashlynne

"Energy and intent," replied Michele. "But these are western magical practices, and not what I normally do. I will need some time to work on this—as well as find out where Papa Legba fits since he has decided to be involved in the situation. Can you two come back in a week?"

"Yes!" said both in unison.

"And I think we can all research," said Andrew pulling the notebook from Ashlynne's bag. "I can look into candles and magic. Ashlynne, why don't you do some research on magic circles? And Michele, you find out how Papa Legba will be involved. Sound good?"

With all three in agreement, Ashlynne stowed the book, the notebook, the stone, the spool of thread, and the ball of twine back into her bag and hoisted it over one shoulder.

Michele returned to her store to unpack new incense. Ashlynne and Andrew began the walk back to their own houses as the late-February sun shone its feeble warmth down onto their heads.

Chapter 23

For anyone looking in on the three friends' lives, the days following their meeting at Michele's botanica passed in a blur of work obligations and Mardi Gras events. Andrew drove to and from his job as a manager of a large retail store in the suburbs during the day and attended Krewe Balls and parades with Chris in the evenings. Ashlynne worked at the vampire lounge, doing double duty as both Reader and Cocktail waitress to keep up with the steady stream of Mardi Gras visitors, and Michele—off the beaten track of the tourist trade—continued to serve her community with cleansings, fixed candles, and amulets to meet their spiritual needs.

What the public wouldn't have seen was the research done by each that was beyond the normal, even for them.

Andrew searched the Internet from his office while on his breaks, trying to learn all that he could about candle magic. Shapes, sizes, and colors all vied for attention across the monitor's screen as he tried to narrow down the huge amount of information into the smaller bits they would need for their work.

Ashlynne spent her afternoons before work re-reading the books stashed around her house that had anything to do with energy, magic, or magical circles. Over the years she had collected a decently sized esoteric library without being aware of it. She had a bad habit of purchasing whatever book grabbed her attention which had resulted in books ranging from the autobiography of a woman who studied chimpanzees to a lengthy tome detailing western magical subjects. She was very grateful for her poor impulse control as the necessary information began filtering through her quick scans of pages, and her notes filled several sections of a blank notebook she had purchased to avoid using

Andrew's.

Early in the week, Michele closed her shop before the scheduled time and retreated to her back room. Once situated in her comfortable chair, she closed her eyes and began chanting. Lyrical and musical, the words wound up and around her, calling and cajoling the Spirits to attend her. The elaborate altar, normally hidden from view behind a curtain, was alight with candles and oil lamps and decadently adorned with flowers, cakes, and bottles of liquor.

When she felt the Spirits' arrival, Michele approached the altar and lit a cigar. She took several deep drags from the pungent leaf-wrapped bundle, blowing the smoke above her head.

"Ah, Papa! Ah, Papa! Look what I have for you—your favorite cigar! It is strong and sweet, and I know you will love it. Talk to me and tell me what I need to know, and I will give you cigars every day next month!"

She laid the lit cigar in an ashtray on the

altar then produced a handful of hard candies from her pocket.

"Ah, Papa! Ah, Papa! Look what I have for you—candy! So sweet and so tasty! Talk to me and tell me what I need to know, and I will bring you candies every day next month!"

After arranging the brightly wrapped candies in a bowl next to the lit cigar, Michele stood silently in front of the altar breathing deeply in through her nose and exhaling gently from her mouth. As the smoke of the cigar blended with the rising smoke of the incense, images began to float past her closed eyes, stopping and starting at random like an old-fashioned movie. A large oak tree with a red car smashed next to it. A pack of dogs. A dark-haired young woman offering a man dead leaves and sticks then receiving a key to a hotel room.

Next, she was flying over the French Quarter, her sisters in flight next to her, cawing and laughing as the sun shone brightly in the blue Louisiana sky. She could see pockets of disease and decay throughout the Quarter that, old and dirty as the neighborhood was, were not supposed to be there. The diseased spots bloomed and spread out from the lower part of a small house just outside the Quarter proper, flowing in and out of bars, shops, alleys, and parks. It glistened an ugly-black with swirls of sickly-green. From her perch high above on a slick slate roof, she could see that humans walked into the blackness and out again, not seeing it at all. The effects were there, though, as a strange angry frenzy took over the oblivious pedestrians and spread person to person throughout the Quarter.

"This is very bad for us," said the thin black man sitting next to her on the roof's peak.

Michele looked down and saw she no longer had iridescent black feathers but was once again in her own skin—darkly brown and shiny with sweat, but no feathers. She was also naked and thought in a removed way that this should be bothering her more than it was.

"What is happening down there?" she asked the man sitting next to her.

"There is an energy here that does not belong. It has come for no other reason than to cause discord and dis-ease, and it calls others to itself to continue its work," the old man replied as he continued gazing down at the neighborhood that he had loved so much. "You must send it back to where it came from. It caused a great imbalance in its arrival to this world and that must be righted."

"I don't know how to do that," said Michele sadly as she watched the spread of the moldy black and green below them.

"It is from a place next to and yet apart from here."

"Ashlynne and Andrew call it a Faerie," interrupted Michele.

"That is one name for this type of being," he agreed, lighting a cigar, and inhaling deeply.

Michele smiled at the man sitting next to her, honored and happy that she was gifted with a visit from Papa.

"Its magic is strong," he continued, "but it is not from here. The river and the bricks do not heed its call and the Spirits in the Cities of the Dead turn away from it. We are from here; this is our place. The river knows us and sings to us. Our dead talk to us and drink with us. You will send it back to where it belongs using what is strongest from here."

Papa Legba stopped talking and resumed his enjoyment of the cigar that Michele had gifted him. They sat in companionable silence for several minutes; he smoked while Michele watched the skyline with its mix of modern office buildings and older gabled roofs.

"You will need to bring a red candle, water from the river, a silver knife inscribed with my sign, shells from the grounds of The Dead, the name of the Faerie, and the dog to the base of the oak tree in the park. Do not speak the Faerie's name until the circle is made and the candle is lit. Everyone must remain in the circle, except Ashlynne and the dog — they will travel with me."

"How will I know which oak and in which park?" asked Michele in a small voice. She was suddenly very much afraid of what lay ahead of them.

"Ashlynne will know," was the response that came from next to her, though the only thing there was a brightly wrapped piece of butterscotch candy.

Michele opened her eyes and did several deep squats to wake her legs back up; she wasn't sure how long she had been standing there but it was long enough for her legs to stiffen up and her feet to have fallen asleep.

Once the pins and needles had subsided, she plugged in her kettle for tea and rummaged around in her desk drawer for a pen and a notebook. It was time to get their plan of attack down on paper, and Michele, for one, was very anxious to get all of this over with.

Andrew grabbed his phone off his desk when it let out its loud *ping* alerting him to a text.

Have you found anything about candles yet?
It was Ashlynne.

Andrew: *Lots. Maybe too much, how about you? Do you know what a magic circle is yet?*

Ashlynne: *Yes, I think I have a good idea of it. Better yet, I think I can make one. We'll talk about it with Michele. When are we meeting again?*

Andrew: *This is Wednesday, so I think Monday. I'll ask her, hold on.*

Andrew found Michele's name in his phone and sent her a text asking about the planned meeting time and place. Her response was immediate and concerned Andrew a little bit.

Michele: *We can meet now. I have everything I need. Bring what you have.*

Returning to the screen with Ashlynne's picture on it he typed out the response and planned to meet everyone at Michele's shop after work.

"It's go-time," he muttered to himself, fighting down the fear that threatened to bubble up from his chest.

Michele flipped the open sign to closed, switched off the lights in the retail section of the shop, and locked the door. She followed the other two into the back of the building and prepared herself for a long evening.

Andrew smiled to see that each of them now had a notebook, as he took a long swallow from his coffee procured from the coffee shop around the corner. He had come straight here from work and was beginning to feel the effects of their metaphysical sleuthing, one too many Mardi Gras cocktails, and full days at the store.

"Let's get started, shall we?" began Michele. She spoke firmly and with purpose, and Andrew's sense of unease from the first text grew more pronounced.

"I heard from Papa."

"Um, you what?" asked Andrew.

"I said I heard from Papa," stated Michele again with an annoyed look in Andrew's direction. "And," she continued, "he's told me what we need to do and how to do it. Mostly."

"Mostly?" asked Ashlynne, speaking up for the first time.

"He showed me what this Faerie is doing and gave me a list of things we need to send her back." Checking her notes, she read, "a red candle, a silver knife that we need to inscribe with his veve or mark—"

"His what?" interrupted Andrew.

"His veve. It's his personal symbol. It calls him to us," explained Michele.

"We also need river water and shells from the cemetery," she finished and looked at the other two. "So, I did my part. What did you two find out?"

"I found out I have too many books," began Ashlynne with a smile, "but luckily for us, I have books on magic and books on how to make and use a magic circle. It's called *casting*, and I'm certain that I can do it. I practiced a little at home."

"I found out I will never look at a candle the same way again!" laughed Andrew, "and I'm not too sure how it all works, but if I understand it correctly then we need to choose a color that matches what we want to happen. There are shapes and figures, too, like female and male figures, penis shapes, and—"

"OK, we got it!" laughed Michele. "We don't need to go find a penis candle, though. Papa said a red candle, and I have those here."

"Why does he want a red candle?" asked Andrew.

"His colors are red, black, and gold. I guess he decided that red is the color he would work with for this job," said Michele with a shrug.

"Alright, we have a list but how do we put it all together?" asked Ashlynne.

"I've been thinking about it, and I think I

know the basics," began Michele. "The circle will be made with the shells from the cemetery, then Ashlynne can cast it around that so we have a double barrier—the shells and the energy of the magic circle. Inside the circle, we need to light the candle and call Papa to join us. Andrew and I can do that part. Then we need to say the Faerie's name like the charm from the book tells us to."

Ashlynne and Andrew sat watching Michele, waiting for her to continue.

"And? Then what?' asked Andrew.

"I'm not sure," admitted Michele. "I haven't worked it all out yet."

"What is the purpose of the circle?" he asked.

"It's to contain energy inside but also protects anyone in it from energy outside of it," reported Ashlynne as she checked her notes.

"Then what are we containing and what are we being protected from?" Andrew asked her.

"Papa said we cannot say the Faerie's name

until we have the circle done, and that will call her to us. So maybe we are to trap her in the circle with us?" suggested Michele.

"Well that doesn't sound like any fun at all!" exclaimed Andrew while Ashlynne nodded her head rapidly in agreement. "What the hell are we supposed to do with her once we're stuck in a circle with her?"

"Calm down," said Michele as she double-checked her notes. "This is new to me as well. I don't do magic circles and Faeries, remember?" She scanned the notes that were scattered here and there over five notebook pages and then found what might be what they were looking for.

"Here!" she said, jabbing her finger at the space on the page that held a scribble of notes. "I think once she's in the circle is when Ashlynne and her dog travel with Papa Legba. And I think it has something to do with the tree…"

"Whoa! Wait a minute! I'm traveling where with who?" squeaked Ashlynne in alarm. "And what tree?"

"'Bring all of the supplies to the base of the oak tree in the park. Everyone must stay in the circle except for Ashlynne and the dog, they go with Papa,'" read Michele from her notes. "Do you know what tree and what park? Papa said you would," she asked Ashlynne.

Ashlynne and Andrew exchanged a glance, and she replied, "Yes, I know exactly what tree we need to go to. It's a portal—I saw the real Amber in it when Andrew and I went to the Celebration in The Oaks this past November. I think he means that we will be going into the tree to get Amber." she finished in a whisper. While Ashlynne had been aware of and seen these portals all her life, she had never actually gone into one and had never wanted to. Having her dog and a Voodoo Spirit with her didn't make it sound any more appealing, and she said as much to her two friends.

"When Spirit calls, we answer, Ashlynne. That is the way of it. Papa Legba has chosen us, and your dog, to send this Faerie back to where she belongs. Her presence here is causing pain and dis-ease to our neighbors; not to mention that she stole someone's body, and that person is stuck god-knows-where. We have to do this. There's no other way."

Ashlynne nodded and knew that what Michele said was true, but it didn't stop her from wishing that anyone else, anywhere else, could take care of this and not them.

Andrew stood up and began arranging the items that they had collected so far: the holey stone, Mimi's book, the spool of red thread, the ball of red twine, and the glass-encased candle that Ashlynne had taken from the front of the shop previously.

"We still need river water, shells from the cemetery, and a silver knife. Do you think it needs to be real silver?"

"Yes," replied both women at the same time, causing them to laugh for the first time in days.

"Well, we can figure that one out a little later, but for now how about we go for a walk?"

"A walk?" asked Ashlynne

"Yep, a walk. We need to stretch our legs and get some air, and we need river water and shells. May as well kill several birds with one stone," said Andrew as he headed to the front door.

Michele winced at the words but grabbed a small plastic bottle that used to hold drinking water and a fabric bag she normally carried to the market and walked out behind them. She stopped briefly to lock the door then jogged after her friends as they headed in the direction of Armstrong Park and St Louis #2 Cemetery beyond that.

Chapter 24

The three friends were lucky enough to find the gates of the cemetery still open given the lateness of the hour. Whether it was just an oversight or the influence of greater powers that left the wrought iron gates to St Louis #2 open was up to debate and Ashlynne listened as Andrew and Michele did just that.

Letting their words flow over and around her, Ashlynne trailed behind them trying to decide how she should handle the graveyard. Normally she shielded herself to not be bombarded with wayward spirits and errant energies, but she wasn't sure if that was appropriate for this visit.

"Why are you doing that?" asked Andrew as Michele laid three coins at the base of the pillar of the front gate before walking through ahead of everyone.

"Because we plan on removing items. I must leave payment so that we are not indebted to The Dead, as well as it being honorable; nothing is free, Andrew."

"But we're only taking shells from the walkways, nothing from actual graves. If the shells are trucked in as gravel, then how is it wrong to take it?"

"This isn't about right or wrong. It's about balance. But you are correct in that we are taking nothing from graves. That would not only be dishonorable but legally and spiritually dangerous."

Ashlynne decided to not close out the energies of the place in case there was a spirit that had information that might help them. Having made the decision, she became immediately aware of whispers and footsteps that floated along on the breezes that wafted among the miniature stone mansions which housed hundreds of remains from hundreds of years of the city's history. It was overwhelming, and she fought the impulse to close it all out.

"You OK?" asked Andrew.

"Yeah. It's just a bit much in here," she replied with a small smile in his direction.

"Well, let's get moving then. It's getting dark, and we don't want to be in here too long," said Andrew as he bent down to gather oyster shells from the middle of the walkway.

"Do we need whole shells?" he called up to Michele who was collecting further up the path.

"I don't think so, but we need enough to ring a decent sized circle so whole shells will mean we have less to carry," she called back over her shoulder.

As Michele and Andrew gathered oyster shells in varying degrees of wholeness, Ashlynne was seeing the cemetery in an entirely different way than they were. To her left, at an intersection of pathways, stood an elderly man holding a bunch of flowers. His baggy brown pants and scuffed wingtip shoes paired perfectly with his white cotton shirt and suspenders that marked him as having been alive in the nineteen forties or fifties. He was thin except for a noticeable paunch around the middle. Ashlynne's heart broke a little at how lost and confused the man seemed, but when she stepped up to talk to him, he abruptly turned away from her and walked off, eventually disappearing entirely.

As she watched the man become dimmer and dimmer, then winking out from view, a small voice to her right said, "Have you seen my momma?" She turned to see a very young boy of perhaps four years old wearing a long nightshirt that had been white at some point but was now covered in stains of yellow, dark brown, and black.

Vomit, blood, feces, Ashlynne recited morbidly in her head while rearranging her face into a look of bland welcoming for the child spirit.

"No, I haven't seen your mom," she said in a gentle voice.

Ashlynne watched, horrified, as the young boy's eyes began to turn the color of old newspapers and his skin grew gaunt and jaundiced. His lower jaw dropped, and Ashlynne braced herself for a screech that only she would hear. But instead of a scream, blood bubbled out of the child's mouth and ran in rivulets down his chin and onto the front of his already filthy nightshirt. His eyes rolled back in his head as his mouth opened wider and wider seeming to take up his whole face. Ashlynne forced herself to look away from the death scene, reminding herself that this child had long ago passed on to whatever waited in his afterlife; this was nothing more than a looping vision of the trauma that was suffered hundreds of years ago. Whether this was the fragmented memory of the young boy or that of his mother, she would never know. As she turned away from the image of the dying child, she caught sight of a young man peeking out from behind an elaborate tomb. Ashlynne waved to him but he moved back to hide behind the massive stone edifice.

"Are you going to help us or not?" demanded Andrew as Ashlynne walked up to where he was crouched in the path filling a small bag with shells. "You are totally empty-handed," he said as he watched his friend's eyes scan the cemetery in the growing gloom of the evening.

"I'm sorry," she said, all the while watching half-formed images and figures flit in and out of view between the monuments and stone angels. "It's just that there's an awful lot going on in here."

"I think we have enough," said Michele with no small amount of sympathy for the sensory overload that must be making the other woman want to run out of the cemetery and into the well-lit street beyond.

Ashlynne smiled gratefully as Andrew stood and stretched his back and tucked the small bag of shells under his arm.

"Let's get out of here then," he said, and he took Ashlynne's hand and escorted her outside the cemetery gates that were thankfully still open. He didn't want to contemplate what the effects of being locked in would have on his friend.

"I'll catch up!" called Michele as she added more coins to the base of the pillar that marked the boundary between the world of the living and the world of the dead.

After a stop for pizza and drinks just outside the French Market, the three friends made their way to the darkly undulating waters of the Mississippi River. Her currents appeared deceptively gentle in the rising moon's light, but each of them was grimly aware of the fate of anyone who fell into her waters at night. While appearing gentle on the surface, the currents were swift and fast just underneath and would pull a grown man under and downriver before help could even hope to arrive.

Ashlynne moved carefully down the piled rocks and boulders with Michele holding onto one of her hands while she was, in turn, held and anchored by Andrew. This arrangement had been discussed and debated at length over their dinner and finally agreed upon based on the strength and weight of the friends. Ashlynne was the smallest and lightest and Andrew, his history of football and current gym regiment apparent, the strongest and tallest which left Michele in the middle of the human safety chain.

She scooped the muddy water into the plastic bottle and stood up, planting her feet firmly on the rocky out-cropping.

"I'm good," she panted and let go of Michele's hand as she handed the plastic bottle of river water up to Andrew. Glad to have both hands free, she climbed back up the embankment, wiped her hands on her jeans, and shuddered to think of the slime, goo, and rat droppings that she had just crawled through.

"Do we have everything we need?" she asked Michele.

"Yeah, we've got everything we need.

Thank you for crawling down there."

"De nada," she replied breezily, despite having been scared to death of falling in and drowning.

"Let's head home," said Andrew as they walked back up over the levy and descended into the French Quarter, the moon rising higher and higher into the purple night sky.

"So, when does 'Operation Go Away Faerie' begin in earnest?" asked Andrew as they strolled down Royal, dodging costumed Mardi Gras revelers and groups of conventioneers pulling rolling suitcases headed toward Canal Street.

"I think we should wait until after Mardi Gras," replied Ashlynne as she stepped around a lone man's dress shoe laying in the middle of the sidewalk.

"We need to do it in March—March 20th," declared Michele.

"March 20th? That's three weeks away!" cried Andrew. "Why that long?"

"It's one of Papa Legba's feast days, and it's the Spring Equinox. This will be a day of great power and will make reestablishing balance much easier. It's best to wait."

Andrew groaned loudly at the thought of three more weeks of no sleep, while Ashlynne could only think about the lone shoe lying in the middle of the sidewalk.

"Who loses one shoe and just keeps walking?" Neither of her friends answered her, too caught up in their own thoughts about what lay ahead of them.

Chapter 25

"**W**hat are you doing with my knife?"

"Oh my God, Mimi! Don't do that!" yelped Ashlynne.

"I'm sorry, I forgot to announce my presence again," replied Mimi with enough snark to make Ashlynne look up sharply.

"Yeah, you did. And I'm polishing it."

"Well, I can see that, Dear, but why?"

"We need to use it to send the Faerie back."

"How will my butter knife do that?" asked Mimi, her brow crinkling up on the other side of the mirror.

"I'm really not sure. Michele said that Papa Legba came to her and gave her a list of things we'll need to send it back to where it came from and bring Amber back here. One of those things was a silver knife, so I thought I'd use yours. You don't mind, do you?"

Mimi lit a cigarette and inhaled deeply, "No, I suppose not. I know I can't use it any longer, or the matching fork, but I was so very proud of them. I still am, I suppose. Will you remember how much it means to me while you're using it?"

"Of course, I will!" Ashlynne exclaimed, wishing again that she could hug the older woman in the mirror. "I'm hoping that having some of the items that meant so much to you when we have to do this ritual, or whatever it is, will be like having you with me. I'm kind of scared to do this, Mimi."

"You're going to be fine," Mimi declared firmly.

"Can you be there with me, or do you need a mirror?"

"I can go wherever I choose, for the most part, but I have my own bit to do on this end that will keep me busy."

"I would rather you be with me," sulked

Ashlynne. Mimi was surprised to see the pouting return; it was a trait she thought her young friend had left behind when they embarked on this journey so many months ago.

"We all have our parts to play, Ashlynne. You have yours based on what you are skilled at, and I have mine based on the same. If you or I side-step what is needed to be done, then this will fail. And if this fails the real Amber is lost to us and the Faerie will continue to destroy everything that it encounters simply because it enjoys doing so. So! Stand up! Square those shoulders and do what you can do to set this mess to rights."

Ashlynne watched as the cigarette smoke bloomed outward obscuring the mirror's surface.

"I guess I've been dismissed," she grumped to herself as she resumed polishing the sterling silver butter knife. She knew Mimi was right, but the rebuke stung and didn't help to make her feel anymore strong or capable than she had before the verbal reprimand.

The silver knife gleamed, showcasing the beautiful baroque floral pattern that encrusted its hilt. Ashlynne held it up to the light to admire the antique craftsmanship and was surprised to see the details within the floral pattern that she had missed before; the roses and leaves entwined around not a branch as she had originally thought but a key—an ornate skeleton key. She laid the knife down and went to get the fork that was still wrapped in the bundle she had taken from Mimi's house. After a quick polish, the fork revealed that it, too, had a skeleton key hidden in its floral pattern.

"Interesting…" Ashlynne muttered as she grabbed her phone. She sent Michele a picture of the knife with the accompanying text:

'See the key?'

She placed the silverware on the living room's mantel on her way to the kitchen to get something to eat.

Ashlynne pressed the button down on the

toaster and watched the two slices of bread descend into the red glow of its interior. As the bread toasted, she paced in circles around the table, antsy and at odds. Tomorrow was March the 20th, and as the clock tick-tocked closer and closer to the time of the ritual, her nervous energy increased to an almost unbearable level. At the *pop* of the toaster, she jumped and banged her knee painfully on the leg of the table as she made a third trip past it in her pacing around the room.

"Dammit!" she cursed angrily as she hobbled over to the counter. She buttered the toast and added a sprinkle of cinnamon then went outside to sit in the sun.

The Calico cat was laying on a spot of sun-warmed flagstone when Ashlynne stepped outside, headed to the iron table and chairs.

She took a deep breath trying to settle her nerves and watched as the once-tiny kitten stretched languidly then got up and walked over to wind itself between her ankles, purring loudly.

"Hello, my lovely," Ashlynne purred back

at the beautiful cat. The notched ear showed that the neighborhood's monthly donations to the care and maintenance of the cat colony has been used to spay the now-adult female. The lack of scars and wounds showed that she had been fully accepted into the community by the other felines, and the sleek coat and muscular body attested to her ability to catch and eat the rodents that always threatened to over-run the downtown neighborhoods.

"Aren't you just the prettiest success story that ever was?" Ashlynne crooned after the cat who had wandered off, having found something much more interesting to occupy herself along the edge of the brick wall.

Ashlynne munched on her toast and watched the crows fly over and around the neighborhood while mentally ticking off what was going to be expected of them all tomorrow. "Red candle, shells, river water, red twine, pen and paper, holey stone, knife, Mimi's book, and Murphy," she recited in her head as the crows called overhead.

"Call the Faerie into the circle and go through the tree with Papa Legba. What could possibly go wrong?" she joked to herself as she stood up, brushed the toast crumbs from her lap, and went inside to get the dog—it was time to walk off this nervous energy.

Ashlynne and Murphy turned left after leaving the house, walked into the Tremé, then turned right onto Henrietta Delille Street. The late-afternoon sun was warm on her bare arms as she watched Murphy nose around amongst the overgrown edges of a mostly vacant lot and laughed when he emerged with a large and overly ripe lime in his mouth.

"Give me that, you goof!" she laughed as she held out her hand for the greenish-yellow fruit that had fallen from the large tree at the edge of the sidewalk.

Murphy dropped it at her feet, his wiggling and wagging behind declaring better than words his happiness at giving her a present.

"You're a good boy, Murph, the best boy ever," she said at the bundle of happiness at the end of the leash.

"C'mon, let's go," she commanded, and they set off up the street past the Tremé Backstreet Museum, home of Mardi Gras Indian and Baby Doll costumes and artifacts as well as being a cultural hub for the surrounding blocks. It was a place she had always intended to go into but had so far never made it over during its open hours. She sketched a wave at an elderly man sitting on his porch and pulled Murphy in on a short leash in response to the large dog lying next to him. She was grateful to see that neither Murphy nor the older man's dog showed any interest in each other and once past the porch, let up on Murphy's lead allowing him more room to roam. They turned left and crossed the street at the corner of Governor Nicholls and continued up to the corner of Saint Claude and the venerable Saint Augustine Catholic Church. She pulled Murphy in again on a short leash and entered the garden at the front of the building and The Tomb of The

Unknown Slave. The large cross, tipped on its side to rest on one arm, consisted of large links of chain with smaller links at its base and paid homage to those people held in bondage who died before Emancipation. The location for the cross was chosen by the parishioners specifically because it was the location of the Tremé Plantation where so many enslaved people were kept. Eventually the plantation was sold and split up to become the neighborhood that she lived in today.

The air was heavy and warm under the oaks as she stood gazing at the huge iron cross. Ashlynne loved to visit this site, the weight of centuries of strength and faith that settled around the monument left her awe-struck like few places in the city could. Whispers of past songs floated around her as the voices of the community claimed its place here in the first African American Catholic church in the country. There was sadness and anger here too, and she tried hard, in her limited ability, to feel and honor those emotions which had settled in and around the garden; anger and frustration from centuries past flowed through to the injustices of the present. What never failed to bring the goosebumps to her arms, though, were the songs raised in victory and faith and love that sang alongside those that cried for justice. This place held them all, safe and secure among the sacred structures and beautiful oaks within this amazing community that not only endured, but celebrated, its history and its future. Ashlynne was honored to call it her home.

Chapter **26**

The morning of March the 20th dawned gray and humid, the smell of the river hanging heavy in the air as Ashlynne and Murphy made their way down to the coffee shop on Saint Philip street. Ashlynne carried her canvas shopping tote filled with Mimi's silver knife and book, her holey stone, her notebook, the shells from the cemetery, and the bottle of river water. For good measure she also tossed in a sweatshirt for herself and a package of Murphy's favorite treats. She wasn't sure how long the ritual would take but the sweatshirt was a silent nod to Mimi and the treats a 'thank you' to her dog that, so far, had had no choice in the role he was being asked to play.

Passing the familiar houses of the

neighborhood, still dark and shuttered in the dreary early morning, Ashlynne ran through the events that were planned for the day; the three friends agreed to meet at the coffee shop for fortifications and to ensure that everyone had brought the supplies that each was in charge of. Once the necessary caffeine and sugared pastries had been consumed, they would go to Michele's shop. She had closed it for the day in anticipation of what needed to be done. At the shop they would use the stone to reveal the Faerie's name. Papa Legba had warned Michele that they could not, under any circumstances, say the name until they were in the magic circle. Because of this, they had all agreed to reveal the name immediately before heading to City Park and the giant oak tree that would be the site of their ritual. Ashlynne had run through the sequence of events hundreds of times over the past few weeks and was feeling tired of the whole thing; she would be very glad to have something else to think about after this evening.

As Ashlynne and Murphy walked down to the coffee shop, Michele was finishing up her offerings and prayers to Papa Legba. Today was one of the Spirit's feast days, so certain observations were required of her, but Michele added extra chants and gifts to the already full altar in anticipation of the day's ritual that would require his presence and participation. Beautifully wrapped candies, expensive cigars, and extravagantly decorated cakes and cookies were displayed and presented for the Spirit's approval and use. Having lit another stick of incense, Michele stood back and closed her eyes. She drew in a deep breath, held it for the count of three, and then let it out slowly. She thought she would offer a heartfelt and eloquent prayer to the Spirit who had so graciously visited her and offered his help but only individual words and short phrases made it through the fog of images swirling in her head *"..Please help.... Give us the strength.... What if this fails? Thank you for helping ... Keep us safe..."*

Andrew finished loading the last of the dishes into the dishwasher, kissed a still-sleeping Chris goodbye, and walked out the door into the damp and gray morning. Though the coffee shop was only a couple of blocks up from his house, he got into his car to drive there rather than walk because their next stop, City Park, was much further away. Tossing his bag onto the front seat, he started the car and turned the radio down—he wasn't feeling the music this morning. Truth be told, Andrew was exhausted and terrified. It had been months since he and Chris had gotten a decent night's sleep with the noisy invasion of the neighbor from hell's parties and brawls. To make matters even worse, the filth from the lower apartment invaded just as the noise did; mold, roaches, and rats had become a daily presence in their once spotless home, causing the two men to become stressed, argumentative, and increasingly unhappy. Chris wanted to move and had valid reasons for doing so. Andrew's insistence on staying made no sense to Chris since Andrew had opted to not tell him most of the situation because he knew he would never be believed.

Andrew knew that the Faerie had to go, for all their sakes, but he had lost many night's sleep over the past few weeks worrying about what would happen to them all if they did this ritual wrong. He could hear the Faerie's maliciousness and its abuse of the other beings down there, so he knew how cruel she could be. The thought of being trapped in a magic circle with her terrified him more than he let his friends know. Shaking his head to clear away the run-a-way thoughts, he checked his bag for the hundredth time that morning—the red twine, his notebook, his travel bottle of water, his phone, and some crackers. Unsure how to pack for a Faerie removal ritual, he opted for those items he might need for an afternoon hike. Shrugging out of his sweatshirt and adding it to his bag, he put the car into drive and drove the few blocks up to the coffee shop.

"Let's do this thing," he muttered to

himself in a bad imitation of an action hero in a blockbuster movie.

Andrew held the door for Michele who was walking into the small restaurant while he was.

"Good morning, baby," he smiled, and she leaned in to kiss him on the cheek.

"Good morning," she replied just a little too loudly so that Andrew took a closer look at her. Dark circles, pursed lips, and clenched hands gave away her nervousness, and he felt better about not being the only one to be afraid of what the day held for them.

The pastry case and counter sat at their left with a small scattering of tables and chairs and several upholstered sofas to their right. Beautiful black and white photography of the neighborhood and its native Second Line groups adorned the walls, with the occasional pop of color from whimsical original paintings. The coffee shop was clean, cozy, and welcoming and one of their favorite places in the neighborhood.

"Coffee with cream and a bagel with cream cheese, please," said Andrew to the young woman behind the counter who rang up the order and ran his card. She handed him his coffee and told him his bagel would be just a few minutes.

"I'll have a coffee with cream, too, and a honey bran muffin," said Michele in response to the questioning look from the clerk.

Taking their coffees out to the patio where Ashlynne was already seated with Murphy, they settled in amongst greetings, hugs, and smiles. There seemed to be a silent agreement between the three of them to go about their own business since collecting the last of their supplies, and aside from an occasional text, they hadn't seen each other since their walk home from the river.

Andrew got up to collect his and Michele's breakfast at the call of his name from within the building as Ashlynne took a drink of her coffee and smiled at Michele.

"Are you ready?"

"About as ready as I'm going to be,"

answered Michele with a weak laugh. "I've got the supplies I'm supposed to bring," she added, pointing to the bag at her feet.

"Me too, on both counts," smiled Ashlynne, gesturing to her own bag slung over the back of her chair.

"Looks like Andrew has his supplies too," said Michele as Andrew approached their table with the bagel and muffin.

"I brought everything on my list plus some water, some crackers, and a sweater," he told the other two as he settled into his chair.

"Crackers and water?" asked Michele. "Do you think you might get hungry?" she laughed.

Shooting her a wounded look he said, "It just seemed like a good idea," and turned his attention to his breakfast.

"Hey, I brought extra stuff, too, and cookies for Murphy, so I think we're all pretty much on the same page," smiled Ashlynne as she laid her hand on her friend's arm. It bothered her that he was so easily hurt, and she added it to her list of one more reason the Faerie had to go.

The three friends passed the next few minutes in silence, each lost in their thoughts, while Murphy nosed around the hedge looking for interesting things to smell or eat.

"OK! We need to come together or this will never work!" said Michele with a firm clap of her hands that snapped the other two out of their mental wanderings. "Let's get our coffees to go and get back to the shop, we need to get the first part of this done so we can get to City Park while it's still early. I don't think any of us wants an audience for what we plan on doing," she said with a smile, and they gathered up their bags, dishes, and cups to bring inside.

Ashlynne handed her cup to Andrew to refill for her as she walked out to the sidewalk and around the front with the dog. The sun hadn't completely crested the horizon yet, and she shuddered to think of how much more humid it would be by the time it rode high in the sky at midday. She was glad they had agreed to an early start; the sooner they were done the sooner she could be home with a cold drink and a safer neighborhood. She accepted her re-filled coffee cup from Andrew and gladly relinquished her bag to his outstretched hand. Trying to juggle the dog, the coffee, and the bag was a recipe for disaster, and she was glad he had noticed and made the offer to take one of the things out of her hands.

Michele moved on ahead of them as the three walked the next couple of blocks to her shop and the first step of the ritual.

The bodega welcomed them, its cool interior a comforting respite from the heavy damp air outside. With the door securely locked, the three friends made their way into the more private rooms at the back of the building.

"Is that a Ouija board?" asked Andrew, approaching the table in the center of the room.

"I borrowed it from my niece. We need this to get the name of the Faerie," answered Michele as she dragged chairs up to the table.

"Where are the stone and the twine?"

"Here's the stone," said Ashlynne, having pulled it from the depths of her bag as Andrew passed the twine across the table.

"Andrew, do you want to write down what letters come up?" asked Michele.

"Yeah, I can do that," replied Andrew with considerably more enthusiasm then he felt as he retrieved his notebook and pen.

Andrew and Ashlynne watched as Michele cut a length of red twine and set the spool down on the floor next to her chair. She then threaded one end through the small hole in Ashlynne's stone and knotted the end making a necklace of sorts. She balanced her elbow on the table and held the stone suspended over the playing board.

"Are you ready?" she asked them, her voice soft.

Ashlynne nodded and Andrew picked up the pen ready to write down whatever came from the stone and board, though he honestly had no idea how this was supposed to work.

"Creature of the North Born by The West Reveal the Name of the One We Request. Spell the Word for Us to See, That We May Rightly Name the Faerie."

Gone was the soft voice of their friend, replaced with the strong and forceful voice of The Priestess. Michele repeated the chant over and over, indicating with her free hand that the other two should join in.

Matching her tone and cadence, Andrew and Ashlynne joined in with Michele, repeating the rhyme over and over again—the goose flesh showing on all their arms as the energy they raised grew more and more potent. Suddenly, Michele brought her hand down with a smack on the table, and Ashlynne could see the sparks of energy released to fly about their heads, zips and zaps of thundercloud blue, bright red, and sparkling gold, as they all abruptly stopped the chant.

As all three watched in silence, the stone began to spin in clockwise circles, slowly at first but faster and faster within short order. Michele carefully moved her elbow closer to the board and looked pointedly at Andrew who lifted his pen, ready to write.

The rock stopped its circular movement and began to move back and forth, swinging in higher and higher arcs until it sliced the air over the first letter in the name.

"M," said all three at once, and Andrew wrote the letter down on the paper.

As if it could hear them and knew they had understood the first letter, the stone resumed its circular motion. On and on it went, gathering speed at each round until it began moving in the swinging back and forth way again. Michele gently scooted her elbow in the direction that the stone swung to most, and it responded by swinging straight and strong over the next letter.

"O," they all whispered, and Andrew dutifully wrote the second letter next to the first.

Michele understood now how the stone indicated the letters they would need and adjusted her elbow at its request.

"R," breathed Ashlynne.

"A," said Andrew as he bent to write it next to the others.

"Mora?" asked Ashlynne in a quiet voice.

"There's more," whispered Michele as the suspended stone continued its series of spins and swings.

"G," they all said as they watched the pendulum lose its momentum and hang docile from the twine, just a stone on a piece of red thread once again.

"M-O-R-A-G," spelled Andrew as Michele quickly shushed him from saying anything more.

"Remember! We cannot say the name out loud until we are in the circle! Then we say the name to call her to us like the charm says in the book. You brought Mimi's book, didn't you, Ash?"

"Yes, I have it right here and I marked the

page with the charm on it," said Ashlynne, indicating the bag that held most of their supplies.

The room was silent as the three sat and stared at the name spelled out on Andrew's paper. No longer 'Amber' or 'the neighbor from hell' or 'The Faerie,' but Morag. They had found her name, and now they would send her back.

Mimi moved within the mists of the In-between, drawing close to the opening that swirled with black and green light. She stood to the side and watched as The Faerie peered inside the mirror, looking beyond and around Mimi, unaware of her presence. Turning to look at what it was seeing, Mimi saw the image of Ashlynne and her friends seated around a table in a darkened room. The view was situated from above so that what was visible was the tops of the three friends' heads and a game board in front of them. There must be a mirror somewhere on the wall above them. "You really need to pay attention, Dear," scolded Mimi at Ashlynne's head.

As the ghost and the Faerie looked on, the young Haitian woman threaded a stone with red twine as the man picked up a pen to write in a notebook. From their vantage point, the energy in the room began to grow thicker and sparked through with dark blue and red as the woman with stone began chanting. The low growl from the Faerie alerted Mimi that it was time for her bit part in this play, and she lit her cigarette. She inhaled deeply to produce a glowing red tip then exhaled, blowing the smoke at the image of the group as it began the second stanza of the Priestess's chant. Repeating her inhales and exhales quickly, Mimi obliterated the image of the group from The Faerie who's screams of anger and fear could be felt throughout the In-between.

Somewhere off to her right, Mimi heard an elderly man chuckle in amusement and the tap-tap-tap of a staff to the counterpoint of his footsteps as he walked further away into the swirling gray mists.

Chapter 27

Ashlynne climbed out of Andrew's red VW with Murphy in tow while the other two retrieved the bags that held their supplies.

Conversation was sparse as they made their way through the park to the ancient oak tree that would be the location of their ritual.

The day was still new, and the gathering daylight showed that, aside from the lone jogger along the bayou, the park was essentially empty. Ashlynne was very glad about this. New Orleans could be fairly forgiving of its citizens' eccentricities, but she wasn't sure if their planned activity would land them all in jail if they were seen.

Murphy led the way, spurred on with the mingled scents of squirrels, picnics of times past, and goose droppings. Trailing behind, more afraid of the chore ahead than tired, were the three humans.

"Here it is," said Ashlynne warily, not sure if she wanted to look directly at the oak tree or not.

The other two had no such reservations and eyed the old tree brazenly.

"It doesn't look like much of anything, aside from a big ass tree," acknowledged Andrew in response to Michele's visual let down.

"Yeah, that's what it looks like to you right now," countered Ashlynne. "Look through the stone and tell me what you see."

She handed the holey stone to Andrew who held it up to his eye, squinted, and looked through at the oak. The formerly nondescript tree had a swirling hole in its trunk the color of bright green frog's eggs. The hole was large, about three feet tall and four feet across. He took the stone away from his eye, blinked several times in succession, and then opened his eyes again. The tree was just a tree.

370

Michele watched all of this with amusement, and when he saw this, Andrew scowled and handed her the stone.

"OK, comedienne, you try and then see what's so funny."

Michele held the stone up to her eye and squinted through the tiny hole.

"Oh, my Gawd!" she whispered. She lowered the stone and saw the plain tree. She looked through it and saw the portal glowing in its bright green glory again.

"Not so funny, huh?" asked Andrew, and he took the stone back from her as she stood staring at the tree with her mouth slightly ajar.

"Not funny at all! It's amazing! Is this what you see Ashlynne?"

"I don't know what you saw," she reminded the two of them with a smile, "so I'm not sure. But what I see is a large hole in the tree that starts with glowing green swirls. The longer I look, the more the swirls move away, and I can see inside to where Amber is."

"This is just amazing," mumbled Michele as she emptied the bags and sorted the supplies.

She moved the bags to a bench a few yards away and said, "OK, this is it. Ashlynne, once we lay the shells out in a circle then it will be time for you to cast the magic circle. Once that's done, we can't leave it until we're finished, understood?"

Andrew found a large fallen tree branch, heavy enough to scratch a line through the hard-packed dirt under the tree, and used it to draw a circular pattern from one side of the tree's trunk out roughly 5 feet and back again with the opposite side of the trunk closing the circle. After emptying the bag of shells from the cemetery into the center, he laid one after another along the scratched line, forming the circle as Michele instructed.

While Andrew drew and laid out the circle, Michele gathered the red candle, a lighter, the bottle of river water, and Mimi's silver knife. She knelt in front of the tree and set the glass-encased candle down with the knife laid horizontally in front of it. The bottle of river water was set to her left and the holey stone to her right. Mimi's book, opened to the chant, was positioned in front of all of these with the whole set up in a roughly equal-armed cross formation.

Ashlynne called Murphy back from his inspection of a pile of Spanish moss and handed his leash to Andrew to ensure the dog didn't wander off again. She gathered their stash of extras—water, dog treats, crackers, sweaters, and sweatshirts—and laid them off to the far edge of the ring of shells but still within the circle.

"Are you ready for me to start this?" Ashlynne asked Michele quietly.

"One moment," Michele whispered as she picked up the river water and poured a small amount into the palm of her hand. Using one finger that was moistened with the murky liquid, she picked up the silver knife and began to trace a pattern onto the hilt of the knife, then repeated it onto the blade.

"What's that?" asked Andrew peering over her shoulder.

"The veve of Papa Legba," she replied, returning the knife to its position on her make-shift altar and screwing the cap back onto the plastic bottle containing the muddy water from the Mississippi.

Michele stood up, wiped her hands on her jeans, and nodded at Ashlynne.

Ashlynne stood facing outward at the right side of the oak tree's trunk. Closing her eyes, she envisioned bright blue energy rising from the ground and into her feet. As it continued up through her body, she raised her right hand, and with her palm outstretched in front of her, moved the flow of energy out and into the shells that Andrew had laid down. Andrew and Michele watched as Ashlynne opened her eyes and moved clockwise, hand outstretched, as she conjured their circle. When she reached the far-left side of the tree trunk she stopped, took a deep breath, and moved to the center of the ring with the other two.

"I think it's good," she said in a breathless voice.

Michele then picked up the bottle of river water and, beginning where Ashlynne had, removed the cap, and sprinkled the shells with the water as she moved clockwise toward the other side of the tree trunk.

Very softly she chanted the words that had come to her during her weeks of meditations, "River run and river flow, the life and blood for those who know. Shells that gather Spirits near, your voices now we wish to hear. All that draw forth at my call, stand with us and be our wall."

Michele stopped in front of the tree trunk and whispered a heartfelt *'thank you'* to the ancient tree and then turned to face her friends, "It's time to call it."

Michele lit the candle and called to Papa Legba, "Papa Legba! Papa Legba! Open the Door! Papa Legba! Papa Legba! Open the Gates!"

The humid air stirred gently in a cooling breeze as Michele continued her softly chanted words, imploring the Spirit to open the way and join them.

"He is here — read the charm, Ashlynne."

Ashlynne saw the small black man dressed in rags step from behind the tree's massive trunk as he approached the small group. He bent to pat Murphy on the head, and the small dog wiggled in joy. Papa Legba smiled affectionately at Michele, but she was watching the Spanish moss dance in the breezes signaling his arrival and could not see the Spirit who had joined their circle.

Andrew held Mimi's book open for Ashlynne who began to read, "Circle 'round and flame a' bright, say the name to set it right! Say the name again times three to send it far away from thee!"

Joining hands, with the candle and Murphy in the middle of their small circle within the larger circle, the three called out loudly, "Morag!"

At the first call, the breezes ceased to blow,

and the Spanish moss hung silent and sullen.

"Morag! Morag! MORAG!"

The three friends called the Faerie's name three more times as the charm had instructed and waited in the heavy morning air.

"Nothing is happening," whispered Andrew. "Is she supposed to just pop into the circle from thin air?"

"Keep chanting!" instructed Michele, and Ashlynne saw Papa Legba nod in agreement.

"Morag! Morag! Morag! Morag! Morag!"

Over and over and over again the three, hands clasped, chanted the name of the Faerie as their clothes grew wet from the sweat running down their bodies, and their voices began to grow scratchy and rough.

Many city blocks away in a small ground floor apartment, the Faerie Morag screamed in anger and fear. The apartment was alive with swirling winds and the scents of the river. The most peculiar sensation ran up and down her human body as if the skin were threatening to unzip and send her flying away on the muddy-scented breeze that had invaded her home. She paced up and down the small space, squashing slow-moving beetles and roaches between her toes as she wrapped her arms about herself trying to stay in one piece despite the feeling of being wrenched apart.

Her attempts at trying to find out what was happening by using the mirror were of no avail due to the never-ending swirl of gray that permeated the interior of the glass. In a frenzy of frustration, she grabbed the small-framed glass and hurled it against the tiled floor, shattering it into thousands of shards. The hated gray smoke rose up and out of the ruined mirror, filling the apartment with the overpowering scent of cigarettes.

The three friends continued their chanting at the base of the old oak tree in City Park, though their pace was slower and their voices weak. On and on they went, hands clasped as the damp air below the arched branches of the oak tree settled silent and heavy.

Ashlynne wasn't sure how much longer she could go on and desperately wanted a drink of water; she knew Andrew had brought some, but she was afraid to break their small circle to get it.

Michele squeezed her hand, and she worked harder to keep pace when suddenly the cool breezes swept into their circle, lifting her damp hair and making the moss that dripped from the branches over her head swing and sway.

It was just the relief they needed, and their voices soared with the name of the Faerie, offering it to the cooling wind that blew around them.

The wind began to blow harder and the temperature dropped ten — then fifteen — degrees as the previously sweltering friends began to shiver in their circle. The moss blew like so many windsocks, and the dead leaves and small twigs rolled past them as the wind grew stronger and stronger.

Murphy let out a low, menacing growl, and

Ashlynne looked to see what had upset the dog. Maintaining her chant, she squeezed Michele's and Andrew's hands and pointed with her chin at what had alerted Murphy; headed their way was a swirling mass of twigs, leaves, and dead bugs. As the mini-tornado moved closer, Ashlynne could see banners of dark hair whipped from the edges and an arm or leg that tried to escape the whirling mass before being pulled back in by the centrifugal force of the winds.

The spinning funnel of air slammed into their circle with such force that Ashlynne saw sparks and ribbons of her blue energy shoot out at the impact zone. She dropped her friends' hands and moved to close the circle but stopped in her tracks as a small, stooped woman stepped up from and out of one of the shells carrying a kitchen broom. Ashlynne stood gaping as the old woman, dressed in a flowered dress with a frilly apron, the only thing defining her waist, began to sweep the scattered bits of blue light back into place. Once she was satisfied, she nudged the shells back into position, stepped back into the one that she had come from, and sunk out of view.

While Ashlynne was watching their ancestral housekeeper set their circle to rights, Michele and Andrew were huddled together, staring at the inert form that the winds had dropped into their space. The woman lay sprawled in an extended fetal position, her dark hair spread over her face, one arm draped over her head with the other cradling it like a pillow.

"Is she alive?" whispered Andrew.

"I think so," replied Michele. "Is that the neighbor? Is this the woman we called?"

Andrew had not considered up to that point that Michele had never seen their neighbor and marveled at the woman's ability to work on faith alone.

"Yeah, that's her," provided Ashlynne who had stepped up to the other two, convinced that the circle needed no help from her after all.

"She doesn't look so awful," said Michele.

"Oh, she's awful. Believe me. Here, have a look," and she bent down for the holey stone and handed it to Michele. "You next, Andrew. You've never seen her as she truly looks."

Michele peered through the stone and gasped. Gone was the pretty dark-haired woman, and in her place lay a creature from a nightmare: gray-green skin and matted hair that looked like it had leaves and bugs stuck in it. The stick-like arms were unnaturally long, and her hands very thin with the fingers looking like a cross between fingers and opposable claws. Looking closer, she gasped again and asked, "Are those horns?"

"Yes, those are horns."

"Holy shit. That is the most disturbing thing I've ever seen. Here, Andrew, you need to look at this."

Andrew squinted through the hole in the stone, and the color drained from his face. He handed the stone back to Ashlynne and said, "Let's send her back."

Chapter 28

Responding to the grim determination in Andrew's voice, the two women acted quickly. Ashlynne grabbed the water that Andrew had brought along and took a long drink, bathing her parched throat in the blessedly cool liquid. She handed the bottle to the other two and looked at the glowing portal in the tree. The green swirls of light, just like the places that opened for her when she sent the creatures away that Morag had called to roam the French Quarter, eventually lightened in color and thinned, leaving a murky view into the horrifying forest that lay beyond. The predator trees were silent and still for the time being, and Amber—the real Amber—was lying in a mirror image of her physical body on this side, an extended fetal position, one arm cradling her head and one arm over her face. She was still dressed in the jeans and purple shirt that Ashlynne had originally seen her in.

"Do you know what to do?" she asked Andrew.

"It's here in the notebook," he replied, flipping quickly through to the page she had marked. "When you and Murphy go through the tree, we wait until we see you come back with the real Amber then seal the portal with the silver knife."

"How will we know what's happening and when you're coming back?" asked Michele as she stooped to pick up the knife.

"Use the stone," said Ashlynne as she took Murphy's leash and tossed him a treat. "Ready, Murph?"

Michele tucked the knife into the back pocket of her jeans and moved toward the still form of Morag.

"C'mon Andrew, we need to get this done before the park fills up with people or this thing wakes up."

Andrew bent and grabbed one of Morag's arms and the corresponding ankle with Michele doing the same on the opposite side.

"You'll tell us when we're close?" panted Andrew as they began swinging Morag toward the tree's trunk. "We can't see where the portal is."

"You're right in front of it. When I say so, swing her hard and let go," said Ashlynne as she looped Murphy's leash over her wrist and held her right hand out toward the oak tree.

Ashlynne planted her feet firmly on the packed earth and moved her hand in a clockwise motion until the bright green swirls once again appeared in the trunk of the tree. She was acting on pure instinct, attempting to recreate how she sent the creatures back while hunting in the Quarter. Morag was a much larger catch, and Ashlynne hoped desperately that the process would still be the same.

The portal swirled, and Ashlynne felt a tug; it was pulling energy into itself. She had never had this happen before, and she wondered if it was due to the power of the Equinox as Michele had suggested.

"Now!" she cried. And, as Andrew and Michele swung Morag into the portal, she grabbed Murphy and leaped in after her as bursts of bright green light flickered dizzily around them all. Ashlynne's stomach dropped alarmingly as she tumbled around and around, the feeling of being pulled and pushed in so many directions both terrifying and strangely exhilarating. With a bone-jarring *thump*, she dropped onto a bed of dry leaves and twigs with Murphy landing squarely on her outstretched thighs.

"Are you OK?" she whispered, frantically checking the dog for injuries. Though definitely stunned, the small terrier seemed no worse for wear, and Ashlynne breathed a sigh of relief.

"I would not allow him to come to harm," said a creaky voice over her shoulder. Ashlynne looked behind her to see that Papa Legba had come through the portal with them and was standing behind her, a smile playing on his thin face.

Ashlynne stood and looked around at where they had crash-landed. There were two Ambers with them: the real Amber, dressed in the purple t-shirt and jeans, and the Faerie, still encased in the form of the human, dressed in black leggings and a long gray tunic. Both figures were completely still.

"Are they alive?" she asked Papa Legba.

"For now, both spirits live, and the body is bruised but alive. The spirit of the human is growing weak. It has spent too much time in this place and has eaten the food here. Without help, this would mean that she could not leave."

"But we can help, can't we?"

"Yes," the old man smiled. "The three of us can establish the balance that the Faerie disturbed when she stole the human form."

"The three of us?" asked Ashlynne, looking around for a third person.

"You, me, and Murphy," replied Papa Legba.

Ashlynne looked down at the little dog and noticed that the small key-shaped mark on his head glowed a bright gold in the purple twilight. Murphy looked up with a sloppy doggy grin that hurt Ashlynne's heart.

"I will not let him come to harm," Papa Legba repeated as he watched the play of emotions across Ashlynne's face.

Andrew squinted through the tiny hole in the stone and saw Ashlynne, Murphy, and the two Ambers along with a tall, elderly man standing in a foreboding forest. The image was wavy and slightly distorted as if he was looking through the wrong end of a telescope underwater.

"Who is that with them?" he asked Michele as he handed the stone over to her.

Michele held the stone up to her eye and looked through the hole and into the portal beyond.

"Papa is there," she said with a smile. Having such a powerful ally was both a blessing and an honor. She made a mental note to leave candies and cigars for the Spirit for the rest of her life if they made it out of this mess in one piece.

"What do we do now?" asked Andrew.

"We wait until they come back," replied Michele sitting cross-legged at the edge of the circle.

"Cracker?" asked Andrew with a rueful smile as he handed the box to her.

"Don't mind if I do!" she said with a tired smile, helping herself to a handful.

The two friends passed the box of crackers back and forth and shared the bottle of water as they sat watching the tree's trunk. The sun continued its rise into the morning sky, and a small breeze lightened the heaviness of the humid air. For anyone walking past it would have been a completely normal scene, even with a circle of shells and the lit glass-encased red candle. It was, after all, New Orleans.

Murphy began to growl a low, threatening noise from the back of his throat. Despite his small size, the sound left no doubt as to the ferociousness that could be produced if the terrier or his human was attacked.

Ashlynne looked into the forest to see what had alerted the dog and froze in terror to see the dark, hunched shapes of at least a dozen or more hounds. They were massive in size, and their eyes glowed a sickening yellow in the gloom of the place. She pulled Murphy in so that he stood directly at her heels as she watched the large canine shapes flow out from the shadows of the forest.

"You must act quickly, Ashlynne," said Papa Legba in his soft, yet creaky voice. Despite his calm demeanor, Ashlynne caught the undercurrent of urgency and took a deep breath.

"I don't know if it will work!" she cried.

"It has worked before, and it will work again. But Murphy and I cannot do our parts until you do yours. Please begin, Ashlynne."

As the dark shapes of the hounds moved toward them, melting into the shadows of the trees then back out again, Ashlynne took a deep breath and mentally moved through the steps that needed to be done to set this situation back to rights. It amazed her that what confounded her here had been second nature in the French Quarter, but then again, in the Quarter she wasn't being stalked by phantom dogs and urged on by a powerful Voodoo Spirit.

"OK, here we go," she said in a firm voice that belied her fear and stepped over to Morag-as-Amber. She held out her left hand, palm out, over the still form feeling for the place of power at the top of the head. Ashlynne's heart began to beat furiously—she couldn't find it!

'Stop this, Ash. Every living creature has this, and it will be there. Just stay calm,' she counseled herself as the rustling behind them indicated that either the hounds were moving closer or the trees had woken up. Neither of those scenarios helped alleviate her fear, but she took a deep breath, planted her feet firmly on the alien land, and felt outward again for

the place at the top of the body's head that would open for her.

Just as her arm began to shake and quiver from remaining extended for so long, the center of her palm tingled and she saw the swirl of energy pulse and glow at the crown of Morag-as-Amber's head. Ashlynne connected with the small portal of energy there and, using her right hand, reached into it and yanked. She shook the Faerie out and away from her with the same revulsion that one would have reaching into a bag of grapes and pulling out a cockroach.

Once her right hand was free of the Faerie, Ashlynne grabbed the spirit of Amber, as it slept on in its self-imposed dreams of a happier place, by the top of the head and shoved it forcibly through the opening being held open by her left hand.

Morag opened her eyes to see that she was back in her own world.

"Nooooooo!" she screamed as the trees woke and began their whispers,

'Ouurrrsssssss. Baaacckkkkkkkk.
Hoooommmmmeeeeee.'

With the sickening sounds of wet, sucking earth, the trees began to pull their roots free and clamber toward the errant Faerie who lay sprawled in the piles of leaf mold and dead branches on the forest floor.

Morag, knowing full well the danger of the trees that approached, crab-walked backward away from their approach and clambered to her feet standing at her full and imposing height.

"Stop!" bellowed the formidable Faerie, holding one hand out to halt the advancement of the forest. While the force of her will was enough to stop the trees' advancement, it did nothing to deter the hounds from their silent approach. The Sluagh Sidhe knew their Mistress had been returned, and they would not be deterred from exacting their justice. While she may have led The Hunt, her power was not absolute. When she abandoned them and her role, she became prey.

The Hunt moved in, as silent and as steady as the Ocean's tides, both born by the strength of the moon. Murphy watched with his head hung low, his growl deep and steady at the back of his throat. The old man had told him that the hounds would come for The Monster but that he mustn't let them near the humans.

Amber woke from the strangest dream; a long table filled with beautifully decorated cakes, piles of exotic fruits, and beautifully cut glass goblets filled to their rims with delicately colored wines. She was dressed in a gossamer gown that draped over her shoulders with a fitted bodice and a skirt that floated around her bare ankles as if she were underwater, though she was not. The other guests were dressed just as decadently in gowns or suit coats of bright greens, deep purples, or silvery pinks. The conversation was lively and enchanting, and she thought that staying right here would be the most wonderful thing ever. Then the lavender sky turned a deep and bruised purple as the storm

394

blew in, snuffing out the candles that lit the long table. The guests who had, just seconds before, been engaged in frivolous chatter and tinkling laughs now murmured in low and threatening tones as the darkness settled in around them. Just as she began to ask what the matter was, a tremendous burst of light exploded behind her eyes, and a pain like nothing she had ever felt before erupted in her head. Gone was the candlelit dinner party and the beautiful guests. Gone was the delicate floral wine and tart, exotic fruits. Instead, Amber found herself being hurled through a tunnel, black as pitch, except for sparkling lights of blue and white that shot out from the edges as she slid down and down and down.

She came to rest feeling nothing but pain; her head felt like it would crack in two, and her arms and legs felt as if they had been dislocated and her back was bruised beyond anything she had ever experienced before. Amber carefully opened her eyes and moaned in dismay as she recognized the toxic forest that she had tried so hard to dream herself away from.

Ashlynne dropped to the forest floor, exhausted and shaken from the massive movement of energy that she had just facilitated. She heard Murphy continue his low growling but was too spent to see what he had focused on.

"Who are you?"

Ashlynne opened her eyes at the question. The honey-sweet southern drawl that had previously been used by the Faerie Morag was now thin and weak. Amber, the real Amber, was back.

Though she felt as old as the hunting trees in this god-forsaken forest, Ashlynne pulled herself to her feet and moved over to where Amber sat looking lost and dejected.

"Hi, I'm Ashlynne," she said, holding her hand out because she couldn't think of anything else to do in the situation. Miss

Manners hadn't covered the proper etiquette for how to greet a body-swapped human trapped in a haunted forest.

"Hey," replied Amber very softly, afraid the trees might hear them. "Did you bring me back here?"

"Yes. I'm also going to bring you back to our world. Do you think you can stand up?"

"I think so," winced Amber as she carefully got to her feet, every part of her body feeling bruised and beat up.
"What's happened to me?"

"That's a long story. How about we agree that you've been dreaming?" said Ashlynne, keeping one eye on the approaching hound-shaped shadows.

"I remember driving through town with Rodger, and then I was here. Then I was at the most beautiful dinner party and then…"

"We don't have time, really," said Ashlynne curtly, cutting off Amber's bewildered ramblings as the hounds moved in closer and closer. While they were most interested in

Morag who was standing imperiously demanding that they stop, Ashlynne didn't want to stay in this awful place any longer than necessary.

"Look, I need to get you out of here so you will need to do exactly as I say, do you understand?"

Michele peered through the stone at the tree that bounded their circle relaying to Andrew what she was seeing.

"Morag is standing off against a bunch of big black dogs. She's been commanding them to stop, but they keep moving toward her. I think she's toast."

"Well, good. There's got to be some kind of punishment for stealing someone's body, right?" asked Andrew around a mouth full of crackers.

"Who knows? The little bit of reading I did on Faeries didn't go into a lot of detail on rules and laws. Either they don't have any or we don't know about them," replied Michele as she continued to watch the scene unfolding in a world not their own.

"Where's Ash?" asked Andrew

"She's talking with the real Amber. Amber seems kind of out of it, and Ashlynne is looking a little scared."

"I would be a little scared too," shot back Andrew in a mocking tone.

"Don't be like that; you know what I meant," said Michele gently. The stress of the previous months was getting to be too much for all of them.

"Yeah, sorry."

"OH!" gasped Michele. "I think we might have trouble!"

"What? What's happening?" cried Andrew reaching for the stone.

Michele ducked out of his way and continued her reporting of the situation unfolding somewhere beyond them.

"Ashlynne and Amber are standing forehead to forehead. I'm not sure why, but their eyes are closed. There's a big black dog that has moved away from the main pack and is circling towards them—its eyes are bright blue, but the other dogs' eyes are yellow. This can't be good," she finished in a whisper.

Andrew's fists clenched in frustration and fear. He couldn't see anything that was happening and couldn't help in any way. He had never felt so helpless in his life.

Murphy watched as one dog-shaped shadow slipped from the rest of the pack and crept along the tree line toward Ashlynne and Amber. His growls turned to whimpers of fear when he saw that the hound's eyes were bright blue, not yellow like the others. He moved quietly toward Ashlynne, staying low and out of sight, matching the movement of the blue-eyed hound.

Ashlynne took both of Amber's hands and leaned in, touching forehead to forehead.

"Close your eyes and relax," she whispered, and Amber gratefully accepted the invitation to shut out the terrifying forest.

Ashlynne reached into Amber's mind,

searching through the disjointed memories that flickered in and out of view like a film reel. Amber at five with a new bicycle. Amber at twelve, scowling into the mirror at her mouth full of braces. Amber at fifteen, kissing an awkward boy behind her school.

"Ahhh... There we are..." whispered Ashlynne as she watched the images of Amber sitting next to a good-looking boy as he sped down a deserted highway a bright red sports car. He looked over at Amber and smiled, his brilliant blue eyes flashing. Ashlynne continued to watch the images in Amber's memory; the moon rode high, the radio was blasting, and then, there! There it was—a lone oak tree just off the highway.

"That's where it happened, and that's where you're going," she said gently to Amber.

Papa Legba stepped up to the two young women and laid his hand on Amber's brow. He watched the scene of the accident unfold as it had happened so many months ago.

"I will open the gates for this woman," he said to Ashlynne as Amber opened her eyes in surprise at the sound of his voice.

Ashlynne stepped aside and watched as the old man seemed to grow not only younger and stronger, as he lifted his walking stick, but much, much larger. The full enormity of the Spirit's strength left Ashlynne feeling weak, and her knees buckled. She had finally hit her limit, physically and emotionally, and as she dropped to the forest's floor and her eyes fell shut, she thought she heard Michele cry out far away from her.

Murphy continued to stalk the hound as it made its way in a slow circle until it was just to the left of the woman who looked like The Monster. The old man stepped up as his human fell. As much as Murphy wanted to go to her, he was told to watch the hound with the blue eyes, and that is what he would do. As he watched, the old man grew larger and larger as he moved the stick in a circle, sending out glittering colors of red and black and gold that swirled together, looking like the hole that Ashlynne had pulled them through. As the new hole grew bigger and bigger, Papa Legba took the dark-haired woman by the shoulders and began to push her toward it. At the same time, the movement just beyond her made Murphy turn to look as the dark shape of the blue-eyed hound bounded out from the tree line and launched itself at her.

Whatever was left of Rodger watched in a state of heated hatred as Amber was being pushed back into their own world, away from this awful place. Why should she be allowed to go home while he was stuck here, tethered to a pack of hounds hunting every drunk and degenerate human that bumbled into their path? He was destined for so much more than her and yet she was to be saved? His envy and resentment propelled him forward as he leaped out from the forest and launched himself at the woman he had nearly killed so many months before. If he had to stay here, then she would too.

Murphy saw the blue eyes of the hound narrow as it focused on the woman that Papa Legba was pushing toward the swirling black and red opening. As the colors moved around and around, he could catch glimpses of fields and a large tree: *home.* As the black hound pounced, Murphy jumped and slammed himself into the back of the woman sending them both hurtling through the portal and into the hot Alabama sunshine. He stood, shook himself off, and turned in time to see the way back at the base of the old oak's trunk close tight. By the time he had run up and scratched in a futile attempt to reopen the way back to Ashlynne, Amber had stood up and bent down to lift him gently and hold him tight.

"Thank you so much, you sweet little guy! I'm not sure how this happened, but you're safe with me."

Murphy threw his head back and let out a howl full of sadness, grief, and fear as the

woman he had saved continued to hold him
and whisper soft words of comfort.

Chapter 29

Michele let out a wail of despair as she watched Ashlynne collapse just as Murphy launched himself at Amber, propelling them both through Papa Legba's portal and out of the doomed forest. The black hound, who was at one time Rodger, slammed into the place that had offered his escape and dropped to the forest floor. As Michele watched in amazement, the bright blue eyes became murky and dull, turning to the dismal yellow of the other hounds. With his attempted revenge a failure, all hope of ever returning to a human form evaporated. Rodger was gone.

"What? What's happened?" demanded Andrew in a panic. Not getting a response from Michele, he forcibly removed the holey stone from her grip and looked through, trying to see for himself what had occurred.

Ashlynne lay in a heap on the ground with Papa Legba standing, legs akimbo and staff raised, next to her. Further off stood Morag in full Faerie regalia as a large pack of hounds slowly moved in toward her.

"Where's Murphy? Where's Amber?" he yelled at Michele who had not moved, her face slack as she stared off into the distance. "What happened to Ash? C'mon, Michele! Snap to it, damn it! What the hell happened in there!"

Responding to the sharp tone and the sharper shake of her shoulders, Michele took a drink of water and relayed to Andrew what she had seen before he took the stone.

"So, Murphy and Amber are where?" he asked once she had finished up her version of events.

"I'm not sure. Somewhere in our world, but I'm not sure where exactly."

"And Murphy went with her, why?" continued Andrew, drilling the exhausted woman with question after question.

"Murphy saved Amber from the other large dog that had blue eyes. But after they both went through Papa Legba's portal, the black dog's eyes turned yellow, like the rest of the packs."

"What happened to Ashlynne, then? Why is she just lying there?"

"I don't know, Andrew!" yelled Michele stepping forward, nose to nose with him. "I can only tell you what I saw, and I don't know why it all happened just yet. Back off, already!"

Morag spun in circles trying desperately to keep the Sluagh Sidhe in sight as it moved out of the forest and began to surround her.

"I said STOP!" she screamed at the black hounds as they continued their slow advance toward the Faerie that had deserted them.

The trees, while heeding the Unseelie's command to stop moving, decided that they could safely continue their malignant whispering, adding a terrifying backbeat to the deadly dance of the hounds.

'*Bbbbacccccckkkkkk, sheeeee'ssss baaacckkkkkkkk!*' they hissed, one to the other as their branches swayed overhead. '*Ouuuurrrrrsssssss, bbbeeee ooooouuuurrrrrsssssss!*' the trees whispered as Morag fought down the terror that threatened to wash over her. She was used to standing aside as these beings moved in on those creatures that she had hunted; being the hunted was beyond her ability to understand.

Papa Legba watched as the trees continued their deadly song and dance and the massive, yellow-eyed hounds moved in closer and closer to the once-powerful Faerie. He felt no sympathy or remorse. Each world and realm was held in the most delicate balance, and this being had knowingly and willingly set that all awry with her selfish theft of the young human woman's body.

He caught the movement at the edge of the forest before the hounds did; a tall horned figure melted out from the shadows and strode toward the circling canines and the cornered Faerie. The Horned One was large and muscular and held a massive bow in one hand with a quiver of arrows slung behind his wide shoulders. He nodded to Papa Legba, and Legba returned the greeting with a low bow at the waist that acknowledged The Hunter's sovereignty within this realm. The Sluagh Sidhe, sensing the approach of one more powerful than their former mistress, stopped their slow advance and turned, whining at the Horned Hunter that stood outside their loose circle.

Morag froze in terror as the huge figure approached from the line of trees. She knelt and began babbling her apologies and excuses, begging to be dealt with gently.

The whining of the hounds and wailing of the terrified Faerie roused Ashlynne who came to stand behind Papa Legba, her eyes wide and her body shaking with the effects of prolonged terror.

The powerful Voodou Spirit reached out to the shaken young woman who had been through so much and gently turned her away as the Horned Hunter gave a nod to the Sluagh Sidhe. In one fluid movement, they pounced on the kneeling Faerie who disappeared under the heaving furry shapes, alive with grasping claws and snapping teeth.

Ashlynne saw none of this, but the screams of terror and the high-pitched yelping of The Hounds would stay with her for the rest of her life.

After the harsh words with Michele, Andrew stood by himself, still in the circle but close to the tree's trunk. He watched the scene within the other realm with both amazement and terror. Seeing the subtle but mind-blowing interaction between the massive horned man that stepped out of the forest and the thin elderly man holding the staff was beyond anything he could have ever imagined. The mutual respect and acknowledgment that each gave to the other was incredible.

"If only humans could be so gracious," he said to himself as he continued to watch the goings-on through the tiny hole of the stone that his best friend gave to him.

"Hey! It's happening! Michele—bring the knife!" yelled Andrew as he watched Papa Legba turn Ashlynne gently away from the gruesome scene and move her toward the tree. The images within grew more and more distorted as the inky, black swirls with blood-red accents moved faster and faster within the portal.

Michele ran to his side, holding the knife at the ready as sparkles of gold suddenly shot from the trunk of the tree, and Ashlynne fell face-first onto the ground at their feet.

Andrew grabbed his friend's arms and dragged her away from the tree as Michele laid the anointed silver knife at the base, sealing the portal closed.

Andrew held his friend as she sobbed

heart-wrenching tears of loss, fear, and exhaustion. She kept telling him that she needed to go back for Murphy, that the small dog had been left behind, but Andrew said nothing and simply held and rocked her until her deep sobs subsided to silent tears, then defeated silence.

"He's gone, isn't he?" she asked in a tired voice.

"No, baby. He's not gone. He went out of there with Amber. He's not in the forest anymore."

"But he's not with me, and I don't even know where I sent Amber or if she made it!" cried Ashlynne, hot tears welling up in her eyes and flowing unchecked down her chin.

Andrew looked over her head at Michele, completely at a loss as to what to do for his friend.

"Darlin', Papa said the dog was protected by him. Papa Legba keeps his word, so you need to keep the faith, my friend. We'll get Murphy back," she declared with more assurance than she felt.

Chapter 30

Ashlynne lay in her bed, the room dark and cool with the shutters drawn and the window AC unit cutting any outside noises. She had been here for days, lost in a half-sleep where she went over and over the events that happened in City Park.

The cleanup was mostly a blur; she vaguely remembered removing the magic circle and Andrew gathering the shells for their eventual return to the cemetery from which they had been gathered.

She assumed that the ride home was uneventful because she had no recollection of it but did have a blurry image of Andrew bringing her into her house. She remembered Mimi watching from the mirror as she removed her filthy clothes and threw them into the garbage next to the sofa. Mimi's eyes were big and sad, and Ashlynne wondered if she had seen what had happened.

Andrew wrapped her in a blanket, turned the coffee pot on, and ran warm water in the deep claw foot tub. When the water was ready, he gently walked her into the bathroom and closed the door, trusting that even in her current state she would know to remove her underwear and get into the tub.

She assumed that she washed and got out of the tub since she was wearing a clean T-shirt and had on clean underwear. She might have had some coffee, or she might not have. She didn't really remember and didn't care at all.

Her phone buzzed with the arrival of a text message, and she glanced over with the barest of interest; it was Michele. From very far away her brain reminded her that her friends were probably very worried about her, but she really couldn't muster enough interest to care. She ignored the text and closed her eyes, watching the never-ending events from the other world's forest play out again and again in her mind.

"Ashlynne! Ashlynne! Wake up! C'mon!
You need to get out of bed and snap out of
this!"

Andrew's voice grated on her nerves, even
given the obvious concern. She didn't want to
wake up, and she sure as hell didn't want to
get out of bed. If she stayed right here then
maybe she could watch the looping visions
that went on and on behind her closed eyelids
that showed her Murphy's last minutes at her
side. She didn't see how getting up and
'snapping out of it' would help her to get him
back.

"Go away, Andrew."

"No."

She cracked open one eye to glare at him.

"What do you mean, no?"

"Just that, no. I won't go away, and you
will get up. I think we can find Murphy."

Ashlynne sat up with a start, her hair in a
tangled, matted mess and her eyes red and

puffy from crying.

"What? How?"

"Well, we knew Amber was from Alabama, right?"

"Right...."

"So, how many young women do you think just suddenly appeared next to an oak tree on a rural highway carrying a small dog?"

Ashlynne threw her arms around Andrew and began crying again, this time with tears of hope.

"That might work! I know I had Murph micro-chipped when I took him in to the vet, so if we can find out where Amber showed up, we can find my dog! C'mon! Let's go!" she yelled, jumping out of bed and rummaging around for some clean jeans.

"First thing first. You go brush your teeth, now. You've been lying here in this bed for days. Deodorant too, please," added Andrew in response to her glare.

"Fine, then we look for Amber."

"No, then you have coffee and food. I've brought my laptop over. While you eat, I'll search for news articles about strange women and dogs showing up on Alabama highways."

Though she insisted she wasn't hungry, Andrew watched in amusement as his tiny friend put away four slices of toasted bread, three scrambled eggs, a bowl of fruit, and a glass of juice.

"Find anything yet?" asked Ashlynne after she refilled their coffee cups for the second time.

"Actually, yeah—I think I have. Here," said Andrew, pointing at the screen that held an online news article about a young woman believed to have died in a car accident showing up several months later at the scene of the crash, very much alive.

"That's got to be her! Get the information, Andrew! I need to call my vet!"

It had been the longest two days of his life, and while Andrew was very happy for his friend, he thought he would sure-to-god slap her if she didn't stop jumping up and down on his back seat.

"Stop it and sit still! What are you? Four years old?" he grumbled at her from through the rear-view mirror.

Michele shot him a look from the passenger side, "And what are you? Forty?" she laughed as Ashlynne continued her nervous bouncing behind them.

"I just can't believe it took them so long to find him!" she rattled on from the backseat.

"Ash! Seriously, it took the vet 48 hours— what were you expecting?"

"I was expecting, Andrew, to not have lost my dog in the first place!" she shot back at him.

"Papa Legba said he would keep Murphy safe, and he did. He didn't say he would keep him with you," Michele said from the front. The fact that she was looking out the windshield kept her from seeing the absolute anger that washed over Ashlynne's face.

Andrew saw it from the rear-view mirror, though, and quickly changed the topic.

"OK, we're here!" he said in an overly cheery voice as he guided his car into the nearest parking space next to the vet's office.

The car was barely in park before Ashlynne jumped from the back seat and sprinted up the sidewalk. As their friend disappeared into the small building, Andrew and Michele looked at each other; neither one had to be psychic to know what each was thinking.

"God, I hope that's the right dog," muttered Michele as she followed Andrew up the walk.

Chapter 31

Ashlynne finished her cup of coffee as she watched the Calico cat creep up on an unsuspecting lizard that was basking in the sun on a large banana leaf next to her chair. With an apology to the huntress at her feet, she gently flicked the bottom of the leaf, sending the small lizard scurrying up the tree and out of sight. Glaring at her with equal parts annoyance and betrayal, the cat stalked away in search of other amusements.

Ashlynne breathed in the warm air of the early-April day, delighting in the less than normal humidity. It was going to be a great afternoon.

She tossed a piece of her toast to the small terrier laying in the shade and smiled as he caught it in midair.

"C'mon, Murph. Let's get out of here and see what trouble we can get into, shall we?"

The shaggy brown dog with the funny smile bounced at her feet, always up for a walk with his human. He ran in ahead of her, turning in circles and waiting for the magic words.

"You're a Good Boy, Murphy!" said Ashlynne as she bent down to kiss the small key-shaped scar on his forehead.

She clipped the leash onto his collar and headed out the front door.

"Don't forget your sweater, Dear!"

"Got it!" she called back over her shoulder to the older woman who was blowing elaborate smoke rings in the full-length mirror in her living room.

~The End~

February 20, 2020
East Jordan, MI

Lightning Source UK Ltd.
Milton Keynes UK
UKHW011041150821
388855UK00001B/138